# LATE TO THE PARTY

# LATE TO THE PARTY

MIDDANG3ARD™ BOOK TWO

RAMY VANCE

MICHAEL ANDERLE

## LATE TO THE PARTY TEAM


### Thanks to the JIT Readers

Misty Roa
Diane L. Smith
Jeff Eaton
Dave Hicks
Deb Mader
Dorothy Lloyd
Jeff Goode

*If I've missed anyone, please let me know!*

### Editor
The Skyhunter Editing Team

# DEDICATION

*This book is dedicated to Buffy the Vampire Slayer (read the Author Notes to find out why)*

*—Ramy Vance*

*To Family, Friends and
Those Who Love
to Read.
May We All Enjoy Grace
to Live the Life We Are
Called.*

*— Michael*

# 1

-----

Beneath the streets of Eleshier were catacombs that stretched far beyond the reach of the city. It was said that they were created thousands of years before the elves moved to the realm.

They'd been carved out by creatures who slunk in the darkness, etching their likenesses into the cold, wet stone, groping about in the darkness as if they were looking to find some kind of meaning or perhaps create their own.

The catacombs were left untouched for thousands of years, the smell of death festering in their walls as those who were entombed rotted away, along with the subsequent civilizations that had risen and fallen. The current residents of Eleshier avoided the catacombs.

They dumped their shit in them and left it at that.

It was this shit that the Mundanes were trekking through. Robert "Suzuki" Fletcher led them down the claustrophobic corridors. He held a torch that cast a flickering light across the smooth sandstone.

He wore tight-fitting leather armor he had picked up a few weeks ago that was decorated with two sets of runes.

The purpose of the runes had been lost on him, but he had been told they might be helpful. His helmet hid a scarred and burned face covered in stubble. His short sword was chipped, and his shield was covered in basilisk hide.

Stew followed closely on Suzuki's heels. He was a hulk of a man whose true nature was betrayed only by the softness of his acne-scarred face. His eyes rapidly searched the darkness, and he gripped his torch so tightly that his fingers were nearly as white as the sandstone walls. He wore hardly any armor, only a steel kilt. His chest was covered in myriad deep, long scars. What he lacked in armor, he made up in weaponry. Throwing daggers were strapped to his war-painted chest, and short swords, longer daggers, and a great sword hung from his waist.

The barbarian seemed more jittery than Suzuki, and he puffed out his chest as if to prove to himself that he wasn't afraid. Still, his free hand hovered over the hilt of one of his short swords.

Behind Stew was a young woman named Sandy, whose long hair was pulled back in a braid. She did not carry a torch. Instead, a flame flickered in her open palm. She wore no armor, only an ornate set of robes with embroidered arcane symbols . Her feet floated a couple inches off the ground, her toes lightly scraping the stone floor as she glided forward.

She didn't seem to care much about the narrowness of the walls. In her free hand, she held a book which she winked at every time she wanted to flip the page.

Stew jogged to catch up with Suzuki. "How much longer are we going to be slogging around down here?" he whined.

Suzuki sighed and looked at Stew. "We all spent long enough staring at that bullshit map. You couldn't make any more sense of it than I could. But if you would prefer to be the one leading the way into the caverns of darkness, please, be my guest."

"Dude, you know I have that whole dark thing."

"You mean being afraid of the dark?"

Sandy closed her hand, and not only did the flame in her hand go out, but so did the light from their torches.

Stew yelped.

With a snap of her fingers, a small fire burned from the palm of her hand, illuminating the dark corridors again. "Nyctophobia," Sandy chimed in with a devious giggle.

"Yeah, that," Stew said.

Suzuki turned his head so Stew couldn't see his smirk. "Kids are afraid of the dark. You are not a kid. You're a big-ass, manly man, right?"

Stew looked down at his boots. He sighed and nodded his head. "Yeah. I'm a big-ass, manly man."

"You know," Sandy cut in, "it says that the people who used to live down here once conducted human sacrifices to communicate with their gods. The elves say that when they first disturbed the graves, they unleashed an army of spirits who possessed the first villagers and made them turn on each other. And that was when they started to hear the voices coming from the catacombs, telling them to—"

Suzuki turned to Sandy, his lips pursed. "Sandy, will you cut it out with all the history lessons."

Sandy floated closer to Suzuki and Stew. She closed her book, and it vanished. Another fireball snapped into existence in her open hand.

"Why?" she leaned forward menacingly, the flames of the fire casting shadows across her face giving her a corpse-like appearance. "Are you getting afraid, too, Suzuki? That maybe, just maybe, whatever was locked down here..."

Sandy whipped her head around suddenly. "Did you guys hear that?"

Suzuki sucked in a deep breath. "Not funny." He was happy that his helmet was on. He was pretty sure that he had just dropped three shades of color in his face.

Sandy's smile widened, and all the menace in her face was replaced by a smile far too cute for where they were. "You both need to chill out. These catacombs have been abandoned for hundreds of years, which is why we're stuck with basic groundskeeper duties."

Suzuki shook his head. "This is not groundskeeper duty. We are on an important quest."

"Dude," the barbarian chimed in. "We're killing giant rats. How many times in the last week have we been sent to dank places like this to kill a nest of giant rats?"

Suzuki sighed. "Actually called a 'mischief' of rats. I told you that last time. But these are undead rats, so would it still be a mischief? Maybe something like a 'macabre' or a 'naughtiness' of rats, or—"

"Suzuki, nobody cares what the rats are named."

Suzuki looked at Sandy for support. Even in the dark, he could see the apathy on her face. "You don't care about the historical significance of the caverns we're exploring or the fact that we might be the first people to uncover its secrets in at least five hundred years. But you *do* care about what a herd of rats is called. Priorities, man. Priorities."

"Mischief," Suzuki muttered, "*Mischief* of rats." But they were right, killing a bunch of rats, whatever they were called, was shitty work, work that Suzuki hoped would give them what they needed to accomplish their real mission: saving Beth.

Stew cocked a thumb in Suzuki's direction. "This guy is hopeless. Can we just get back to walking?"

The Mundanes started down the dark, winding underground tunnels again.

Suzuki was keeping quiet. He didn't want to disclose how frustrated he was getting with the journey. Stew and Sandy were right. These quests, if you could call them that, were nothing more than vermin extermination. Granted, the exterminations were of very large, dangerous vermin. But in the grand scheme of things, they weren't heroes.

They were pest control.

Their skills weren't being put to use. And to add insult to injury, it didn't seem that any of this was helping him or the rest of the Mundanes figure out a way to save Beth.

It almost felt as if the MERCs were intentionally wasting their time.

Suzuki couldn't imagine why they would be doing that, though. Milos, a high-ranking dwarf MERC, had vouched for them on multiple occasions. They were one of the few new recruit parties who were qualified to hit the field without any veterans watching over them.

And they hadn't suffered any casualties worse than a few sword wounds or burns. Yet here they were, walking through another set of catacombs with yet another terribly-drawn map, looking for rats. At least they were just rats this time. Suzuki was still trying to scrub the smell of basilisk shit out of his armor.

Stew scraped his daggers against the stone wall, causing a screeching noise that cut through Suzuki's musings. "Do you guys remember that one raid we did? The one with all the Wyrm Sisters?"

Suzuki nodded. "Yeah, why?"

"Remember how it wasn't nearly as boring as this?"

"Fuck, Stew if you're just going to—"

"I'm just joking. Just joking. Seriously though, I was

asking because you brought it up last week. You said you wanted to see if we could find footage for some nerdy ass reason."

Suzuki wished he wasn't wearing a helmet so he could pinch the bridge of his nose in aggravation. "I wanted to review the video and take some tactical notes. There's nothing nerdy about wanting to make sure that I don't get us killed."

Stew flexed, but his muscles were lost in the dark. "Just point me in the direction of whatever you want dead, that's how we're going to keep from getting killed. Anyways, I got the video last night from a homeboy. I DMed it to you earlier if you want to take a look at it."

"Thanks, Stew."

If Suzuki could see his face, he'd note that the barbarian was smiling, in a devilish way. "And I was thinking... You know, since I did you such a solid, you know, like a good friend does, maybe I'd get the first crack at any of the loot?"

Sandy and Suzuki chimed in unison, "No."

The fire lighting their way flickered, threatening to go out, "No way," Sandy said. "You got the first crack last time. Besides, I'm up."

"Come on guys, you know I need—"

"Nope. As your fearless leader, I've been keeping tabs. We all agreed to the rotation. Sandy has first dibs this time. And you're not allowed to say anything until three days afterward. I'm tired of you guilting everyone into giving you what you want."

"If you guys weren't so soft, you wouldn't feel so guilty."

Sandy floated closer to Stew and when she was next to him, floated up, bridging their height difference. Once she was face-to-face with him, she gave him a peck on the cheek. "Soft for you. When you're hard, that is."

"Oh, baby."

Suzuki groaned. "Guys. Get a room." And before Stew could say anything, Suzuki added, "*After* the mission."

The Mundanes came to a fork in the tunnels with one veering off to the right and the other to the left. Suzuki consulted his map. "There's no fork in the map," he murmured.

Stew scoffed. "So what I'm hearing is you got us lost."

"Sandy, you need to control your man."

"He wouldn't be my man if he was controllable," Sandy purred.

"Why don't you just use that Find Target thing you're always using?" Stew asked.

"One," Suzuki started, "I don't think it's a good idea to always be relying on magic to figure out how to accomplish things. What if we end up in a non-magic area? What are we going to do then? Secondly, I want to conserve my mana so we don't have to spend a couple of days down here trying to get back home. And thirdly—"

The barbarian lifted his hands in surrender. "All right, all right, I get the point. So, left or right?"

Suzuki walked over to the left opening. He strained his ears, but he couldn't hear anything. "Your guess is as good as mine."

Sandy came up beside Suzuki and pulled out her book. She flipped through a couple of pages and stopped. She pointed at the opening on the right. "If either of you jack-asses had been listening earlier, you would have heard me tell you that the crypts were always built to the right. The split in the tunnels was to confuse looters. Every turn we're supposed to take is going to be a right. There's a lot of them. I guess the idea was that people would eventually get fed up and try a left and get lost."

Suzuki looked over Sandy's shoulder, trying to make heads or tails of the scribbles on the page. "What language is that written in?"

"Don't worry, I've been using that Cypher SD that Diana gave me last week. It works pretty well. I'm thinking about splurging to have the Chipmaster upgrade it if we get a good haul on this one."

"Why don't you pump some cash into something more useful?" Stew asked.

"I dunno, honey. That Smell-o-vision SD that Suzuki got a while back has been pretty useful. Plus, I'll get to read more. And more reading means more spells. You've been liking the spells I've been learning, right Stew?"

Stew laughed nervously and cleared his throat. "Yeah, they've been fun."

"Gross," Suzuki cut in. "All right. Right turns it is."

They took the right turn and the tunnel instantly descended, the roof shortening so that the Mundanes had to crouch to continue moving forward.

It was not easy going.

The floor was muddy and covered with brittle things that Suzuki thought would be best to avoid looking at. Instead, he focused on the darkness beyond what their torchlight illuminated.

Suzuki let his mind wander as Sandy made her way to the front of the queue, guiding them through the next series of tunnels. It was nice to sit back and let Sandy take care of something.

Over the last couple of quests, she had started to take a more assertive position in what was being planned. It was greatly easing the general stress that had been building in Suzuki's head about planning every step along the way. When Sandy knew something, she would speak up and help out, providing things that Suzuki wouldn't have been able to see on his own.

Even Stew was trying his hand at different aspects of questing. The fact that Stew had gone out of his way to hunt down a video specifically for tactics was proof that he was learning to prioritize, even if the extent of his knowledge was defined by how to get the best loot for himself.

The Mundanes were not the same group they had been just a few months ago. The hours that they used to spend plugged into *Middang3ard* VR seemed like a lifetime ago. Suzuki didn't even feel he resembled that person who had played that game for years. Even the initial recruitments with the military and their eventual poaching by the hands of the MERCs seemed like a distant memory.

There was just the here and now.

And *now* they were crunching bones and shit beneath their boots as they hunted a mischief of undead rats.

"Maybe a perversity of rats," Suzuki muttered to himself, "That might work better than—"

"Drop it, Suzuki," Sandy interrupted. "Do you hear that?"

Suzuki was silent. Sandy pointed down the tunnel. There was a sound of teeth gnawing wood, and a few screeches and squeals.

Stew started down the tunnel. "Sounds like rats to me."

Suzuki grabbed his arm, stopping him from moving forward. "Remember what we talked about."

"Yeah, yeah. Save the Leeroy Jenkins shit."

Suzuki nodded. "Yep. Save the Leeroying for later. Come on. Let's check it out. Slowly."

The Mundanes walked down the tunnel. The walls were built farther away from each other here, and the ceiling opened up so that they no longer had to crouch. After a few feet, the tunnel opened up to a large crypt. Suzuki rested his hand on the wall. The sandstone had been replaced with brick.

Suzuki pointed his torch. "Sandy, can we get a little bit more light."

A handful of small, non-flammable blue sparks floated out of Sandy's hands. The sparks took an orb shape and floated down the tunnel, shedding light on the catacomb's dark crevices.

Suzuki had been right. The walls were brick. What he hadn't noticed though was that there were crypts dug into them. Thousands of skulls were stacked on top of each other. Their blank eyes stared out as if they were meant to watch whatever was coming to pass. The floor of the crypt's open area was covered in bones, some more decomposed than others, although many of the bodies still wafted the fumes of the dead.

Among the skeletons and rotting corpses were rats. They were scuttling about, ignoring the lights that flickered over them. Each rat was nearly five feet, long, and they were indeed undead. Most of their flesh had rotted off and what was left was green and toxic-looking. Their hair had mostly fallen out, and the remainder was knotted up in mangy tuffs.

The undead rats gnawed at the flesh of the decomposing carcasses, occasionally snapping at each other. Their teeth, visible from behind their gaunt cheeks, never ceased moving.

Suzuki looked closer. He could see that there were even more rats than he had initially expected. Much of what he had thought were the bones of humans were nothing more than smaller rats piled on top of each other. The floor looked as if it were waving back and forth because of the unceasingly moving, ironically dead bodies.

Sandy peered over the edge of the ledge. "Well, there's your mischief."

Suzuki sat at the foot of the tunnel and looked out at the crypt beneath him. " 'Mischief' does not do justice to how disgusting that is."

"Can't we just have Sandy drop a firebomb or something?" Stew suggested. "All of those rats are pretty close. The whole thing would probably go up in flames."

"Not a bad idea, Stew. Not a bad idea at all."

Stew looked extremely proud of himself. Somehow, he was flexing as smugly as he was smiling.

Suzuki waved away Stew's celebratory mood. "Unfortunately, decomposing bodies release methane gas, and this crypt is probably filled with it. And the rotting undead. They're surprisingly explosive."

"So?" Stew stopped flexing. "That's a good thing, right?"

Suzuki gave Sandy a troubled look before returning his attention to Stew. "Maybe if we weren't miles and miles underground. You ever see the movie *Backdraft*?"

Sandy made an exploding gesture with her hands.

"So, I guess not." Stew was deflated. "So if I understand you correctly, what you're saying is that we have to go down there and kill everything."

Suzuki nodded. "Yep. Any Area of Effect spells from Sandy are pretty much out of the question 'cause it'll be too cramped."

Sandy pulled out her staff and spun it. "Guess it gives me a chance to try this."

"Might as well," Suzuki said. "Let's go."

"Wait, you don't have a plan or something?" Stew asked.

"I was thinking we could just wing it. See what happens."

Suzuki stepped to the side, holding out his arm as if guiding Stew over the edge of the ledge. "Stew, please, be my guest."

Stew cracked his knuckles and looked around, with a smile as wide as an anarchist's on being introduced to his first pipe bomb. His eyes settled on an empty crypt to their right. He reached in and dislodged a hunk of a wooden beam that was being used to support the bricks.

The small crypt collapsed in on itself, skulls and other wooden planks falling and shattering against the ground. Stew held up his plank and surveyed it closely. After he was satisfied, he grabbed a few other planks and started working. When he was finished, he had somehow managed to connect each of the planks together so that they made a large square.

He scrolled through his HUD, selected hemp fabric that instantly materialized in his hand and stretched the fabric over the frame he had built, before hammering it to the frame. "Sandy, could you cast Stoneskin for me?"

Sandy raised her hands, and they took on the consistency of rock. "No problem." She waved her hands over Stew's impromptu sleigh and the fabric hardened.

Stew picked up the sleigh and looked down at it, satisfied with his work. "Looks good to me." Then he jumped on the sleigh and, holding on, leapt off the tunnel's ledge. He sailed through the air for a few seconds before he fell to the ground, still standing on his structure.

The sleigh hit the ground with a sickening thud, sending rat guts and body parts flying through the air as Stew swung his greatsword, cleaving through the closest rats.

"That's what I'm talking about, Stew," Sandy shouted. "That's my man!"

Stew skewered three rats on his sword, then held it up for Sandy to see. "Hey, babe, it's a rat-kebab!"

A giant rat leapt from the mass of screeching rodents beneath and knocked Stew into the sea of claws and teeth.

Suzuki sighed as he unsheathed his sword. "Guess that's our cue. I will hand it to him, though. It did look pretty cool."

Sandy raised her hand to her face and pulled her hood over her head. A stone mask with sullen eyes and a mouth drawn into a grimace shimmered into existence. "It was pretty sick. Not very effective, but pretty sick."

Suzuki leapt from the ledge and landed on top of Stew's sleigh. He reached down and grabbed Stew's leg, which was barely visible beneath the massing bodies of fur which covered the crypt's floor.

Sandy floated down behind Suzuki and helped him pull Stew out of the river of rodents. A couple of undead rats still clung to Stew's chest hair, and Sandy knocked them off with her staff.

A couple of small rats ran by, and Suzuki kicked them off the sleigh. "All right. The room isn't that small. Everyone clear a path to the walls. Take care of the big rats and try to ignore the small ones."

Stew was still pulling rats off his body. "Yeah, you try to ignore these fuckers."

"You know what I mean. We clear a path and take care of the big ones, and then we can mop up the rest. For honor."

"For glory!"

"For XP!"

Stew was the first one to charge in. *Hardly surprising*, Suzuki thought. What was surprising though was how efficiently Stew was doing it. He had leapt to the far side of the room and was clinging to the wall, looking down on the rats beneath him.

The larger rodents were sniffing around for Stew. Even though they were undead, it seemed they still retained the basic instincts of the animal they once were.

Since Stew was above the rats, they couldn't get a good look at him. Instead of jumping into the fray, he was taking potshots at the undead vermin with his throwing knives. He had already noticeably cut down on the number of rats near him.

Beside Suzuki, Sandy was twirling her staff, casting non-flammable magic missiles at the larger rodents who were fighting to crawl over their smaller brethren and overtake the little wooden island Stew had provided.

Suzuki could tell that Sandy was bored. The staff didn't seem to be all that it was worked up to be. He didn't know much about it other than that Sandy had traded away a good chunk of her loot from their last quest to get it.

An undead rat soared through the air at Suzuki. He held up his shield and was able to block it in time. The rat rolled around on its back, its jaws jabbering uncontrollably as it hissed louder than a king cobra.

Suzuki impaled the rat with his sword and kicked it into the growing pile of recently extra dead undead creatures. "How do you like the staff?"

Sandy shrugged and listlessly knocked a deranged rat over the side of the sleigh. "Eh. It's all right."

"You know, I noticed you've been kinda bored recently... with the quests." They were having a casual conversation while killing undead rats. *Look at how far we've come*, Suzuki mused.

"It's not the quests. There are just only so many ways I can blow stuff up. I mean, look at Stew."

Sandy pointed at Stew, who was hanging upside down, his face almost completely overrun by rats, hacking away while occasionally doing a sit up and laughing maniacally. Sandy hung her head and shook it like a child disappointed by her birthday presents. "That man always finds a way to keep himself entertained."

Stew grabbed one of the larger rats by its tail and swung it against the wall. The rat exploded, sending entrails and rotting flesh flying everywhere. "Hey, guys! If you grab them, they pop! Guys! Guys! Check it out!"

Sandy sighed and hit a rat with her staff. The rat instantly incinerated, and its ashes fell in a neat clump before her feet. "Remember when I used to laugh insanely? When was the last time you heard me laughing?"

Suzuki nodded. "True. It's been a while. Why don't you try something new?"

"Like what?"

"I don't know, you could try some of the stuff that you've been reading about."

Sandy shrugged. "Everything I'm reading is necromancy. And you can't use necromancy against things that are already undead."

"Says who? Didn't Niv and Diana say that it's mostly your imagination?"

"Huh. Yeah, I guess so."

Suzuki thought to himself, directing his internal monologue to the eldritch imp residing in his body. *Fred, do I have enough mana for some holy spells?*

The imp was roughly the size of a small man with red scales, wings, and an intimidating smile showing razor-sharp fangs. Suzuki rarely saw that, though, since Fred preferred to stay inside of Suzuki and only came out when it was necessary.

Fred stretched his intangible, invisible wings and sneered in a way that made Suzuki's skin crawl from the inside. *Holy spells? If you wish to cast such banal and simple magic, yes, you do have enough mana to go 'hog wild' as the muscled imbecile says. And you will still be able to navigate out of this putrid place.*

Suzuki jabbed Sandy in the side. "May the holy waters of...uh, light wash over you," he said as he raised his sword in the air. Suzuki was no master of warrior-mage magic, but Fred usually helped him muddle his way through those spells. He made a note to himself to ask Sandy for some books when he got back because he was not getting the hang of free-styling spellwork.

Sandy laughed and smashed another rat with her staff. "Is that the best you got? That was terrible."

"Why don't you show me how it's done?"

Sandy raised her hands and floated higher into the air. Lightning jumped between her fingertips. "Let my enemies be drowned in the depths of my power!"

The caverns shook, and Stew looked up from the rats he was killing. Small, swollen clouds had gathered above the rats. Rain came crashing down from the clouds. In a matter of moments, the small room began to flood.

Suzuki grabbed Sandy and turned her around. "What are you doing?"

Sandy tapped the side of Suzuki's neck. His skin started to itch, and he scratched it. In the open space between his armor and helmet, he could feel gills on his neck. Then she leapt over to Stew, grabbed hold of the wall, and planted a fat kiss on his neck "Making this interesting!"

Stew groaned and tried to push Sandy away. "Ew, that hurt, babe."

Sandy grabbed Stew's hand and pulled him into the water before he could object. Suzuki watched them as the water continued to rise.

Swimming in a pool of rotting, maggot-infested rats sounded utterly disgusting. It also sounded more fun than just hacking at them for another half an hour. However, given that he had no choice in the matter, Suzuki jumped into the water.

Beneath its surface, he could see Sandy swimming back and forth. She had a mermaid's tail and she was throwing what looked like icicle tridents at the rats, pinning them to the wall. Stew had almost forgotten about the rats. He was doing backflips underwater.

Sandy was right.

This was making things more interesting.

---

The Mundanes stood around a fire in the middle of the room, tossing the bodies of the undead rats into the firepit. The smell of charred, rotting flesh was almost unbearable, and Suzuki constantly had to work to keep himself from gagging. They had been killing for nearly an hour and were finally down to the last three huge rats.

Stew reached down, picked a rat up and cast it upon the fire, watching as the flames consumed the carcass, quickly reducing it to bones.

Sandy raised her hands and the flames jutted out like tendrils, engulfing the last two rats. "You know, that was more fun than usual, but I don't see how it's helping us get to Beth."

Suzuki hit his HUD and pulled up the map of the area. A percentage of success blipped across the HUD's screen. The area they were currently in read 90%. He swiped through his HUD to a map of the island. The area was darkened; there was a lack of information because it hadn't been explored. At best, it gave a vague impression of wherever Beth was. The success rate dropped to 0.007%.

Suzuki shut down the HUD's map. "It doesn't look like it's helping us at all."

"We need to get an army," Stew muttered.

"We tried that," Suzuki growled. "And a fucking lot of good that did us. We sent all the proof we had to everyone and anyone...the repeated message, its signal, the HUD's location, everything. And what did they say?"

"Fuck off," Stew muttered.

"Fuck off." Suzuki pursed his lips as he mentally ran through the last conversation he'd had with them. The officer who had been patient the first seven times Suzuki contacted him had eventually lost his shit, saying that it was probably some orc fucking with him.

"Orcs don't send emails," Suzuki had said.

The officer responded by ending the call and blocking Suzuki from being able to contact him...and apparently the entire World Army. He'd been blacklisted.

So had Sandy.

Stew was the only one at the time who could contact them, and that was largely because he'd only tried once and —uncharacteristically—was full of "Yes, sirs" and "No, sirs," sitting perfectly rigid while on the phone.

"Military brat," Sandy said, "His dad was a marine."

But even Stew's charms weren't enough and eventually he was blocked too, for over-calling. Not that it mattered. No one believed them about Beth, which meant that her rescue was left up to them.

Stew sat down on the crypt's floor and shook his head. His disappointment was evident. "Yeah, I don't get how cleaning up rats every other day is going to get us any closer to helping Beth. And we're still not sure that—"

"I'm sure."

Stew crouched down next to the fire and watched the flames. "I know Beth meant a lot to you...to us...but we got to be real. We still don't know for sure that she's out there."

Suzuki clenched his fists tight. "I know."

"Getting a repeating message doesn't prove anything, Suzuki. It could be just a glitch in your HUD or the message center. It's hard to accept but—"

Suzuki raised his hand and cut Stew off. "I'm not going to accept that she's dead. She wouldn't accept that we were. And if anyone of us was going to survive, it'd be Beth. If we're still here, so is she. So let's see if we can find anything to boost our chances of surviving wherever the hell she is."

Stew shrugged as he walked off to complete his task. "All right."

The last of the rats had burned. The crypt looked much larger without the mischief of undead rats crowding the floor. It gave the impression of something large and ominous waiting for you, very fitting for a crypt.

Suzuki pointed to the piles of graves. "If we're going to find anything, it's going to be in one of those. So let's get looking."

Stew grumbled and walked over to the walls. He started pulling bodies out. Some of the skeletons turned to dust the moment they were touched. "So glamorous. Now we're robbing graves. Isn't that going to cause a curse or something, Sandy?"

Sandy was already climbing through a pile of skulls, kicking them to the ground to make more space for her to slide through the tight openings. "Nope. There were no curses here. Niv checked when we first got in."

Suzuki searched around the crypt. He noticed a lever in the corner of the room. It was broken. He wedged his sword into the open space where a wooden piece was meant to connect and jimmied the lever until it moved, and he pushed hard against it. The lever snapped back, and the walls in the room groaned. Suzuki stepped back as the rest of the Mundanes came and crowded around him.

"Did you trap-check it?" Sandy asked.

"Uh, yeah," Suzuki murmured. In truth, he'd forgotten, not that he could do anything about that now. If it was booby-trapped, he'd be fucked. Or maybe he'd get lucky, not that he was having much luck anymore.

In the center of the room, the floor opened up. And nothing popped out, exploded, or shot poisonous arrows at them. "Perhaps my luck hasn't completely run out after all," Suzuki thought.

A small platform rose from a compartment underneath the floor. A plain wooden chest sat in the middle of the platform.

Stew rushed over to the chest and flung it open, his eyes wide and waiting. "Sweet."

Sandy shook her head as she walked over to the chest. It was mostly empty, but there was a set of leather gauntlets, a dagger, and a wooden mask. Suzuki's eyes were drawn to the mask. He didn't know why. There was nothing remotely interesting about it.

Suzuki picked it up and looked it over before tossing it back in the chest. "This chest is a bust, but at least the payment for the quest was pretty high. We'll probably be able to get some better gear. You can still have first dibs if you want, Sandy."

Sandy picked up the mask. She held it up and stared into its eyes. A gust of cold wind blew through the room, instantly sending a shiver up Suzuki's spine. Sandy pulled her robes closer until the chill passed. The Mundanes all looked at each other.

"That's a bad sign, right?" Stew asked.

Sandy pocketed the mask, leaned over, and kissed Stew. "Not as far as I'm concerned. I'll have Diana look at it when we get back. Doesn't look too dangerous."

"Yeah, neither did that Ax of Intent and Homing that Stew picked up last month," Suzuki noted. "You remember how that turned out, don't you?"

Sandy nodded. "I'll have Diana give it a thorough check. And I won't use it until then. Scouts honor."

"All right."

Stew had already snatched up the daggers and added them to the collection that hung from his kilt.

"You know, maybe we should do more underwater missions. That was pretty fun. And there are probably sea rats that need killing."

"I think those are called seals," Suzuki said. "And I don't want to make a career out of killing seals. They're cute. Abnormally cute."

Stew kicked the chest over, satisfied there was nothing of further interest. "Yeah, I'm not sure about killing cute things. Well, Suzuki, could you do us the honor?"

Suzuki held up his sword. A beam of light shot from it, went up the tunnels they had just come through, and disappeared into the darkness. "Might as well head back."

The Mundanes set off to follow the trail Suzuki had cast, and as they walked, Suzuki considered things. Sandy and Stew were right about these small quests. This wasn't getting them any closer to Beth, and it was starting to drive Suzuki out of his mind.

He knew she was out there somewhere. He watched the last video she had sent him at least three times a day. Beth had been so calm. Bored, almost. That wasn't the face of someone who believed she was going to die. He was going to find a way to get to her.

## 2

The Red Lion sat in a swamp infested with mosquitos and bathed in the amber glow of the sunset. It was a modest tavern that magically stretched to nearly triple its size on the inside. The doors opened and closed as MERCs came and went, either returning from or leaving for adventures. Members of multiple races showed up, shook hands, and shared drinks with each other.

A party composed of elves, gnomes, and humans sat outside the Red Lion, sharing a long pipe among them as they sipped on their beers. The slender elf looked outward with her pale silver eyes and stared into the marshlands in the distance. She puffed the pipe, letting a cloud of smoke drift up to the steadily-darkening sky as she hefted her tankard, which was empty. She kicked the chair of a gnome sitting behind her, knocking him to the ground.

The gnome growled, but stood and went into the tavern. He returned in a few moments with a tray of beers, dropping them down on the small patio table amidst cards and gold pieces.

The small party of MERCs continued to drink, staring off into the swamplands.

Out in the distance, it seemed as if the swamp itself had come alive and was shuffling toward the Red Lion. As the mass of moss and swamp sludge got closer, the party sitting outside the Red Lion laughed.

Slowly, the Mundanes approached. They were nearly as green and filthy as the swamp. They pulled themselves up onto the floating pathway that the Red Lion and the rest of the MERC settlement rested on.

The elf MERC laughed and offered her pipe to Suzuki. "How was extermination duty?"

Suzuki waved the pipe away, grabbed the elf's beer, and downed the drink. "How does it look like it went?"

"I believe you owe me a beer."

"Just tell Wendy to put it on my tab," Suzuki muttered as he pushed open the Red Lion's door and walked inside.

The rest of the Mundanes followed him, both Sandy and Stew in noticeably irritable spirits.

Suzuki hit his HUD and his armor disappeared, replaced by a loose-fitting cloth tunic. The dirt and muck still clung to him. He wiped his forehead and tossed the filth onto the floor.

A dwarf slipped in the pile of mud, tossing his beer into the air. Sandy reached out and caught the drink before helping the dwarf to his feet. Damn, she was fast. The dwarf laughed cheerfully. He was obviously just as impressed as Suzuki was at her dexterity and speed.

Once inside, Stew stumbled to a booth and collapsed into a seat. He sighed heavily, tapped his HUD, and looked down at the state of his tunic. He tried to wipe some of the mud off on the side of the table. "You'd think that they'd have found a way around this."

Sandy sat next to Stew and leaned her head on his shoulder. "Magic can't solve everything. At least we aren't the ones who have to clean it all."

"Who cleans it?"

"Someone lower on the totem pole than us. I'd prefer not to think about it."

Suzuki raised his hand to catch the attention of the barmaid walking past him. "Three ales, please?"

The barmaid nodded and walked off as Suzuki leaned back and plopped his feet on one of the nearby chairs. "I don't think that my feet have ever hurt this much in my life."

Stew looked at Suzuki's boots with disgust. He picked up a fork sitting on the table and pushed Suzuki's feet away. "Someone has got to figure out a better fast travel system. This whole 'portal one way, walk back home' thing is not working for me. It feels like every day is leg day."

Sandy grabbed Stew's thigh hard under the table. "But it makes your legs look so good."

Stew yelped and slapped Sandy's hand away. He raised the fork and pointed it threateningly at Sandy. "My legs always look good. This is just making them tired. And thank you."

One of the barmaids dropped off the ales and the Mundanes raised their drinks, clanking their tankards together.

No one spoke for some time, and the silence was something Suzuki was grateful for. The nightly festivities for the new recruits was turning into an endless parade, and he was getting sick of welcoming more newbs. Still, it was an indication that the war was heating up.

It meant that more MERCs were needed, which meant that there were more missions floating about. Manny, the MERCs recruiter, must be working overtime.

But there was no one new to welcome today, and Suzuki found it much more agreeable to be able to sit down without being bothered after a grueling quest.

And the quests had been grueling.

Nothing that the Mundanes had been assigned over the last ten days had been particularly difficult, but each quest had taken up time and energy.

Suzuki drank his beer and stared off, letting his mind drift. He absentmindedly watched the barmaid filling a dwarf's tankard of beer. She caught his eyes, and Suzuki quickly looked away. He had been imagining pouring Beth a beer and wondering what she was drinking right now.

Sandy interrupted Suzuki's burgeoning fantasy. "How are we doing on funds right now?"

Suzuki pulled up his HUD, scrolled to his inventory, and selected his coin purse. He checked through their collective coin stash and looked at the pending transfer. "Looks like we got enough from this haul to cover the week in room and board. We might have to take it easy on the booze, though."

Stew coughed awkwardly and took three quick sips from his beer before he started picking at his face. "I got the booze covered. Me and Wendy worked something out."

Sandy's eyes widened, and she grabbed Stew by the cheek. "And what exactly is it that you worked out with Wendy?"

"Nothing, nothing. Jesus."

"Just like nothing with you and that orc?"

Stew lifted his hands up defensively. "Nothing happened with that orc! She was trying to chop my cock off to take back for a trophy."

Sandy pursed her lips. "So she thought you had a trophy dick?"

"You are missing the part about her wanting to give me an orcish circumcision. The most important part."

Sandy pinched Stew's cheek hard enough to leave a mark. "You know I'm just giving you a hard time. But seriously, how are you getting free drinks?"

Stew hung his head, still picking his face as if he would unearth an answer beneath his zits. "Dish duty for the week. Only two hours a day. She showed me the set-up. It looks horrible, but we gotta start saving money."

Suzuki closed down his HUD and leaned back in his seat. He sighed. "Never thought that my adventure in Middang3ard would consist of being more broke than when I was home."

"Yeah, but at least you're not still working customer service."

Suzuki raised his tankard. "I can drink to that shit."

Sandy clanked her beer to Suzuki's. Stew sheepishly looked down at his own beer.

Suzuki clapped Stew on the back. "Cheer up," he said. "At least you can work for booze and food here."

"Yeah, beats trying to pay off a student loan any day."

Sandy looked over her shoulder and checked the floating chalkboard near the front of the bar. A list of meals for the day was etched on it: Erymanthian Boar Steak with a side of Hydra Eyes. Kelpie Hoof Stew. Kraken Calamari. "You guys down to split some stew?"

Stew and Suzuki checked the chalkboard behind them. "Sounds good," they said in unison.

Sandy walked away, calling over her shoulder, "I'll go grab it."

Stew and Suzuki both drank some of their beer. Suzuki watched Stew, who suddenly started shaking his head as if he were reacting violently to something being said.

"Uh, Stew? You doing okay over there?"

Stew lifted a finger to his ear. "Wait. I was just talking to GB."

"Everything okay?" Suzuki asked.

"Yeah. GB just wants to do another, you know, spell type of thing."

"You mean, for your dick?"

"Yeah. For my dick."

Suzuki gave Stew a worried look. "I thought you were done with that whole thing."

"Oh, yeah. Mostly, I mean. Not like I'm super nervous or anything, but, you know, it's nice to spice things up here and there."

"Too much info." Suzuki returned to his drink.

"But GB's been really weird about it recently. Then I remembered, the dude is actually in my body. So what if he feels the things I feel? Like, what if he's getting off on the idea of Sandy and me being...intimate?"

"That is between you and your familiar, buddy."

Sandy sat down at their booth in a flourish of puffed robes and dropped a basket of bread in the center of the table. She eyed Stew and Suzuki, both of whom were sitting and chuckling like a bunch of schoolgirls. "What is it?"

Suzuki snatched a roll of bread from the basket. "GB's trying to get a threesome going with you two."

Sandy whipped around and glared at Stew. "Goddamn it, Stew, I've told you before. We'll know when it's time to have an extra sexy friend."

"No, no, babe, that's not what I was—"

"Nope. Not tonight. Also, I don't trust that donkey gargoyle familiar of yours. He's too quiet. You can't trust anyone that quiet. Not anyone. Now, if we're done talking about our fuck schedule, I'd like to talk about what we're going to do about Beth."

Suzuki nearly dropped the bread he was shoving into his mouth. "I thought you guys didn't believe me?"

"I mean, I have my doubts. But I trust you. So does Stew."

Stew smiled and nodded. It was a comforting sight for Suzuki. He had been worried that the two of them assumed that he was crazy.

"You don't just jump to conclusions," Sandy said. "Most of what you think is pretty well researched or well-founded. So if you think there's a reason to believe that Beth is alive, we're both behind you. What do we do from here? What's the plan?"

Suzuki took a deep breath. The plan. It was something he'd been working on for a while, and it was still far from perfect, but now was as good a time as any to let them in on what he had so far. "What did we used to do when we were out-leveled? I mean, it can't be a whole lot different than what we would have to figure out in *Middang3ard*."

"We'd just grind." Sandy shook her head in frustration. "Grind for skills, advantages, loot. We'd take any mission we could to find that one magical item or NPC or whatever to give us the edge we needed. Just like we're doing now. It'd be like that time we were trying to run that golem-hunting mission. Do you guys remember that? Every time we broke into the dungeon, we'd get our asses handed to us within a couple of seconds. And the only thing that we could do was grind XP out in the valley next to the dungeon because it had a better gear-drop rate than the rest of the area. We did that for a week! Six hours a day for a whole week! But I *do not* want to grind here. Partly because it's not the same here as in the game, but mostly because it's exhausting, and it's not getting us anywhere fast."

Stew laughed and clapped his hands. He was nearly crying from laughing so hard. "Remember that time we had to farm blue ember crystals so Suzuki could upgrade his armor? You know, that upgrade he had a hard-on for so he wasn't so weak against Dark Creatures? He didn't want to give up that chest piece, but if a vampire or something touched him, he'd be nixed in one hit."

Suzuki took another bite from his bread roll chuckling at the memory. "How did we end up getting the crystals?"

"We found this cave where they were spawning, and you did this conversion ratio to find out how many times we'd have to walk in and out of the cave for the embers to respawn. We must have walked in and out of that cave a thousand times in the first day. I ended up paying my baby sister to do it for me."

Sandy snatched a roll, munching down hard on it. "I remember that. And then we got jumped by a horde of giant ravens—"

"A conspiracy of ravens," Suzuki corrected.

"Whatever. A conspiracy. But Stew wasn't even there to help. His sister didn't know the controls, and Stew's character perma-died."

Stew said as he raised his tankard, "RIP Leeroy the First."

Suzuki, Stew, and Sandy clanked their tankards together as they shouted, "May he rest in peace!"

"We could find a dragon. There have to be dragons here. And they've got to be loaded with a shit-ton of loot."

"I don't know. If we can't handle a new zone, we probably couldn't handle a dragon."

Stew pinched his fingers together. "Maybe a baby dragon. A teeny-tiny baby dragon?"

Sandy shook her head as she bit down on her roll. "I am opposed to killing baby animals, even if they're dragons. It's unethical. Someone has to think of the whole ecosystem and shit."

"What do you know about Middang3ard's ecosystem?"

"I know enough about what an ecosystem is to know you don't kill the babies. You kill the adults."

"But who makes the babies, then?"

Suzuki waved his hands, signaling he was done with the way the conversation was going. "We could find a real dungeon."

"Haven't we been running dungeons for over a week? Technically what we just finished was a dungeon."

Stew drummed a beat on the table. Then he clenched his fist and mimed two people walking toward his fist with his index and middle finger. "Oh! There's that herd of giant man-eating hippos in the South Plains. Those things are huge. They gotta be worth some kind of XP."

"No, we're thinking about this all wrong. You remember what Fred said? The whole XP thing doesn't work like that here. It's not like we level up and suddenly get more HP. We have to get more proficient in combat, but it's not going to change our chances at survival. We need to actually get better at this, like we'd have to on Earth." Suzuki put down his tankard. "However, actually improving our skills is going to take a shit ton of time— time Beth doesn't have. So our best bet is upgrading our gear.

He stood and ran his hands through his hair. Suzuki started to pace, something he did when he was trying to figure out a problem that didn't have an obvious solution.

"I mean, think about it. Our HUDs can't possibly know

how good we actually are at swinging a sword, and since we haven't input any plans of attack, it must be making its calculations on whether or not our gear can stand up to what's there. We don't need to be focusing on getting better at fighting, we need to be focusing on getting better gear."

"Well, we can't afford better gear," Sandy responded. "All of our money is going to paying our bills."

"Yeah, that is a problem."

Stew looked down at the bottom of his empty tankard. "VR was so much easier than this. At least the real Middang3ard has good beer!"

Suzuki nodded as he finished his beer. Out of the corner of his eye, he saw a familiar shape hobbling toward him—a stout dwarf with a wispy white beard and fiery brown eyes. Milos. The dwarf was using a pair of crutches to walk, and both of his hands held a beer. How he was using the crutches without hands was a mystery. The Mundanes sighed as Milos approached them.

Suzuki raised his hands as if he could ward off Milo. "Not now, Milos. We don't want any more quests from you right now."

Milos plopped into the seat next to Suzuki and forced his way into the Mundanes' booth. He placed both of his beers on the table and belched loudly. "I didn't come here with a mission for any of you. Not after the last one. Flooding an ancient crypt that you were just supposed to clear out? I lost money because of you three!"

Sandy shrugged. "You said to get rid of the rats. We got rid of the rats."

"I didn't think you were going to flood the damn place. You were getting rid of those rats so some researchers could come in and study the place. Do you know how pissed off they were when they showed up and all those mummies were soaked to the bone? No, I ain't got nothing for you three right now."

Stew pulled out the measly pouch of coins the Mundanes had collected from the quest. He tossed it onto the table, drew a dagger, and pointed at the pouch. "Not that it matters anyway. We're not getting anything from any of the quests you give us. Hardly any money, and even worse loot."

Milos looked at them, confused. "If you guys are looking for better loot, you should be trying quests and not missions." He spoke as if he were reading from the *Middang3ard 101 Handbook*.

"What the fuck is the difference?" Stew growled.

Milos leaned in and twirled his spindly beard. He plopped his feet up on one of the empty chairs and groaned loudly as he adjusted his feet. His pain did nothing to disseminate his aura of smugness. "You don't know the difference between a mission and—"

Sandy absentmindedly levitated a few bread rolls and flicked one at Milos. "No, Milos. We do not know the difference between a quest and a mission. Will you please explain to us with your all-knowing wisdom what the fucking difference is?"

Milos glared at Sandy, the fun obviously taken out of his explanation. "The differences between the two are numerous. First and foremost, missions are broad, easy-going little shindigs that can be taken care of by the least experienced adventurers. Think of them as entry-level jobs. You can do them. I can do them. But it would make more sense for you to do them since I have the experience to warrant spending my time in other more interesting venues. You could say that it would be a waste of my time. Quests, on the other hand, are generally much more specific, require a shit-ton of know-how and offer larger rewards. They're generally assigned by veteran MERCs who see that you have the skills to get the job done or are invested in your personal growth, much like I am invested in you three."

Suzuki watched Milos suspiciously, the dwarf squirming under the pressure of his judgmental gaze. "Then why do you keep giving us shit missions?"

"As one of the purveyors of the Shire, I've got a backlog of missions." He chuckled. "Better you than me. Besides, not everyone wants to wake up at the crack of dawn and go fight a pack of undead rats."

"A dead-chief! You know, like a mischief but dead!" Suzuki shouted. "So let me get this straight. You're pawning those missions off on us because they're beneath you?"

Milos nodded. "But you get your cut."

"Cut?" Suzuki felt indignant rage bubbling up, making him want to do things to Milos that would go against his personal code of ethics. "We're not even getting paid for the full mission?"

"Well, I take a percentage for setting it up."

Suzuki jumped up from his seat. His mouth was moving before any sound came out, and he had to take a deep breath to calm himself. "How much?"

"How much what?" Milos asked.

"Your cut. How much?"

"Thirty percent."

"What the fuck are you, an app store? We want that thirty percent. Now."

Milos considered this before clearing his throat and tapped his crutches irritably on the ground. "I'll give you fifteen."

"Twenty-five." Suzuki folded his arms over his chest.

"Twenty," Milos countered.

"Twenty-five, or I'll show you another meaning for blue balls." Sandy cupped her left palm and lightning danced between her fingers.

"Fine, fine, twenty-five percent. Check's in the mail." Milos smiled like a used car salesman who just gave them the deal of a lifetime. "Anyway, if you want a quest, a real quest that'll give you the kind of loot you're looking for to upgrade your gear to be able to withstand some of the harder areas, you're going to want to talk to one of the older MERCs. They usually have a couple lying around that need to be taken care of."

"Why can't we just get one from you?"

Milos' eyes narrowed until they were rat-like and nearly lost behind his bushy eyebrows. "You whelps ask a lot of questions of a guy who's just trying to do you a solid," Milos growled, before he stood up, drained the last of his beer, and started to hobble away. "Next time you ingrates have any questions, direct them to someone else."

The Mundanes looked at each other with confused expressions. "We didn't ask you. You just came over and told us this shit," Suzuki said.

"Ingrates," Milos shouted as he walked off.

One of the barmaids came by carrying a tray of food. She dropped it off at the Mundanes' table without making eye contact and went on taking other orders.

Sandy looked warily at the plates of steaming food before grabbing a set of chopsticks and digging into the meal. "So, I guess we just have to bug some cool kids until they give us a shot at the glory. I'll check with Diana. I need her to take a look at my mask anyway. What about you guys?"

Stew shrugged. "I don't really know anyone."

Sandy patted Stew on the back and pushed the plate of

food toward him. She smiled in a sickeningly sweet way and spoke with a thick Texas accent. "Guess you're making friends today, buddy."

Stew grimaced, picked up a fork, and started eating. "Sounds fun." He groaned. "How about you, Suzuki?"

"I'll check around too. It's worth a shot, I guess."

The Mundanes looked around the bar as they tried to determine which MERC they were going to talk to. It was fairly obvious who the veterans were. Anyone with interesting armor had obviously been out in the field for a while. Now all they had to do was convince someone to give them a chance.

## 3

Suzuki stood up and stretched. "OK, new plan. Everyone's got until the end of the day to find a quest. We meet back here tonight. Sound good?"

"Good enough for me." Stew scanned the bar. "Sandy, babe, how about you and me team-up and find us one ultimate fucking quest. You in? You wanna come with me?"

"You know I'm in, babe," she said.

Suzuki left Sandy and Stew to figure out what they were going to do. He had no idea who to talk to about getting a mission. José and his party? Suzuki didn't want to actually approach José's party, the Four Horsemen, because, to be frank, he was intimidated by them.

The last time Suzuki had any real interaction with José was when the skinny, bearded MERC complimented him on his smell-altering dongle. José had pointed out that most predators hunted with their noses and that being able to mask or change your smell could make you into the ultimate assassin.

Suzuki had used that advice when fighting a gang of krampuses by changing his smell to that of a baby krampus and using the darkness to sneak close enough to one of the beasts to stab it.

It had been golden advice, proving José's worth.

Which meant Suzuki was now completely in awe of José and the thought of fucking up some quest José assigned terrified him.

There were a lot of MERCs who looked like they had their shit together, but the Four Horsemen were on a completely different level.

They walked around as if they owned Middang3ard, and they looked the part as well. "Intimidating" was not the word for the Four Horsemen. They were an example of what could be accomplished in Middang3ard.

He couldn't approach them, not for his first quest. So Suzuki thought about other MERCs to approach before remembering someone who hung around the Four Horsemen but wasn't actually one of them.

She was a sleazy-looking elf who seemed to always be standing within earshot of the Four Horsemen. Always nearby, but always apart, too. Suzuki had never heard her speak, but he assumed she was a veteran from the gear she wore. It was nothing like what the rest of the recruits were walking around in.

Suzuki started looking for her.

Across the bar, Sandy and Stew were still looking around for someone to talk to. Stew would approach a table, clear his throat, and wait for someone to say something. The MERCs sitting at the table generally ignored him or awkwardly coughed until he moved on to the next.

After visiting a couple more tables, Sandy motioned for Stew to follow her to a corner of the bar. "We could just go talk to Diana. I want to ask about the mask anyway."

Stew shrugged his shoulders and tried to avoid Sandy's

eyes. He didn't speak until she grabbed him by the jaw and forced him to look up at her. "She gives me the creeps. Besides, we can figure this out all on our own."

"What about her is creepy?"

"The whole magic skin thing. It's real fucking creepy."

"You know, that might be what happens to my skin...eventually."

Stew coughed theatrically and pointed over to a group of MERCs. "Hey," he suggested, "I think those guys might be a good place to start."

The MERCs Stew pointed out were sitting at a table in a corner of the bar. They were all human and were trading their loot back and forth. Stew and Sandy walked up to them, and Stew cleared his throat until the MERCs stopped talking amongst themselves.

"We're looking for a quest." Stew tried to sound like he was there to do them a favor.

One of the humans leaned forward. He was a lanky man with greasy hair and a thin mustache. His eyes were sunk deep in his skull, but somehow, when he smiled, it was nearly angelic.

"Oh, you are?" the greasy MERC asked. "And you knew that we were just the folk for you to come to, aye?"

"Aye."

"Well, what level of work are you looking to put in?"

"We're looking to upgrade. So whatever will help us do that."

The greasy MERC appraised Stew and Sandy's armor. After a few moments, he leaned forward and spit into his tankard of beer.

"I think we got the quest just for you."

Suzuki had found the elven MERC sitting by herself near the front of the bar where the barkeep Wendy doled out drinks. The elf wore the robes of a mage, but they had been upgraded in the way that only veterans were able to afford. The robes were so finely made that if Suzuki were to look closely, he could see each individual stitch linking each piece of cloth to the next.

Suzuki took a seat next to the mage and tried to keep from stammering as he spoke. "Excuse me."

"Yes?" The elf didn't look up for her drink.

Suzuki offered his hand. "Suzuki."

"Adeline." She spoke in an absentminded way, as if she were deep in thought. Or stoned. It occurred to Suzuki that she might be on drugs.

"Um, I was wondering if you had any quests that needed to be fulfilled?"

Adeline laughed and tossed her hair to the side, looking at Suzuki for the first time. "You're asking me if I have any quests?"

"Yeah. You know, I'm just checking around like us new recruits do."

"That is ideal," she said, snapping her fingers, "Because I am looking for someone to take care of something for me. It's personal, which is why I haven't talked to any other MERCs about the whole subject. But there is something I do believe I can use your services for."

Suzuki let his guard down a little and leaned over the table. He wanted to look certain of the skills he had to offer, but not over-eager. This felt like a good middle-ground for him.

"Well," he said, "how can I be of service to you?"

"It's a very, very personal quest. We'll need to talk in private."

The greasy MERC led Sandy and Stew out the back of the Red Lion. He extended his hand to Stew. "Jerry. Nice to meet you."

Stew and Sandy introduced themselves. They stood in silence for a few moments as Jerry looked over his shoulders at the Red Lion and then up to the moon and the stars. "So, how do you like the booze in there?"

Sandy shrugged and scrunched her face as she tried to figure out what Jerry was getting at. "Uh, it's good."

"Yeah. Good. Just good. Nothing exceptional. Nothing amazing. Just good. What if I told you I had access to great beer? Not just great. Life-changing."

Stew nodded in appreciation. "I'd ask why you hadn't opened up a bar yourself."

"Well, that's the thing. I had one a long time ago," Jerry said. "But you know, it didn't pick up like I thought it would. It eventually got bought out. This is where you come in. My special batch of booze is still at the other bar. I need someone to sneak in and get me a keg of that beer. I can tell you exactly where it's at. You just need to sneak into the bar, grab it, and bring it back to me. Then you get your cash, and I'll...I'll even make you part-owners. You'll get equity."

Sandy narrowed her eyes dubiously at the greasy MERC. "I need to consult my associate," Sandy said as she walked off and motioned for Stew to follow her.

"So, I'm your associate now?"

"Oh, shut up. Do you want me to introduce you as my boyfriend to everyone?"

Stew shrugged. "Yeah, sort of. I mean, it would be cool if you did but yeah, whatever..."

"You are so obnoxiously cute when you're jealous. What do you think about this guy? Sounds kind of sketchy to me."

"I thought so too, but GB says he knows the guy. He's definitely a veteran. And Milos did say that it was the vets who had the good quests."

Sandy pursed her lips. "I don't know about this. I mean, what kind of loot are we going to get from bringing back some beer?"

"Who knows? You would have thought we would have got some kickass loot from exploring an ancient crypt, and you saw how that turned out."

"Yeah, guess you're right. So we're doing this?"

"Hell, yeah." Stew's face lit up in that way it did when he was about to do something stupid and knew it. "Plus we get to see what else is in this weird-ass village. It'll be kind of like a date."

Sandy and Stew returned to Jerry and agreed to take the mission. Jerry clapped his hands together and pulled out a map. The map detailed the layout of a bar a couple miles down in the MERC encampment. "Here's a map of the whole city." He pointed to a series of parallel lines on the map. "All of these pathways go through the city. Some of the older MERCs own houses around here. It doesn't make sense to be renting every night if you can afford to live someplace. There's a mages' guild on the other side of the encampment next to the fighters' guild. Then there's a temple for the religious folks. And right next to that is my old bar, The Last Ale."

Sandy mimed drinking a beer and choking. "That sounds a little fatalistic."

"Eh, I was never much for names," Jerry agreed. "But you can make sense of it on the map. Very straightforward.

Very easy to understand. You just gotta get in, grab my batch of booze, and bring it back to me. Easy-peasy, right?"

"Sure, sounds easy enough."

Jerry handed the map to Sandy. She scanned the information into her HUD and handed the document back to Jerry. "All right," she said, "let's get going."

———

Suzuki followed the elf mage to her room. When they entered, the mage quickly walked behind Suzuki and shut the door. Then she went over to the bed and sat down on it, hiking her robes up a bit. Suzuki tried not to stare at her ankles. He tried to pull off a casual cough before walking over to the desk, where there were a couple of framed photographs.

Suzuki picked up one of the frames, but before he could get a good look, the mage jumped to her feet and ran over to the desk, turning one of the photographs over, placing it face down.

Suzuki stepped back and tried to keep his reaction as even as possible. He was freaked out, and wasn't sure exactly what was going on. He wasn't often invited to a woman's bedroom.

Actually, he'd *never* been invited into a woman's room—although this was an elf. Maybe they had different social standards and etiquette. Either way, covering the picture so suddenly was probably weird across cultures.

When the mage noticed that Suzuki was shifting his weight between his feet excessively, she laughed, a nasally high-pitched sound. "Sorry. It's a really awkward picture of me that I forgot was there."

"So, about this quest?"

"Oh, yes. I completely forgot for a second. The quest. I lost something very special to me. It's extremely valuable, and I haven't been able to get it myself. There've been a lot of complications. I'm looking for someone who doesn't mind getting a little bit dirty to help me out."

Suzuki internally sighed to himself. It sounded like another mission that a high-level MERC just didn't have time to do. "I'd love to help, but I'm kind of looking for a quest, not a mission. I'm trying to get some armor and weapon upgrades as soon as possible and—"

"Oh, this *is* a quest. It's not something easy to take care of. It might take all night. Maybe even a day or two. And it is very delicate."

"All right, what is it?"

"I need you to climb into my walls and retrieve my lost pearl," the elf said as if that was the most normal request in the world.

"Uh, climb into your walls?"

"Yes, my walls. Do you think you can do that?"

Adeline smiled sweetly at Suzuki as she removed her gloves and placed them carefully on the side of the bed. Suzuki was even less certain of what was going on than he had been a few minutes ago. He didn't want to read into the situation, but he felt he was getting a ton of different signals. "Yeah, I guess I could do that."

Adeline squealed as she jumped up and clapped her hands. She turned around, and when she faced Suzuki again, she was holding a wand. "Perfect."

"Huh. I haven't seen many of those on Middang3ard."

"You obviously haven't seen many elves, then. Close your eyes."

"Close my—"

"It's going to be very bright, and it might burn a bit."

"Wait, what?"

There was a bright green flash, and Suzuki covered his eyes as the green light filled the room. When he opened his eyes, he couldn't see anything. He stumbled, then reached out to try and get hold of something. Suddenly, he fought a tight grasp on his ribs. It felt as if a giant had reached out and wrapped him in his arms. He struggled to breathe, and then he felt himself falling through the air. His vision was coming back, but it was still blurry. He hit the ground with a heavy thud. The wind went right out of him, and he coughed loudly as he tried to catch his breath.

Something tapped Suzuki lightly on the butt. Then it tapped again, this time more aggressively. Suzuki stumbled to his feet and started to walk forward, still trying to make sense of all the blurry shapes before him. The most that he could see was that he was walking toward some kind of oval opening. He turned around and tried to walk backward, but he felt the giant hand pushing him forward again. It was much stronger than he. The hand shoved him into the opening, and everything went dark as Suzuki tried to breathe. Wherever he was, it was sweltering, and nearly pitch-black inside.

"Perfect," a voice from above boomed.

---

Sandy and Stew wandered around the wooden pathways of the MERC encampment. They were lit by floating lanterns that cast an orange glow over the swamp. Sandy and Stew held hands as they walked.

Frogs croaked and birds chirped in the distance, and occasionally there was a loud splash as something jumped in and out of the water. There were small houses all up and down the paths. Some of the houses were built back from the pathway, and seemed to be floating above the swamp. Their lights looked like giant fireflies in the night.

Sandy stopped walking and leaned over the railing. "You know, this isn't too bad of a date."

Stew put his arm around Sandy's shoulder and nodded. "Nah, it's not. Super chill. It's kind of nice to have some alone time."

Sandy kissed Stew on the cheek, and they started walking again. "I know they're not the same, but it feels like the same shit. The whole reason that I wanted to come to Middang3ard was to be something I couldn't be at home. Now, however, it just feels like we're errand boys. People keep talking about how we're taking on the Dark One, but what have we really done? I've lost track of how many rats I've killed since I've been here. I like rats. I used to have pet rats at home. I don't want to spend all my time out here killing rats. Even undead ones."

Stew pulled Sandy in closer. "At least Beth was out there actually fighting the Dark One. That's what the military says, at least."

"Yeah, I guess. Who knows what MERCs say they're out there doing?"

In the distance, the two Mundanes could hear people cheering and laughing. They followed the sound past the ornate library floating to their right. The bar wasn't too far ahead. It was sandwiched between two smaller buildings.

Sandy pointed at the buildings up ahead. "Those must be the fighters' and mages' guilds. You ever think about joining one of those?"

"Not really. I mean, I did just hear about them. Besides, I don't know. One of the reasons I was always on *Middang3ard*

VR was 'cause...you know, I'm not too good with the whole meeting people thing."

"Oh, really? You were good at meeting me," Sandy said.

"Meeting people in VR was easy. I just pretended I was the kind of person I wanted to be. But it's harder here."

"Yeah, 'cause you're actually out here."

"Exactly." Stew kissed her forehead.

Sandy looked up at Stew, "So you think everything in the *Middang3ard* VR was just an act?"

Stew shrugged as they turned the corner and closed in on the bar. "I don't feel nearly as charismatic," he admitted. "At least in VR, I could just dump experience points into it. Trying to talk to strangers just doesn't have the same feel."

"I prefer you IRL, even if you are a massive, neurotic nerd. Now come on, let's get this beer."

The Last Ale was decrepit on the outside. Its windows were broken, and the rotted wood front door was barely hanging on by its hinges. As Sandy reached out to open the door, a dwarf sailed through the window and landed in a pile of broken glass beside her.

The dwarf stood and shook the glass from his beard. He took out a flask and took a large swig from it, then he turned to Sandy and Stew and stumbled forward. "Ah, newbs. Welcome to the Last Ale. Name's Fyodor. I'm the owner. Come on in."

"If you're the owner, why were you thrown out?" Stew asked.

"A smart-ass, are you? You misbehave, you get chucked out, owner or not. And I was misbehaving." Fyodor staggered to the front door before turning to his side and vomiting off the path. "You might not want to wait for me."

Sandy and Stew stepped into the Last Ale. The

atmosphere was drastically different from the Red Lion. There were fewer MERCs, and many more empty seats.

Most of the patrons were sitting at the front of the bar, talking quietly with each other. There was a dartboard near the bar with a few axes embedded in it. Some of the MERCs looked up when Stew and Sandy walked in. They stared for a little bit before turning back to their beers.

---

Suzuki pulled up his HUD and his armor magically rolled over his body as if it were made out of individual pieces that had a mind of their own. He left his helmet off. Wherever he was, it was too stuffy. He pulled out his sword. *Hey, Fred? I can't really see too well here. Can you help me?*

Fred uncurled in Suzuki's mind. It felt like there was a muscle in Suzuki's head that was tightening and untightening. *Fire, magic, or night vision?*

*Dealer's choice.*

*Very well. Unsheathe your sword.*

Suzuki did as he was told and the blade caught fire. *Good choice*, Suzuki mused, feeling the heat of the flame.

The flame illuminated the small space that Suzuki was standing in. The walls were close to him. He held the flame up to the walls to see what they were made of. A mucous-like membrane covered the walls. Suzuki placed his hand on the membrane.

A trail of mucus stuck to Suzuki's finger as he raised it to his nose to smell. It was nothing that he recognized. *Fred. Do you have any idea what the hell this shit is?*

*I am an eldritch creature who has existed for nearly a thousand generations. Unfortunately for you, I have not wasted my entire existence trying to catalog the various kinds of mucus which you can run across.*

*Okay, well, do you have any idea where we are?*

Suzuki could feel Fred considering his question before answering. *No. I was hit with the same spell as you. Whoever cast it has a high degree of power. It is not an easy feat to stun me.*

*Yeah, yeah,* Suzuki said drolly. *I've heard it all before. You're an all-powerful eldritch demon.*

*Imp. And nigh all-powerful, if you're being specific.*

*Hmmm. Well, wherever the hell I am, I guess I should be looking for that pearl.*

*Next time, you should invest in a contract,* Fred snarled. *I'd hate to think what would happen if you were to find this pearl and not be given your proper reward.*

*Do MERCs always pull this shit?*

*From my experiences, MERCs should only be trusted if there is an obvious thing they can gain from you. But like any other group of mortals, there are some who are trustworthy and others who will take advantage of you. Those tend to be my favorite. A clever MERC is much more useful than a dullard.*

*What did you think of her?* Suzuki asked.

*It would have been a better idea to ask before you agreed. Now, if you will excuse me, all of this transmogrification has tired me out.*

*Wait, what do you mean?*

*You really don't know? Suzuki, we have been shrunk and are roughly the size of a rat at the moment,* Fred said. *Now leave me alone unless you need me for something other than a commentary.*

Suzuki could feel Fred retreating to the far recesses of his mind.

Recently, his relationship with the imp had improved.

This conversation was evidence of just that. Fred had grown more willing to answer questions and, on occasion, engage in conversation. That wasn't important at the moment, though. It was good to know that he could rely on Fred if he needed him, but there were more pressing issues at the moment.

The walls surrounding Suzuki were very close together. If they were any tighter, Suzuki would have had to turn sideways to make his way any further. Luckily, he had lost some weight since he first came to Middang3ard.

All of the running around to fulfill missions had been good for his body. Before coming to Middang3ard, he had had a very difficult time getting out of the house for anything other than the rare, spur-of-the-moment camping trip. He'd been living his life in a VR simulation. Being in the real-world version of the game had necessitated that he get in shape. The missions helped a lot, though. Constantly cleaning out vermin dens and running from giants was ideal for slimming and building cardio.

Suzuki thought about casting Find Target to hone in on the pearl but decided against it. It didn't seem like there were many options of where to go. There was forward or backward.

Casting would be a waste of valuable magic that he might need later. Also, he still wasn't certain where he was, nor did he know what he might be coming up against. It would be better to take his time, get familiar with the situation, and go from there.

This all would have been easier if Sandy and Stew were with him. Even if it was his responsibility to come up with ideas and plans, it was helpful to bounce ideas off of them.

Fred was pretty much useless in that department. So Suzuki was on his own for the first time in a very long time.

He had spent nearly every waking hour with Stew and Sandy since they had come to Middang3ard. He was surprised that he hadn't gotten annoyed by either of them yet. They were not quite friends, not quite family. Something better. That was how he thought of them. He'd never met anyone like Stew or Sandy. Other than Beth.

The walls around Suzuki suddenly vibrated. A pink electric current pulsed through the mucus hanging from them. The mucus shivered again as if the electric pulse had jumpstarted some latent life within it. Suzuki felt the heat of the enclosed space go up.

*I better hurry up and get the hell out of here*, he thought as he made his way through the long corridor, putting in an extra effort not to get any of the mucus on his skin. He put his helmet back on just to be safe.

Another electric pulse ran through the mucus, and this time the spark of electricity ran through his armor as well. He instinctively jumped to the side and fell against the wall. When he pulled himself from the sticky mucus, he could see an imprint of his body. "Gross," he muttered.

"Gross," echoed down the corridor, seemingly gaining more voices as the sound traveled.

---

Sandy and Stew sat down at the bar. The MERCs in the room continued to eyeball them with suspicion. Most were women.

Anytime Stew looked up and met their eyes, they would look away. Sandy didn't seem to notice. She waved over Fyodor, who had finally made his way back into his bar. His eyes were red and very wet as he climbed a stepstool so he could be eye level with the bar patrons. "What am I gonna get you two?"

Sandy held up two fingers. "Two, please."

"You want the regular ale, or you want your Last Ale?"

"What's the difference?" she asked.

"Regular is the same shit they serve over at that sissy bar, the Red Lion. The Last Ale? That'll knock your shoes off, give you halflings' feet, and then burn your hair off."

"Sounds pretty intense."

Fyodor puffed out his chest before suddenly grabbing his mouth and stifling his gagging. Once the urge to vomit had subsided, he breathed a sigh of relief. "Yep, family recipe going back for nearly ten generations. Got a goddamn lineage in each barrel."

"We'll take two of those."

"I'll be back with 'em."

As Fyodor walked away, Sandy leaned close to whisper in Stew's ear. "That's gotta be it. We can get a taste, so we know what we're looking for in the back."

"How are we going to get it out?"

Sandy considered this. "Well, we can't just have you carry it out. It'd be too noticeable. And it probably weighs a ton. I could levitate it out."

"What am I supposed to do?"

"Distract them."

"How am I going to do that?" Stew asked.

"Didn't you say you wanted to work on your charisma?"

---

Suzuki pushed himself through the tightening corridor. He wasn't sure how long he had been walking. His feet were sticky. Whatever mucus was on the walls was also on the ground. Lifting his feet was becoming increasingly difficult. He sighed and told himself it wouldn't be for much longer. He could see a light down at the end of the corridor, and it was only a few feet away.

Another pulse of electricity went through the mucus on the walls and floor. This time it jolted Suzuki with enough energy to cause him to bounce back and forth against the walls. He felt like a pinball stuck on a broken bumper.

Once the shock left Suzuki's body, he started toward the light again. Finally, he pushed out of the corridor. He fell forward, right into a pile of mucus covering a pink, fleshy mound. His helmet instantly clogged with mucus and he rolled to the side and hit his HUD so his helmet would disappear and restore his ability to breathe.

The air was thick and humid. Suzuki tried to flick off the mucus covering his arms and hands, but it was caked on too thick. He accepted that he just had to feel like a walking booger.

The room that Suzuki was in was drenched in the mucus discharge. There were fleshy mounds sporadically throughout the room, and they rose to about Suzuki's waist. They were not only on the floor, but they also covered the walls and the ceiling.

Approaching one of the mounds, he poked it with his sword. The fleshy mound jiggled and swelled.

Suzuki quietly willed his sword to lose its flames before sheathing it. Then he wandered around through the room until he heard a very quiet squeaking. Now that he was in the dark again, he decided it was a good time to use some of that magic he'd been hesitant to cast. "Find Target," Suzuki muttered, and a bright gold light shot out of his chest and zipped around the room until it found its way to the corner of the room where the pearl should be.

Suzuki followed the light, but in the corner, instead of a pearl, there was a rat stuck to the wall of the room, encased in the pink mucus.

When the rat saw Suzuki, it thrashed wildly, its nose twitching excitedly. All that kept the rat in place was the thick layer of mucus covering its body.

Suzuki pulled up his HUD and scrolled through the menus until he came across his scent modifier. It was the upgrade Beth had sent him when he first got accepted into the MERC program. His scent was currently set to "fifteen-year-old scotch." Suzuki focused, and the scent modifier flickered and changed to "rat."

The rat encased in the mucus stopped freaking out. It sniffed the air twice and then looked at Suzuki, who was walking toward it. Using his dagger, Suzuki cut the rat out of the mucus. The rat fell to the floor and scurried around in a circle, sniffing Suzuki three or four times before finally settling down, watching him.

After sheathing his dagger, Suzuki tried to wipe some of the mucus off his body. "You're getting off lucky today. I've killed enough rats for a lifetime."

With the rat free, the find spell light continued into a hole that had been blocked by the captured rat. Suzuki sheathed his sword and squeezed through it. The rat followed him closely. "Great. Gone from killing rats to babysitting them."

## 4

T he Last Ale was served in a tankard that Fyodor took great care in filling in front of the two Mundanes. Once the ale had been poured, Fyodor went to the back and came out with a torch that had a bright blue flame. Sparks circled it.

Fyodor climbed back on top of his stepstool, showing the Mundanes the blue flame. "This fire has been part of my family tradition for longer than any of my tribe care to remember. The fire is added to every time that one of the tribe members die. When we leave our tribe, we take a little bit of the fire with us and promise that we will never let it go out. When I brought the fire here, I started adding a little bit of fuel to it every time a MERC was lost to the Dark One. When you drink your Last Ale, you're part of my tribe, part of my family, just like every other MERC who takes a sip."

Fyodor touched the torch to the tankards, and the liquid's surface went up in blue flames. "Drink up!"

Stew and Sandy looked at each other apprehensively. Then Stew grabbed his drink and downed it. Sandy did the same. They sat there for a moment, and then blue flames erupted all over their bodies. The flames extinguished themselves within a few seconds.

Stew slammed his empty tankard on the table and jumped to his feet. He was possessed by an unknown energy. "Goddamn. Let's drink another one."

"That's what I like to hear! How about you, lass?" There's more whenever you're ready for round two."

Sandy leaned over and kissed Stew on the cheek. "A little too strong for me. I'm going to hit the little lasses' room." Then she leaned over and whispered to Stew, "You know what to do. Use that manly charm you're always talking about."

As Sandy walked off, Stew looked down the length of the bar. The patrons were almost exclusively female halflings and gnomes. Stew swallowed and tried to figure out just what his manly charm was. He'd been saying he had it for years, but this was the first time that he'd ever been called out on it before. There must be something there. It got Sandy to pay attention to him. Now all he had to figure out was how to get everyone else in the bar to do the same.

Stew cleared his throat theatrically and put his hands on his hips. Then he stuffed them into his pockets. "Do you guys have karaoke out here?"

"You gotta drink before you speak."

Stew grabbed the flaming drink in front of him. He downed it in one gulp again.

"You were saying?" the dwarf asked.

"Karaoke. You ever heard of it?"

"Can you kill it?"

"No, it's more like—"

"Can you eat it?"

"No, it's not—"

"Not sure I'm interested. What good is something in a bar that can't be killed, drunk, eaten, or fucked? I'm right, aren't I, MERCs?"

There was a lazy cheer from across the bar as the MERCs raised their glasses and chuckled.

"You might want to check into it," Stew said. "Especially with all the halflings you got in here. Might liven the place up a bit. Maybe get some more business."

"Help improve business, you say? Maybe even give that hoity-toity Red Lion a run for their money? Show this town where the real party is at? All right, boyo, I'm all ears."

"It's real simple. It's kind of like a sing-along."

"Like for children?"

"No, not for kids."

"But children do sing-a-longs."

"Not just kids. Halflings. Halflings do sing-a-longs all the time."

The halfling next to Stew perked up her ears. She leaned over and slammed her beer on the table. "What are you saying about halflings looking like kids?"

"No, no, I was just saying that halflings sing."

"You saying halflings sing like kids?"

"No! Nothing like that." Stew shook his head. This conversation wasn't going to plan. Not that he had a plan to follow. "I was just saying that halflings like to sing."

"Aye, everyone knows that. Why you making a news bulletin about it?"

Stew threw his hands up, visibly annoyed. Then he figured out what he had to do. He turned to Fyodor. "I'll take another."

Fyodor poured another Last Ale. "Good man."

Stew sipped his ale, narrowing his eyes like he thought an old-school bard would have done. Stoke the flames of intrigue. "It's an old human tradition. Older than most. We gather in bars all around the world. After we have a couple of drinks, someone pulls out a guitar, and—"

"Guitar?"

"Or lute. Anything, really. We pull it out and start singing. Everyone joins in, the entire bar. And they keep drinking. People love to sing and drink."

Fyodor eyed the MERCs sitting at the bar. "Yes, yes, everyone likes to sing and drink. Hold on, I'll be right back."

Fyodor stumbled into the back room of the bar. He came back within a few moments carrying a lute. He thrust the lute in front of Stew. "So you gonna show us how this whole karaoke thing works?"

Stew stared at the lute. His heart was thumping in his chest, and the halflings who were sitting at the bar were looking at him eagerly. Stew swallowed the lump that was forming in his throat and grabbed the lute. "Yeah," he said. "I'll show you how it works."

***

Sandy was in the cellar of The Last Ale. She had been sneaking around the bar after her bathroom break and had found a staircase leading down to the dim, dank cellar. The walls were covered with barrels, some which looked noticeably aged from long before her time.

She strolled through the cellar, which stretched as far as the length of the bar. The whole cellar must have lined up with the rest of the bar's floor plan. There were no discerning features to any of the barrels. She had no idea how she was going to pick out which one she was supposed to lift from the rest of them.

"Fuck," she whispered under her breath. "Niv, you think you can give me a hand?"

There was a loud pop, and her familiar stepped out from behind her. Niv was an amaraj, a large rabbit with a foot-long horn in the middle of his forehead. His eyes were blood red, and his fur was as white as snow. He hopped out so that Sandy could see him.

Niv scratched his nose with his back feet. "What can I help you with?"

Sandy knelt so she was at eye level with her bunny-unicorn familiar. "I need you to help me find this beer." She blew into Niv's face.

Niv coughed loudly, and his nose started twitching uncontrollably. "Please, warn me before you overload me with scents."

"Sorry."

Niv sniffed and then bounded into the cellar. Sandy ran to keep up with him. The amaraj hopped through aisle after aisle of barrels, turning corners as fast as he could go. It was all that Sandy could do to keep up with him. Suddenly, he stopped in front of a stack of barrels that stood against the cellar walls.

"Is this it?" Sandy asked.

Niv nodded. "It's the closest to the booze that was on your breath. Is this for the quest you and Stew are on?"

"Yep." Sandy tapped one of the barrels with a spout that connected to it using her Mend spell. "This should be it. Maybe I should test it, just to make sure."

Niv winked at Sandy. "Just to make sure."

"Yeah, just to make sure."

Sandy searched around the cellar until she found a ladle. She grabbed it, dipped it into the barrel, and withdrew a ladle full of ale for herself. She sipped it gingerly, belched loudly, and then covered her mouth in a last-ditch effort at politeness. "Damn, that shit is strong. Even stronger than whatever Fyodor is selling up there."

"Do you think you could get a little for me? Just a nip."

"Sure, little dude."

Sandy scooped another ladleful of ale, knelt, and held it out for Niv to drink. The rabbit guzzled the ale down quickly. "Yep, that's the stuff. How are you getting it out?"

"Well, I only need one barrel, so we'll take the one that we opened. I was going to levitate it out."

"You know how levitation spells work, right?"

"Broadly speaking, yes," Sandy said.

"If you cast a levitation spell, it'll be similar to you actually lifting the barrel. You'll have to focus on it *a lot* to make sure that you don't drop it or spill it all."

"Gotcha."

Sandy raised her hands, and they began to glow. "I cast Levitation."

The ale barrel started to glow. It floated a couple of inches off the ground. Sandy turned to walk away, and her hands suddenly dropped to the ground as if she were being pulled down by a large weight. "Holy shit, that is heavy."

---

Suzuki wandered past the pink walls of wherever he was. At this point, he was no longer concerned about finding out. He had cast Find Target a while ago and was marching after the golden light. The rat was still following after him, nearly close enough to trip over Suzuki's plodding boots. "Quest, my ass."

The light suddenly disappeared. Suzuki checked around. From what he could gather, he was behind something that looked like an electric stove. He turned to look at the rat. "Does any of this look familiar to you?"

The rat stared at Suzuki with unblinking eyes.

"Yeah, that's what I thought."

There were traces of the gold light that led up the back of the stove. Along with the trace of gold, a pinkish skin-textured sludge was pouring out of the back.

*Guess that's where all that junk is coming from*, Suzuki thought to himself. Well, might as well get to it.

Suzuki went to the back of the stove and started scaling it. He thanked whoever was listening that he was stronger in Middang3ard than on Earth. This would have taken all of his strength at home, but now he was able to easily make the climb. That didn't mean that it wasn't tiring, just not as exhausting as it could have been.

The rat scurried up the stove behind Suzuki.

The pink, fleshy, juicy mucus that was coming from the stove gave Suzuki a little bit of extra leverage to pull himself up. It didn't take too long until he came to the opening the pink stuff was pouring out of.

Suzuki pulled himself up and rolled into the stove. The rat came right after him, tripping over him so that they both went rolling around in the dark. Suzuki pulled out his sword, and the blade caught flame. The rat initially recoiled from the fire, but when it saw that Suzuki held the blade, it seemed to calm down. Suzuki instinctually reached out and petted the rat on the head. "It's going to be okay, buddy. We're gonna get through this."

He scanned the room, and his eyes widened in horror. They were inside a stove that had fallen into disrepair. The inside of the stove was covered in the oozing pink slime he had waded through earlier. In the middle was a person-sized mound that had risen from the rest of the gunk.

On top of the mound were three shining pearls, each roughly the size of Suzuki's chest. He assumed they might have been only marble-sized if he hadn't been so small. Suzuki slowly approached the pearls in the center of the room, trying to pay close attention to what was happening around him. He wasn't sure what could have created this kind of mess, but he was certain that he didn't want to be ambushed by whatever it was.

The pearls perched on the flesh mound. Suzuki reached out for them, but stopped when he heard a loud screech from above. He looked up. Above him, in a mass of tentacles and dripping sludge, something stirred. Just as suddenly as Suzuki heard the screech, something large and hairy fell to the floor. Suzuki backed up as the thing stretched out and stood to its full height. It had eight legs resembling needles that were covered in thick, coarse hair.

The top half of this creature was a naked woman, equally covered in hair. A massive head sat on the thing's shoulders. It was part human, part spider. It had a slack jaw that was a mix of a human's mouth and a spider's mandibles, presently dripping thick, pink mucus.

The spider-woman had eight eyes and two arms in addition to the eight legs that held her up. She screeched as she scurried over to the pearls and wrapped them in silk webbing.

Suzuki shouted as he leapt forward. "Oh no, you don't," he cried as he jumped through the air, slashing at the spider-woman. The rat bounded after him.

The spider-woman dodged to the side and slapped Suzuki across the face, sending him flying across the room.

Then she reached out and grabbed the rat, causing the creature to squeak loudly as she snatched it up in her arms and sank her teeth into it. She dropped the rat on the oven floor, where it convulsed, foaming at the mouth.

As the rat twitched, the skin around its stomach started to bubble. Then eight legs shot out, sending blood spewing everywhere. Its jaw broke in two and spider mandibles came through its skin, snapping uncontrollably. Six more eyes opened across the rat's head.

"Are you fucking kidding me?"

---

Stew stood on top of one of the bar tables, gripping the lute in his hand. The halflings and gnomes were gathered around the table, murmuring to each other. Their eyes were shifting. They did not look like they had hope for this "karaoke" Stew kept talking about. Fyodor brought Stew another Last Ale and put it on the table. Stew cleared his throat and turned to the crowd. "This song is a classic tale of the treacheries of love. Please, turn your ears toward me!"

Stew cleared his throat again. What came out surprised even him. Stew sang, his voice floating up and filling the bar as if an angel had come down from heaven with a knowledge of cheesy pop songs.

He belted the opening verse of *Hey Jude*, his voice quivering at first and then rising to a swell as he belted out the chorus, strumming the lute as he sang.

When the chorus was over, he looked down at the halflings and the gnomes. Their faces reflected only disinterest. He turned internally to his familiar, GB, the quiet stone gargoyle with the face of an ass.

*GB, you gotta help me. All I know is human songs. Halflings don't give a shit about human songs. What do you have?*

*There's this ditty I know about the old gnome kingdoms,* his familiar mused.

*Tell me. I'll sing it while you do.*

Stew started strumming the lute again. The tune that came out was slow and melancholy, something like the sound of first love gone sour. He cleared his throat again and started singing again.

*"It was a time before a time we lost*
*When gnomes were known to boast*
*We feed ourselves on beets and roots*
*And leeks and corn and shoots.*
*A maiden was once wed to a king*
*Who felt his power slip and wane*
*He called his court and strode to war*
*Upon the castle walls he—"*

A gnome close to Stew spat on the floor and sneered. "We've heard that one before," the gnome shouted. "What else do you got?"

"Uh," Stew stammered, "how about this?"

GB groaned loudly and started reciting another song to Stew.

"How's this one? An old halfling folktale."

*"There was a ring, we've heard it all*
*Nice and shiny and gold.*
*The ass who held it in his palm*
*Grew stinky, fat, and old.*
*He swore by his wealth*
*It was good for his health*
*But he always had—"*

One of the halflings smashed his tankard on the ground. "Who the hell are you to be poking fun at our ancestors?"

"I'm sorry." Stew fumbled as he turned to face the halflings behind him. The crowd was starting to get surly.

Stew hadn't been in a barfight before, but he could sense one brewing now.

*GB,* he said, directing his thoughts toward his familiar. *You gotta help me out, man. I'm bombing hard.*

*There's a lot of...racial politics that I'm not sure I really understand well enough—*

A gnome was making his way toward the table Stew was standing on. His eyes had murder in them, and he stumbled over his own feet in the way of the experienced heavy drinker.

"Looks like your *karaoke* is just a way to come in here and insult us small races," the gnome slurred.

"No, no, hold on! I got one. This is a classic human song!" And then he belted out the only song that came to his mind.

*"The wheels on the bus go round and round,*
*Round and round, round and round.*
*All through the town.*
*The babies on the bus go wah wah wah..."*

Stew had launched into the loudest, most boisterous rendition of *The Wheels on the Bus* ever sung, belting out the lyrics as loud as he could while he chicken-walked on the table, plucking the strings of his lute so hard he thought they were going to break.

The murmuring in the bar had stopped. The gnomes and the halflings looked up at Stew as if they had just been given a divine revelation. One of the halflings raised his drink into the air. "Hey," he shouted. "Now I like this one!"

The halflings and gnomes were picking up the lyrics as he sang them. They were singing along with him in a matter of seconds. Stew started in on the next verse, hoping that he could remember the entire song.

Suzuki squared off against the spider-woman and her newly created spider-rat. He'd never fought something with so many legs, let alone two of them.

*At least they don't have any weapons*, Suzuki thought . He didn't even want to imagine how many axes and swords could be wielded between the rat and the woman. There were far too many appendages to keep track of. He circled the two creatures, his sword and shield raised high. It couldn't be said who was going to attack first. Suzuki wished that Stew and Sandy were with him. Whatever they were going through, it couldn't be nearly as bad as this.

The spider-rat leapt forward, scurrying along the floor with its grotesquely hairy legs. It slammed into Suzuki just as he managed to use his shield to block the attack. The spider-rat flipped over on its side, and Suzuki moved to stab it through its abdomen. As he raised his sword, the spider-rat shot a wad of sticky silver webbing.

Suzuki raised his hand, and the webbing hit him with enough force to stick his hand to his helmet. He stumbled away, trying to rip his hand from his face. As Suzuki struggled, the spider-rat tackled Suzuki to the ground, where they both rolled around, covering themselves with mucus.

Pushing the rat-spider over with his free hand, he rolled on top of it and drove his shield into the spider-rat's head. He lifted his shield and brought it down again.

Blood gushed from the spider-rat's open wound as Suzuki rolled off the dying creature and ripped his hand from his helmet. He leaned over, picked up his shield, and stared down the spider-woman.

Stew sat at the bar surrounded by the MERC gnomes and halflings. They were buying him drinks faster than he could finish them.

"So what is this 'bus' you speak of?" a gnome asked.

Stew leaned back with a professorial air. The only thing he was missing was a cigar and an open book. "It's like a giant yellow dragon, but it's the dragon's job to take children to school or back home...or anywhere, really."

"And these windshield wipers?"

"Er, those? Those are so the dragon can see in any weather. All across the Earth, buses are feared. No one knows when they are going to arrive or when they're going to leave." This wasn't true, but it made for a great story. "They come and go as they please. And their horns! Their horns are so loud that you can hear them for miles. And it's not just children they eat—"

"Wait, you said they transport children."

"They do transport children. But they have to eat the children first. Then the children, or anyone else that they're taking, sit in the stomach until the bus vomits or shits them out."

"Human children must be very brave," a gnome mused loudly.

"Extremely. To deal with our high school system? Extremely brave."

"What's a high school?"

"Uh, it's sort of like a prison."

"And you feed your children to these buses so that they may take them to prisons?"

"Exactly. Humans are hardcore. We don't fuck around when it comes to child-rearing."

The spider-woman and Suzuki circled each other. Fire spread over Suzuki's blade and shield. The heat caused him to sweat behind his helmet. His HUD read eighty percent chance of success. The spider-woman raised up on her hind legs and sprinted at Suzuki. She came down on him hard, her fists beating against his flaming shield as he tried to slice at her with his blade. She was too large, and there were too many legs. One pair swiped Suzuki's feet from under him.

Suzuki rolled to the side as the spider-woman slammed her feet into the soft, gooey floor. The spider-woman tried to back away, and Suzuki leapt at her, his sword aimed at her head.

He wasn't fast enough, though.

The spider-woman whipped around and smacked Suzuki with her spider ass. Suzuki skidded across the floor, trying to catch his breath. He coughed up blood and raised his hand in the air, willing his sword to appear above her head.

It worked. A golden sword appeared above the spider-woman and came crashing down as she leapt to the side, narrowly avoiding being impaled.

Suzuki doubled over.

He could hardly breathe, and he could feel that something was dislodged in his chest. The spider-woman also looked winded as she spat a wad of silk.

Suzuki rolled his shoulders and cracked his neck, then tore off toward her. The spider-woman answered his call, running toward Suzuki as well. They collided in a mass of legs and arms, Suzuki trying to get his arm around to stab the spider-woman in the back, the spider-woman wrapping Suzuki up in her legs, squirting silk all over his body. Suzuki fought through the silk with his sword and sliced off of one of the spider-woman's legs.

The screams of the spider-woman pierced the air, and she sank her teeth into Suzuki's chest. Suzuki screamed as well, and both of them tumbling around in each other's arms and legs. Silk, sweat, and blood spewed everywhere until Suzuki finally managed to detangle himself from the spider-woman's legs and scrambled to his feet.

The spider-woman swiped at him and knocked his helmet off. Suzuki wiped the blood from his brow and spat as he leaned forward with his sword. The spider-woman stared at Suzuki with murderous rage.

Suzuki sighed, sheathing his sword and raising his hands in the universal sign of "truce." "I'm tired of killing things for the day! Can I just take these?"

He pointed to the pearls in the center of the room.

The spider-woman growled and rose on her hind legs.

"Please? Or we could just keep doing this. I assure you, I can kill a spider."

The spider-woman relaxed. She leaned back on her hind legs and crossed her arms. Her mandibles moved, and something like language came from her mouth. "You...you strong fighter."

Suzuki hit his HUD and brought his helmet back up fast. He didn't want the spider-woman to see him blush. "Uh, you too."

"You good mate."

Was he seriously being hit on by a spider-woman? Middang3ard just got upgraded from weird to bat-shit crazy.

The spider-woman started backing away, pointing at the pearls. "Take them, but only if you come back one day. Soon."

Suzuki went to the middle of the room where the pearls were. "Yeah, will do," he lied. Then he took a good look at her, and now that they weren't fighting, he noted that she was actually kind of hot. Her upper half, at least. Maybe he *would* come back. Then he thought about what she had done to the rat, and he shook his head.

He definitely wouldn't be back.

As soon as he grabbed the pearls, Suzuki felt a fishhook in his stomach as the world swirled around him. When he tried to stand , vomit rose in his stomach. He held it down and looked around. He was back in the room with the elf. He pulled off his helmet and gasped for breath.

Adeline was sitting on the bed, her legs crossed tightly. She leaned forward and the fire in her eyes danced brightly. "Did you get them?"

Suzuki opened his hand. Three pearls the size of marbles were in his palm. "Just like I promised."

The door of the room suddenly whipped open. A woman who looked exactly like Adeline, only older, was standing on the threshold. The older elf dropped the vase of flowers she was holding. Glass and water splattered everywhere. "Saran, what the hell are you doing? And you?" the elf at the door said. "Who the hell are you?"

"Look, Mom," the girl said, holding out the pearls. "I found them. I did good, right? This means I'm no longer grounded?"

"Hell, no, young lady. First off, you were impersonating me again, and secondly—"

The mother elf launched into a rant, completely ignoring Suzuki and his pink mucus-covered body.

Suzuki sighed, sat on the bed, and hung his head. He almost wished he had stayed with the spider-woman. At least that was a relationship that made some sense to him.

Stew left the Last Ale to the sound of halflings and gnomes chanting *The Wheels on the Bus*. He saw a glimmer of light in the distance and ran toward it. Sandy was standing next to a barrel of ale. She was covered in sweat and panting loudly. "Come on. We should get going."

"Are you okay?"

"Yeah, yeah. Levitation spells are just harder than I thought. Let's go."

Sandy and Stew made their way back to the Red Lion. Stew helped to drag or push the barrel of ale that Sandy levitated. As they walked, Sandy mimed playing air guitar. She stuck out her tongue as she gave Stew the rock and roll devil horns. "That was really cute. I didn't know you could sing."

"Really? I sing around you all the time."

"Well, I knew you were capable of singing, I just didn't know that you could *sing*. You have a nice voice."

Stew smirked before breaking into a jazzy version of *The Wheels on the Bus*. Sandy laughed as they lugged the barrel back to the Red Lion. After half an hour or so, they were standing in front of the Inn. Stew opened the door and they managed to get the ale barrel back to where Jerry was waiting for them.

Jerry nearly pounced on the barrel. "You got it."

Sandy took the top of the barrel off, leaned over, and inhaled deeply. She smiled as if the smell of the booze could cure all of the world's ills. "Yep, we got it."

A couple of MERCs had taken notice of Stew and Sandy. They looked at the ale and started snickering. Jerry was struggling to keep from laughing.

Stew looked around the bar at the MERCs, who seemed to be in on some joke. Even GB was laughing. Stew threw up his hands and spun, ready to challenge any MERC who was laughing at him. "Is there something that I'm missing?"

Wendy, the owner of the Red Lion, came out from behind the bar. She looked at the barrel of ale. "What do we have here?"

Jerry sauntered over and rested his hand on the opened container. "Got us a new batch of the Last Ale."

"Finally. I've been waiting all weekend for this, Jerry."

Wendy cast a levitation spell, and the barrel floated off the ground. She gestured toward the back of the bar, and the barrel floated in that direction.

Stew shut his eyes tight enough for them to water and scratched his forehead. "Wait, that was our quest. We were supposed to—"

Wendy turned to Jerry and jabbed her finger at him. "Jerry? Did you pull this shit on a newb again?"

Jerry and the rest of the bar burst into laughter. "I'm sorry. They're just so green. It was hard not to. It makes so much more sense for a bunch of newbs to grab it than to waste my time."

Sandy crossed her arms and electricity crackled off her. "I don't quite see what's so funny."

Wendy shook her head and tried to hide her smile. "I'm sorry, hun. The Last Ale and Red Lion have been stealing these barrels back and forth from each other since we've been in business. It's just a prank, that's all."

Wendy walked off, but not before shoving Jerry out of the way. Stew and Sandy stood there in silence for a few moments as the laughing crowd dispersed.

Jerry shrugged his shoulders, chuckling as he walked away. "Thanks for the help."

Sandy threw her arms up in anger and started to storm

off after Jerry before Stew grabbed her. She shouted, "I should kick your fucking ass!"

There was nothing left to do. Stew threw his arm over Sandy's shoulder and kissed her on the forehead as he guided her to the front of the bar. "Come on. We were had. Let's just go get a beer."

Stew and Sandy shuffled over to the bar, hardly able to hold their heads up. Suzuki was already sitting at the bar, covered in pink slime. He looked at Stew and Sandy as the barbarian sat down with an explosion of air from the old seat cushion. "What happened to you?"

"Met a teen witch who was posing as her mom and spent the last four hours fighting a spider-chick for a couple of marbles."

"Was she hot?" Sandy asked.

"She was a teenager."

"I meant the spider-chick."

"I think she wanted to mate with me."

"So is that a yes or a no?"

"She was pretty hot. What about you guys?"

"Some asshole sent us on a beer run. Stew serenaded an entire bar of halflings, though."

Stew pulled his HUD up and swiped through the inventory. A lute appeared in his hand. "It was pretty sick. Thought I might grab a souvenir at least."

Wendy dropped off the Mundanes' beers. "For yer trouble tonight. A drink on the house."

Sandy groaned, looking down at her beer. Her brow was furrowed. "Fuckin' MERCs."

## 5

The Mundanes sat at the bar for the better part of the night. They licked their wounds and tried to cheer each other up, to no avail. They watched other MERCs come in from their missions and leave on quests.

The bar had the movement of a buzzing bee colony. Wendy occasionally came by and dropped off a few drinks, but the Mundanes were hardly interested in eating or drinking.

The MERCs were generally avoiding the part of the bar where Mundanes were. Their anger was noticeably simmering, and a few MERCs in the corner joked that they could feel heat radiating from the Mundanes.

Suzuki felt incredibly stupid. When he had found out that a teenage elf had hoodwinked him, it took everything he had to leave the room without striking out. It was the first time that Suzuki had actually thought of fighting a MERC.

"So what exactly happened?" Stew asked.

Suzuki shook his head and sighed. Ideally, he would want to avoid going over the last embarrassing evening of his life. "I really don't want to talk about."

"Come on, we gave you all the details."

"Your story was cool. Sandy got to play the thief, and you were a halfling rock star. Me? I just got tricked by a pre-teen."

"You said she was a teenager."

"How the fuck do you tell with an elf? They all look like they're seventeen. And their seventeen is like three hundred on top of that."

"So you're saying she was definitely legal," Sandy joked.

"Honestly, I would have taken the spider-chick over either of them. At least she had the guts to fight her own battles."

"You keep bringing up that spider-chick, dude. Did you really want to fuck her that bad?" Stew asked.

Suzuki shoved Stew and laughed while Stew tried to keep from falling off his chair. "Fuck off. She was pretty hot, though. In a Cronenberg kind of way."

"So now what are we going to do? We can't even tell which MERCs are going to give out real quests."

"I never thought that I would want some goddamn bureaucracy," Sandy moaned. "Just a couple of forms to fill out. Maybe a line to stand in. I'd stand in a five-hour line for a good quest. It would save me some time."

"That's your mom talking," Stew said.

Sandy's hands caught fire, and she grabbed Stew by the collar. "Stew, I've already spoken to you about the times when it is appropriate to mention my mother. Do you remember?"

Stew coughed nervously. "Yeah, I remember. Only when you're—"

"And we mentioned when you were allowed to talk about that, remember?"

"Yes, Sandy."

"Uh, you guys want to, um, do this somewhere else?"

Sandy released Stew, and he straightened in his chair. The collar of his tunic was singed. "No, we're cool. So, what now? Do we just go talk to a new MERC?"

Suzuki waved Wendy over. She came and leaned on the counter. Suzuki tried not to notice her breasts practically spilling out of her top. "Hey, Wendy? Where do the newbs like us get any quests from?"

Wendy poured herself a drink and pulled up a stool to sit on. "Newbs getting quests? Psh, most newbs are lucky if they even get to go on a mission unsupervised. I've been surprised that Milos vouched for you three so quickly." Wendy leaned over and pinched Suzuki's cheeks. "You've just got to bide your time, hon. Kind of like your Sleeping Beauty who set up shop in the stove."

"What the hell are you talking about?"

"You haven't heard? They say she's been pacing back and forth in her web, writing you love poems."

Suzuki slapped Wendy's hand away as she walked off, chuckling. "I'm never going to hear the end of this. Hey, Sandy. You're pretty close to Diana, aren't you? Why don't you just ask her for a quest?"

"We could give that a shot," Sandy said. "The Four Horsemen are supposed to be getting back from the field soon."

Suzuki looked down at his trashed clothes and wiped a bit of dried mucus off his cheeks. "All right, let's give that a try. I'm going to go get cleaned up. A bath sounds like a great idea."

Stew turned his head and pinched his nose. "It could help with the smell."

"What did you say?"

"You smell like baked shit."

"Why, thank you."

Stew laughed and shoved Suzuki away. "Get the fuck out of here. Whenever you stop smelling like ass, we'll be here."

Suzuki left Sandy and Stew at the bar and made his way upstairs. He found his room and locked the door. There was a bathtub tucked into the corner of the room.

He took off his shirt and pants, dropping them in a pile near the bath. His chest was covered in small scars and burns, as were his arms.

He started to draw his bath, checking to see if the water was a temperature he liked. Even his hands were slightly torn up.

He walked over to the full-length mirror and looked at himself. His eyes looked older, and the boyish chub that had once been on his face was gone. His arms and his chest were defined. Muscular, even. He looked good. The best he'd ever looked.

*At the end of the day, being in Middang3ard is doing wonders for my self-esteem*, he mused.

Suzuki had always hated how scrawny he looked, making New Year's resolution after New Year's resolution that this would be the year he'd work out. That had never happened.

Then *Middang3ard* had come out, and the getting-fit plan went out the window.

Still, *Middang3ard* had given Suzuki something to focus on, something that had been all-consuming. *Middang3ard* VR had been like someone had breathed life into all the fantasy worlds he had grown up in.

Now the real thing was kicking his ass. Suzuki traced his hands over a large scar that ran down the middle of his chest. That had happened just a few days ago when a giant had hit him so hard with a club that it had practically split his chest open.

Suzuki examined that scar with pride. It was proof that he was starting to fit in here.

But that was the other thing about Middang3ard. Wounds healed quickly here. On Earth, he would have been bedridden for months. Here, he was ready to go a couple days later. Middang3ard not only made them stronger and faster, but it also made them way hardier.

Still, even though they could take more damage, they could also die here, Suzuki reminded himself, as he dipped his toes in the bathwater. It was hot. He took a deep breath, held it, and then slid into the water.

His muscles instantly thanked him. This was the most relaxed he had felt in days.

He tapped his HUD and brought up a book that Sandy had given to him. It was a history of the Kingdom of Ezrakal. The book was mostly focused on the warrior conclave of the empire. There were detailed notes on the spells that the warrior-mages had created and how they had used them in battle.

The book also included a compendium of battle tactics that had been used by the empire.

Sandy was really investing in understanding the realm of Middang3ard. Suzuki appreciated it, and her enthusiasm was starting to rub off on all of them. Suzuki still hadn't seen Stew pick up a book, but he was starting to ask questions and watch vids. That was good enough.

Suzuki thought about how his whole perspective on Middang3ard had changed so drastically since he'd first arrived. He no longer felt overwhelmed with all of the new rules and physics and shit like that.

He also didn't look up to the MERCs the way he had

when he was back on Earth. Online message boards had been full of stories of the "heroic MERCs." People thought they were Earth's last defense.

Even when he had been recruited, he had been told that MERCs did the hard work that the military didn't want to risk.

Since Suzuki had been in Middang3ard, all he had seen was that the MERC recruits were basically just exterminators. He didn't want to be bitter about having to pay his dues. But after today, it was very hard not to feel that he and the Mundanes were being taken advantage of. Milos had told Suzuki that the MERCs had been watching him and the Mundanes playing *Middang3ard* VR for a few years.

What exactly were they watching for? To see how quickly they could rid a room of mobs? The whole idea seemed extremely bizarre, almost as if the MERCs were intentionally taking advantage of Suzuki and the Mundanes.

That was enough of that thinking. It wasn't getting Suzuki anywhere, and he knew it.

This wasn't helping Beth at all.

Suzuki pulled up the last video Beth had sent him, the one that had for some reason been sent and re-sent to him every few hours. There he saw her face staring back at him. Her face was dirty, and her eyes sullen. She looked exhausted.

Even with a mask of stress, she was still the most beautiful woman Suzuki had ever seen. He thought back to the first time he had seen her. It was outside Myrddin's complex, a couple of days after they had beaten the last dungeon of *Middang3ard* VR. She had called out and he'd turned around—and there she was, more stunning even than she had seemed in *Middang3ard*.

That had been months ago, before she had been accepted into the military and the rest of the Mundanes had been rejected. Beth was the only reason they had all gotten to Middang3ard.

She had pulled some strings, and Manny, the Beholder, had shown up on his doorstep in all his many-eyed glory. Now she was off the grid, and the army had declared her dead.

Suzuki, however, knew she was still out there and that he had to find her. That was all that mattered, not the sophomoric games that the MERCs were intent on playing.

Getting to Beth was what was important.

Suzuki stood up and grabbed his towel. He yelped and jumped back in fear. A giant spider was next to his towel. Suzuki knelt down to get a better look. It was a giant spider with the body of a woman. Her many eyes stared up at Suzuki.

"Jesus fucking Christ," Suzuki said as he toweled off and left the room. He got dressed and went downstairs to look for Sandy and Stew, who were still sitting at the bar. Stew didn't even bother to look at Suzuki when he sat down.

"You guys ready to go try this thing with the Horsemen?" Suzuki asked.

"As ready as I'll ever be to meet Jesus."

Sandy pulled her hair back and started to braid it down her shoulder. "Stew, he's not Jesus. He's just been here forever."

"And he's invincible."

Despite Suzuki's own fanboying over José, listening to Stew fawn over him was slightly irritating. "He's not invincible. I saw him come back a few days ago covered in cuts."

"Okay, maybe not invincible, but unkillable. You've heard what everyone says about him."

"Just because everyone repeats the same rumors doesn't mean that they're true."

"You're just saying that because people are gonna start saying you wanna fuck a spider. Besides, we shouldn't go with Sandy. She'll just embarrass us."

Sandy's eyes went wide with indignation. "What do you mean I'm going to embarrass us? I'm the one who knows Diana."

"You have the hots for José," Stew said. "It's really fucking obvious."

Sandy turned away. "He's just cool. Everyone thinks he is."

"Hardly. Besides, I don't want to go over there and talk to the Son of God. I'm a Buddhist. It goes against my religion."

Suzuki sighed and stood up from his chair. "Stew, you are not a Buddhist."

"How do you know?" Stew asked.

Sandy slammed her hands on the table and towered over Stew. There was a darkness in her eyes usually reserved only for the vermin she crushed under her feet. "Stew, we know you don't believe in the Buddha or anything,"

"I will have you know that I follow all of the Buddha's teachings."

Sandy slapped Stew on the back of the head. "Then you would know that nothing in Buddhist teachings prohibits you from associating with people of other faiths. Even if that person is the God of another faith."

"You seem pretty well-versed in what Buddhists are allowed and not allowed to do. So you're a Buddhist now too, huh? Can't let me have anything to myself."

"I'm not a fucking Buddhist."

"Are you sure? You're always drinking green tea and doing yoga and shit. And, you know..."

Sandy's eyes narrowed as she glared at Stew. She took a step toward him and looked him straight in the eye so close that their noses were almost touching. "Don't you fucking say it..."

Stew smiled devilishly as if he were savoring every word. "You know," he repeated, "'cause you're Chinese."

"God damn it, Stew, I'm Taiwanese," she shouted, as she grabbed Stew by his collar and dragged him out of his seat. "Lead the way, oh fearless leader," she said.

Suzuki nodded and marched ahead of the Mundanes, toward the Horsemen's table.

The Horsemen were quietly drinking. The Chipmaster, a young elf woman wearing a blacksmith's uniform and safety goggles, was tinkering with a HUD that was splayed out in front of her. She puffed on a cigarette while she was working.

It was the first cigarette Suzuki had seen in Middan-g3ard. Everyone else almost exclusively smoked from long, ornate pipes.

Diana was sitting next to the Chipmaster. She was a human mage. Her robes were magically adorned, and ancient runes shimmered in and out of sight. The skin around her neck was cracked, and blue energy could be seen coursing beneath her epidermis.

Across from Diana was José, a powerful man with deep, brown eyes that looked as if they had seen across the course of time. His face was covered in scars, and he had a long scraggly beard that looked as if it hadn't been cut in ages.

The Horsemen weren't alone in their booth. Their familiars all sat beside them, stretching their legs after being inside them for so long.

Diana's familiar was a sleek black cat with bright green eyes that were nearly human. The cat was curled up on the table, lazily pawing at a tarot deck that was spread out on the table. Diana picked up the cards and shuffled them, cutting the deck to make a new tarot spread, without bothering to look up at the Mundanes.

The Chipmaster's familiar was a floating mass of spiritual energy that shifted between foggy white and bright red named Boo. Boo dipped in and out of sight as it meandered above the heads of the Horsemen. An odd humming sound came from his direction.

Suzuki stepped up to the Horsemen's table and tried to clear his throat, only to sound like a congested frog. His neck was burning, and he knew he must have the complexion of a ripe beet. "Uh, excuse me."

"And who exactly is asking?" came a syrupy sweet voice.

Suzuki looked down at José's side. A small lamb with a pure white fleece sat next to José, its head resting in his lap. The lamb looked like it had been plucked straight out of an old pastoral painting. It had soft brown eyes and a nearly cherubic face.

Suzuki raised his eyebrow at the curly, adorable, hooved familiar. "Uh, who are you?"

The lamb got to its feet and spat. "Nines. Now, who the fuck are you?"

"I'm Suzuki. I'm from the new recruit party, the Mundanes. We just—"

Nines pranced closer as if he were frolicking in a meadow. "Holy fucking shit. You just draw so many of these losers in, don't you, José? I'm guessing you pissants want a miracle or a blessing, or some other dumb shit like that? Well, you can kindly just go ahead and fuck off. We're busy. The Chipmaster thinks that I got another quart of beer before I need to piss in someone's mouth, and I think that I can do another five, but if you're willing to sit around, keep that stupid mouth of yours open and see when I need a urinal. You're more than welcome to."

The Chipmaster looked up from the pile of chips and colored wires she was working on. "I'm telling you, you foul-mouthed walking sweater, that the tinkling of piss is gonna be creeping up on that tiny bladder of yours before I get a chance to throw you down and shear you myself."

Nines looked up at Suzuki, its innocent face filled with a heavy dose of malice. "What the fuck are you still doing here? You can't be that interested in a golden shower?"

"Seriously," Suzuki asked, "Who the hell are you?"

José finally looked up from his beer. He stared at Suzuki with a divinely compassionate countenance, sighed, and smiled. "This is my lamb and my companion. We all have our familiars. The Horsemen's familiars just like to spend more time in the bar than others."

Nines muttered as he jumped onto the table and started lapping beer from a tankard. "It's the only way I can deal with these needy-ass humans."

Suzuki laughed and crossed his arms. This pairing was unbelievable! "Your traveling companion is a lamb. Kinda cliché, but I guess it makes sense. How come you didn't go with anything more badass from the Bible? Like a lion or a leviathan or something?"

Nine tipped over his beer on Suzuki's feet. Suzuki stepped back as he glared at Nines. It was starting to dawn on him that José's familiar was one badass son of a bitch—well, son of a sheep—that he probably shouldn't insult.

Nines bared his perfectly white teeth and growled as ferociously as a lamb could manage. "First off, a lion doesn't have shit on me. Because this guy, this tough, bearded son of a bitch I'm hanging out with? This guy isn't Jesus Fucking Christ. Fuck, you humans have so little imagination. One guy doesn't die as easily as the rest of you walking deathbags and you assume that he's your Lord and Savior. So you can just forget about the whole lion of Judah shit. Does this mean, orc-killing machine look like a carpenter to you? He's got soft hands for Christ's sake. And a leviathan? Seriously? I'm not even going to go into how fucking stupid you sound suggesting that anyone get a huge ass whale as a familiar. Like we all want to have a fucking two hundred ton mass of blubber taking up the whole bar. And just so you know, no one is giving you extra points for picking obscure biblical creatures. This isn't a fan club to impress *anyone* with your weird-ass nerd knowledge. So will you please, fuck off. Unless you really want a mouth full of my percolating gold. Cliché. Fucking cliché. You want me to show you a cliché? A cliché is me prancing on your face while I bash your fucking teeth in your stupid ass-eating son of a—"

José raised his arms in a gesture of peace. It was reminiscent of the Last Supper. "Nines. Please calm yourself."

"Me? I am calm. I'm calm as shit. He's the fucker who walked up and started insulting our relationship. Calling it cliché and shit. He's the rude ass mutha—"

"Nines. Please. Just turn the other cheek."

Nines walked the length of the table to sit next to the Chipmaster, who pushed a beer in his direction. "The only cheek I'm turning is my ass."

The Chipmaster went back to working on the dismantled HUD. "I'm telling you, you wee little fucker. One more of those beers and you're gonna be like a Billy goat looking for the potty."

José turned to Suzuki and motioned for him to sit. "You would think Nines was funny if you were a pixie. Pixies think everything is funny though. Anyways, what brings you to me?"

Suzuki launched into the pitch he'd been working through in his head. He tried to explain everything that had happened to the Mundanes up to this point: the trials they had faced and how they had proven themselves, how one of their team had been captured and held prisoner by Orcs even though the military said that she was dead. The Horsemen listened without interrupting. The Chipmaster even stopped working on her HUD to give Suzuki her full attention. Nines was the exception. He snorted derisively throughout the story. When Suzuki was finally finished, Nines jumped onto the table and stamped his back legs excitedly.

Nines chided Suzuki. "You're saying that one of the best intelligence agencies in the seven realms is wrong about your friend? Do you know how fucking egotistical and self-involved that sounds?"

Suzuki's voice raised and cracked slightly when he spoke. "What are you talking about?"

"You know how many people die out there every day? And it just so happens that your friend, out of all of Middang3ard, your one friend who you love so dearly, isn't dead? And you need us to go save her."

"First off, Nines, fuck you. Secondly, I'm not asking anyone to go save Beth."

José leaned forward while the Chipmaster and Diana returned to what they were doing. He didn't seem remotely interested in the story Suzuki had told. "Well, what exactly are you asking for?"

"Beth is in a zone that we're too weak to deal with. We're not asking for any handouts. I don't expect anyone to risk his life based on a theory I have."

"Yet you are willing to risk yours?"

"It's not just a hunch. I know she's still alive."

"So what is that you want?"

"We need to get better gear so that we have a chance to survive out there. We've been trying to get other MERCs to give us some quests so that we can get the gear, but everyone we've talked to is just jerking us around."

"Maybe it's because they don't think that you're ready yet. Maybe they're trying to protect you from your own ambitions."

"I just want to help my friend. She needs us."

José crossed his arms and leaned forward as he spoke. "There are many trials we are given. The trials of Middang3ard are exceptionally difficult. I am afraid this is your cross, and your cross alone to bear."

"What does that mean?"

Nines pranced over to the edge of the table and spit on Suzuki's boots. "It means get the fuck out of here! That's what it means."

José shrugged and turned to talk to Diana. Suzuki stood there for a few moments, trying to find something to say to convince José to give them a chance. Nothing came to him.

So he sucked in his pride and left. The Mundanes followed after him. The Chipmaster and Diana looked up from their work as the Mundanes walked off.

"You didn't need to be such a prick," Diana said.

Nines stuck his head into one of the tankards on the table. He whipped his head back when he pulled out and shook his glossy coat. "Eh, you can fuck off too."

## 6

A few days had passed since the Mundanes first tried to convince José and the Four Horsemen to give them a chance. Suzuki was under all his blankets, pretending that he wasn't moping, his HUD resting next to his head on the pillow.

He sighed, thought about why people sigh, and sighed again, twice as loud as before. It was obvious he was going to have to get up at some point to try and figure things out, but, for the moment, it seemed that all of his problems could be solved by staying in bed.

Besides, there wasn't much else to do other than stay in his room. He was tired of going down to the Red Lion to kill time, and he wondered how all of the MERCs weren't raging alcoholics by now.

*I wonder why* I'm *not a raging alcoholic by now*, he mused, but then he remembered the key difference between him and the MERCs. They were coming back from quests and blowing off steam with their friends. As for him? When he got back from whatever meaningless mission he was on, he would sit at a bar, wishing he had a way to achieve his real objective: save Beth.

Getting José to help had seemed like a solid bet to that end. Now? He had no idea what he'd do.

Suzuki rolled over and groaned theatrically, stood up, stretched, and paced around the room determined to leave this time, only to have his bed call to him again.

His body felt as if it had been drained of all of its blood which had been replaced by concrete. Every small movement took a massive amount of effort. Suzuki worm wiggled his way to his other side, grabbed his HUD lying on the pillow, and placed it over his eyes. He scrolled through his messages and pulled up a screenshot of Beth.

This wasn't helping. Looking at Beth just reminded Suzuki that he was lying in bed, too depressed to even get dressed, and not doing anything to help her. Suzuki couldn't even remember how long it had been since he had received that last message from Beth. Whatever was happening seemed to have cut the loop, and message repeat sending was no longer happening.

Anything could have happened by now. Even if Beth had been alive when she sent this message, it was best not to think about it.

There was a loud scratching from the right side of Suzuki's bed, and he sat up to check on what the noise could be. A hole had been dug in the wall to the left of the foot of his bed that was large enough for a rat to fit through. What walked out of the hole was not a rat, though.

It was the spider-woman.

The tiny spider-woman gingerly stepped out of the hole and walked into the room. She gave Suzuki a sympathetic look when she saw him moping before going about her business. It had been a couple of days since Suzuki had last seen her. Initially, Suzuki thought the spider-woman was stalking him since she seemed to be everywhere. But over the last few days, he'd noticed that she was just going on with her life. She seemed to have a very busy life, but Suzuki wasn't sure what spider-women did. Catch bugs? Mice? Stalk humans?

Still, the two of them had become roommates. The only difference was Suzuki restricted his activities to living spaces, and the spider-woman went wherever she wanted. Sometimes she was spinning webs over Wendy's cash register. Other times, she could be found collecting left-over soap from soap containers. Why? Suzuki couldn't fathom. All Suzuki did know was that he was the only large creature she ever seemed to acknowledge, and usually, she would give him sympathetic looks before shuffling on.

She seemed to ignore everyone else as she went about her business, and that was that.

Suzuki tossed a crumb from the plate of food sitting on the dresser beside his bed. The crumb landed a few inches from the spider-woman and she jumped in surprise, pulling out two large scimitars from her backside and circling the crumb like an enemy.

Suzuki leaned over the side of the bed to watch what was happening. "That's something new."

The spider-woman stabbed the bread crumb. When she seemed satisfied that it was not going to attack, she chopped it up into smaller pieces and gathered them into her arms. She looked up at Suzuki, her eight eyes blinking irregularly. Then she curtsied, smiled, and scurried into her hole.

Suzuki sighed, his heaviest of the day, and lay back in bed, pulling the blankets over his head as he wished for something, anything to help him.

Fred chose then to make himself seen. There was a

loud pop, and the entire room reeked of sulfur as Fred stretched out. He scratched at his goat-like horns with claws that ended in razor-sharp points, stretched his leathery wings, and ruffled his red scales like bird feathers as he flapped and perched on the foot post of the bed.

Suzuki poked his head out from beneath the covers so he could get a good look at Fred. "Go away. No one invited you."

Fred played with his hand scales, moving each scale individually so that he could wedge his claw beneath them. "As there is no one here, human, and I am exceedingly bored, I do not require an invitation."

"Fine, suit yourself. Join the slumber party."

"Yes, it does indeed look like a party. Human, you—"

"I have a name, you know? I can at least—"

"You have been calling me Fred for months because your stupid tongue is incapable of expressing my eldritch regality. You are lucky that I only call you human. Now, human—"

"Name."

Fred growled low under his breath and shot forth a small stream of fire from his nostrils. "Suzuki..."

From beneath the covers, Suzuki smiled. It always felt good to put Fred in his place. "I'm listening."

"When you took me from the Garden of Familiars, there was much talk of glory. Is this what you dustlings believe is glory? Sitting in a smelly pile of blankets, stroking your wounded ego until you...expire?"

Suzuki pursed his lips. "Are you saying... What exactly are you—"

"I am saying that I am surprised that your blankets aren't stiff by now. I have known teenagers who do a better job of keeping their hands off of themselves than you seem to be able to."

"Fuck off, Fred. I'm not in the mood."

The imp shrugged. "And what exactly are you in the mood for? Lying in bed doesn't seem to be...how does the idiot say it? Your style."

Suzuki tossed back his covers and sat bolt upright. He wasn't trying to hide his grin from Fred anymore. He wanted Fred to see it. "Fred, are you checking in on me?"

"No! I am doing no such thing. I do not care about—"

"Are you checking to see if I'm okay?" Suzuki asked, circling his finger as he moved to poke Fred's chest. "Like a friend does? Like someone who has a heart might do?"

"I assure you that I do have a heart, human, and it is not concerned with whether or not you are sad or in a bad mood."

"It doesn't look like it to me," Suzuki said with a chuckle. Fred actually cared, and somehow knowing that went a long way to lifting his spirits. This was the best he'd felt all day. Hell, all week. "Looks like you might care a little—"

"If I care or not is hardly relevant to your problem. And much like sitting in bed, tugging on your meatstick isn't going to solve anything."

"No. You're right."

"Perhaps the spider abomination that obviously has a crush on you could help you with at least one of your problems."

"Dude, I have no idea what you're on about."

Fred flapped his wings and left the bedpost. He flew over to the dresser that sat underneath the window looking out over the swamp. "When I was first born into the world, the cosmos was fresh. There was very little in existence. Only the Elder Ones. I was raised on stories of them. One I was told concerned Alehiiemsaseth, the Creeping Blackness."

"Is this going anywhere?"

"Shut up and listen. The Creeping Blackness had been at war with his mother for nearly a thousand years by the time that I was born. He had tried all of his tricks to destroy her, but nothing worked. Finally, he went to an oracle to search for answers. The oracle rested in the middle of the oldest black hole, and the Creeping Blackness entered the black hole and was not destroyed. Once he found his way through the crushing blackness of space, he stood before the oracle. He asked how would he be able to destroy his mother so that he could finally launch all reality into a night so dark that one would question if it were hell itself. The oracle looked at him for some time, thinking. Finally, the oracle told the Creeping Blackness that he had no mother, that he had birthed himself in the void of time and space. He was in his own mother. Then the black hole collapsed on itself, and the oracle was no more. That was how the Creeping Blackness destroyed his mother."

Suzuki stood and grabbed the robe hanging on the bedpost. He walked over to where Fred sat looking out the window. He pulled up a seat next to the imp. "Fred, I never understand any of these weird-ass stories. What the fuck are you trying to tell me?"

"The Creeping Blackness was his own worst enemy, a lesson you should pay heed to while you're beating yourself up."

Suzuki narrowed his eyes, not entirely sure about the point Fred was trying to make. Still, he was trying. "Huh? I guess that's helpful. For a demon." Suzuki shrugged.

"I am an imp. Demons lack my class and wit."

"Yeah, I can see that."

Fred ruffled his scales and sat up on his hind legs so that he looked like a small dragon. He yawned loudly, his teeth shining brightly. " My point is that right now, you have become an enemy to yourself, and you are the only one standing in the way of your own goals." Then there was another pop, a cloud of smoke, the unforgettable smell of sulfur, and the imp was gone. Suzuki could feel Fred adjusting himself somewhere in the pocket dimension Suzuki's body held. Then there was nothing.

Suzuki stood up to pace again, walking the room's short length one side to the other. He was scrolling through his HUD at the same time, not looking for anything specific. It was just giving him something to do while he thought.

He let his mind wander as his feet hit the ground. The repetition was helpful for his thoughts, not that they were going anywhere.

A knock at the door broke Suzuki's concentration. He crossed the room and opened the door where he was greeted by two small people with yellow hair. The skin of one was blue, and the other was orange. They were roughly the size of a child or dwarf. Their cheeks were a rosy red, and their faces were puffed up as if they were suffering from an allergic reaction.

Suzuki knelt down to be eye-level with the two candy-colored individuals. "Can I help you two?"

The orange one pushed Suzuki out of the way and stormed into the room. "It's me, dude," Stew shouted. "We got Humpa Lumphad-ed."

Suzuki blinked his eyes. "Don't you mean Oompa Loompa-ed?"

The tiny colorful creature that was Stew shook his head. "Humpa Lumphad-ed. Apparently Oompa Loompa is copyrighted."

"Just like Middle3arth."

"Bingo."

Sandy scuttled into the room after Stew. She went straight for the mirror hanging on the wall across from Suzuki's bed. She held her hands out and then looked down at her feet. She spun around and looked at her ass. "Not bad. Got an Humpa Lumphad badunkadunk."

Suzuki took the chair from his desk, flipped it around, and sat on it, leaning over its back to get a better look at Stew. The Humpa Lumphad bore a fair resemblance to Stew. He was unnaturally muscular, like a child forced to lift weights competitively. The acne helped with the image as well.

Sandy hobbled over to Stew and took a seat next to him on the bed. "On a scale of one to ten, how adorable are we?"

"Honestly, you both look terrifying. What the hell happened to you?" Suzuki asked.

"We got sent on another 'not quest.' Some jackass sent us to an Humpa Lumphad brothel, which was fucking awesome by the way." Sandy's voice trailed off as she thought back to the brothel.

Stew jumped up onto the bed. He was trembling with excitement. "Dude!" He wrung his hands and raised them to the sky. "Yeah, I'll say that that brothel was awesome! I have never seen anything like it in my entire life."

"Do you go to brothels often?"

"No, but this was out of control. I guess Humpa Lumphads don't fuck like we do. Or like anyone does. They had all these weird candy things hanging from the walls and the ceiling. And whatever the fuck Humpa Lumphads think is sexy is not like anything I've ever seen. All the brothel workers were walking around, slathering themselves with jam and butter. So me and Sandy got a butter massage. It was fucking rad."

"So how'd you end up all small and weird-colored?"

Sandy sighed. "Uh, we didn't bring enough candy to pay for the massage, so we got cursed."

Stew sat down and picked at his skin. He peeled off a layer of dried butter and flicked it onto the floor. "It was pretty embarrassing," Stew admitted.

Sandy adjusted her overalls as she tried to get comfortable. Then she worked on her gloves. "I can't stop fidgeting. I want my old body back. As awesome as that brothel was, I don't want to be an Humpa Lumphad any longer than I have to be. We need to find someone who can reverse this. Fast."

"How about Diana? You and she are pretty tight, right?" Suzuki asked.

"We might as well check. I really, really want to get some candy—and I fucking hate candy. This is the worst."

"Awesome brothel, though," Stew interjected.

"Yeah, awesome brothel. Anywhoooo, let's go find Diana. You coming?" Sandy said as she rolled off the bed onto the floor.

Suzuki shrugged before nodding. Why not? It wasn't as if he had anything else to do.

Stew jumped down after her and then rolled her across the floor like an oblong ball. Suzuki stepped to the side to allow Stew and Sandy to make their way out of the room.

"Uh," Suzuki started. "You guys—"

Sandy managed to twist her head around for a second before Stew rolled her over to the other side and out the door. "Yes, we know," she shouted. "It feels natural, so we're just gonna go with it!"

Suzuki and the two Humpa Lumphad Mundanes made

their way downstairs in this fashion. The stairs didn't seem to be a problem, and Sandy bounced down them as Stew chased after her like an old-time child playing with a hoop and stick. They were both chuckling under their breath, an odd sound like children laughing underwater. The sound was definitely unnatural, and very eerie. Suzuki tried to stay out of their way as Stew herded Sandy to the bar, where they found Wendy wiping down tables. She was grungy from a full day of work, her hair tied back in a ponytail, and she didn't seem happy to see the Mundanes when she looked up from her work.

That changed when she got a good look at their current orange and blue predicament.

Suzuki grabbed one of the rags on the table that Wendy was cleaning with. "You seen Diana anywhere around here?"

Wendy snatched the rag from Suzuki. She pointed to her own rag and her wiping pattern. "Circular. Don't just move the dirt around. And no, I haven't seen her. I heard she was heading to the Mage's Library. The rest of her crew is out on a quest."

"Why didn't she go with them?"

Wendy jerked her thumb at Stew and Sandy, who were sitting at the bar now, fighting over a bowl of candy. "What the fuck happened to them?"

"Humpa Lumphad brothel."

"That place is still open? Shit, I can see why you're looking for Diana. You know where the library is?"

Suzuki nodded. "Yeah, I got an idea."

"If you run into anyone from the Last Ale, you keep your mouth shut, all right? I got a week to prep for whatever shit they're gonna try and pull."

Suzuki motioned that he was zipping his lips before

locking them and throwing away the key. "Mum's the word, mum."

"Don't call me 'Mum.' It's weird."

"Sorry."

---

The Mundanes arrived at the Mages' Library near sunset. The library was a large ornate building on the other side of the MERC encampment. It was reminiscent of old Greek buildings, white columns next to each other and a massive gold dome on the top. Even with the sun preparing to descend, there were more than a handful of mages walking in and out of the building. None of them seemed to have time to pay attention to the warrior-mage and two Humpa Lumphads making their way up the white stairs of the library.

Stew and Sandy were bickering as they ascended the flight of stairs, but Suzuki couldn't understand them. It sounded like they were speaking another language, and he hoped that this transformation wasn't one of those weird, anime transformations where they would only become more Humpa Lumphad-ish the longer it went on. Trying to finish a quest with them ripping each other apart to find candy sounded like a nightmare.

They were cute in a very unsettling way.

A mage clerk sat at the entrance desk. He looked up from his book as the Mundanes stepped into the building. "Library cards, please," the clerk said.

Suzuki went up to the desk and tried to look casual. It was difficult. Stew and Sandy were holding hands and spinning around in a circle, chanting some nursery rhyme that Suzuki had never heard before. Suzuki turned away from the nonsense that was happening behind him, cleared his throat, and tried to speak with as professional a tone as he could muster. "We're not here to check out books. We're—"

"Why are you at a library if you aren't checking out books?"

"We, uh, we're looking for someone," Suzuki said.

"Is this someone in a book?"

"No. Diana. Of the Four Horsemen?"

"Uh-huh." The mage eyed Suzuki like he didn't believe the warrior-mage could possibly know one of the Horsemen. "You still need a library card to enter the library. There are a lot of important books here. We can't just have anyone walking in and out of the library."

"So you can walk in and out if you have a card?"

"Yep."

"What do I need for a card?" Suzuki asked.

"I just need your HUD. I'll set you up with an account."

"That easy?" Suzuki was wondering why the mage hadn't just volunteered that information right off the bat.

The mage nodded. "That easy."

"And this protects people from walking in and out of here, how?"

The clerk put down his book and closed it very slowly as his eyes bored into Suzuki's. "Do you want the card or not?"

Suzuki removed his HUD and handed it to the clerk. The clerk snatched it and plugged it into the computer screen on his desk, before standing up and riffling through the books behind him. He pulled out a large blue book that had gold lettering on the front and thumbed through it for a few minutes before licking his fingers and dog-earing a page. Then he took a quill from a pile on his desk, turned the book to face Suzuki, and pointed to the empty page. "Sign here, please."

"What am I signing?" Suzuki asked.

"Just a policy agreement."

"What's the policy?" Suzuki was vaguely reminded of Apple's Terms and Conditions, documents that no one read. But on Earth, the worst that would happen was they'd revoke your privileges. Here, Suzuki wasn't sure. For all he knew, he was signing over his soul or agreeing to spend eternity as a bookworm or some shit like that.

"You can check out up to fifty books at a time for two years. Fees are charged if you're late, a copper piece per book per day. If your late fees exceed 100 copper pieces, your privileges will be revoked, and you'll be fed to the dragons in the dungeon. *If* you are fed to the dragons, you reserve the right to a duel with one of the dragon keepers to absolve yourself of your fees. Please be careful with our books because many of them are priceless. Thank you."

So it was worse than selling your soul. "Wait, fed to dragons?"

"It's mostly a formality. We haven't fed anyone to a dragon in, I don't know, a couple years or so. Just make sure to bring your books back on time or get an extension. Thank you."

The clerk handed Suzuki his HUD and went back to reading. Once Suzuki got himself situated, he walked over to Stew and Sandy. They were fighting again. This time it was getting a little vicious.

Now Sandy was hanging onto Stew's arms by her teeth. Stew was laughing and trying to swing her around his head. It looked like a fight, but then again, Suzuki wasn't sure. Both of them were already weird, and that was back when they were human.

Suzuki grabbed them both and pulled them off of each other. Stew went limp like a spoiled child, and Suzuki dragged both of his Humpa Lumphads through the magical detectors that separated the library lobby from the main library. Once they were past the detectors, the library opened up.

Suzuki stood in a massive hall with rows and rows of dark wooden bookcases stretching as far as he could see. The library was filled with lavish couches and chairs. None of the bookcases had any sign of cataloging, and each looked exactly like the other. Mages, mostly elfish, walked back and forth carrying piles of books, sometimes stacked so high that Suzuki couldn't see who was holding them. As Suzuki walked the length of the library, he noticed there were hundreds of tables scattered through the library with mages sitting at them, thumbing through books.

At one of the tables, a group of mages sat behind an alchemy set, their faces buried in separate books. One of the mages held a wand and was levitating a host of vials above the alchemy set. One of the vials tipped over and dripped a small amount of golden liquid into a boiling cauldron. The cauldron suddenly exploded, searing the eyebrows of the mage who was tending to it.

The rest of the mages laughed and kept on with their experiments or reading. The rest of the library was pretty much the same way. It looked as if every mage was immersed completely in his own research.

Suzuki felt a tug on his hand. Sandy was pulling him in the direction of one of the tables. Then she let go of his hand and bolted. Suzuki gasped after her, "Wait, Sandy! Wait!"

Sandy was off, running as fast as her stubby orange legs would carry her. Suzuki groaned loudly. This was more than he had expected. Sandy and Stew were regressing. Whatever the mental age of an Humpa Lumphad was, it was not nearly close enough to an adult for Suzuki to deal with.

Suzuki felt a sharp pain in his foot, and he yelped loudly. Stew had stomped on him and was running away to chase after Sandy. Suzuki took off after them, running through the aisles while the mages looked up from their work and glared at them. Suzuki wondered where the librarians were, but then, with patrons like this, they probably didn't need librarians.

Stew and Sandy were completely out of Suzuki's sight. "Shit," he muttered to himself as he wandered through the rows of books, noting that they stretched to the ceiling.

He looked up at the painted scene on the dome. Elfish, human, dwarf, and halfling mages were standing in a circle with a book in the middle. In the background, there was a black storm, lightning flashing, and a face that could barely be made out in the clouds. *Hey, Fred, what's that painting of?*

*The races uniting their magic against the Dark One.*

*You said that the Dark One showed up without magic, right? Where did he come from?*

*That is a question we have all been asking ourselves for quite some time. No one knows. Not even the eldritch creatures such as myself. He seems as ancient as some of the Elder Ones, but those who agree to speak cannot recall when he came into existence. However, it was his coming into our realms that caused the different races to unite their magical knowledge. Before that, magic was studied in different schools, each race using magic as they had been taught for thousands of years. That has changed since the Dark One came. Now races share their knowledge amongst each other, strengthening their understanding of magic.*

*So he brought people together?*

*If that is how you'd like to think of the war and destruction he has created.*

Suzuki stepped out of the rows of bookcases into another open lobby. He could see Stew's and Sandy's technicolor skin from across the room. They were standing next to a table, gesticulating wildly to whoever was sitting there. Suzuki jogged to catch up with them.

Diana was sitting at the table, listening to the odd runon language of the Humpa Lumphads as Stew and Sandy tried to explain themselves. When Suzuki got to the table, Diana looked up and smiled warmly at him. "I'm assuming you can tell me something about what is going on here."

Suzuki nodded and moved to the side so Diana could see him better. "Yeah, yeah. Sorry to interrupt...uh...whatever you're doing. But something happened to Stew and Sandy. They went to an Humpa Lumphad brothel and came back like this. They were okay, or more okay earlier. But now they're not talking normally anymore and, I don't know, they're just acting really weird."

Diana leaned forward, grabbed Stew's face, and licked her finger before whipping it across Stew's forehead. That done, she stuck her finger in her mouth and sucked. "Hmmm. He does taste a lot like candy."

"Yeah, they seem to really be about candy right now."

Diana nodded, her lips crooked in a devilish way. "One of them must have fucked an Humpa Lumphad, or whatever it is that Humpa Lumphads consider to be fucking. Humans are particularly susceptible to this. We have weaker DNA strains than the rest of the other races; that's why transformations hit us a lot harder than anyone else. It helps when we're trying to transform, though. Ultimately, however, this is just a little virus. We can clear it up in a minute. Come on. Wrangle your friends."

Diana stood and wandered off to one of the aisles of books, leaving Suzuki to grab Sandy's and Stew's hands and follow her. As Diana walked, she would stop at different bookcases, flip through the book she was holding, and start back up again. They walked through the library in this way for some time until Diana took a turn, walked past some bookcases, and came to a stairwell that led downstairs. She took a lantern hanging from the right of the stairwell and descended.

At the bottom of the stairs was a large room that was lit by candles and lanterns. There was a table in the center of the room holding several books and a few unique wands . One was of birch, long and gnarled. Another was deep cherry oak, stout and wide with three holes cut into it. Diana selected one of the wands, a twig-like thing that looked like it could easily be snapped. She grabbed one of the books from the table and thumbed through it for a bit before snapping her fingers and exclaiming softly. "Got it. Your friends will be back to normal in no time."

Diana waved her wand over Sandy's head first, then Stew's. "All is fun with dicks and cum, chocolate and cherry bubble gum, but in the end, this we know is true. Humans must be humans, that's all they know to do."

There was a bright flash of red light, and the room filled with the smell of candied popcorn and Ben and Jerry's Cherry Garcia ice cream.

When the light faded, Stew and Sandy were standing next to each other. Both of them were naked. Suzuki quickly covered his eyes. Stew screamed and covered himself as fast as he could before running into a corner of the room.

Sandy looked up at Diana, folded her arms, and bowed slightly. "Thanks. Ahhh, you got any extra robes?"

Diana scrolled through her HUD, and a pair of robes materialized in her arms. She handed one to Sandy, who threw them on quickly. Sandy took the other to Stew. "We didn't fuck any Humpa Lumphads," Sandy called as Stew got dressed. "We just got a body massage."

"Chocolate is Humpa Lumphad sexual fluid," Diana explained.

Stew's face went white. "Are you saying that they covered us in chocolate jizz?"

"Something like that."

Sandy sat at the table and started to play with the wands. "Kinky. Stew, we just had our first group sex experience. Chocolate *bukkake*."

Stew felt his face gingerly. He smiled and nodded, obviously happy with the results. "I think my acne's a little bit better."

Diana prodded Stew's face with her wand. She was looking him over with the care and intensity of a doctor. "Yes, human skin does respond fairly well to Humpa Lumphad fluids. Next time, just take one of these with you." Diana waved her wand, and a vial of purple liquid appeared in her hand. "Drink it first, and it'll keep your genetic makeup stable."

Sandy grabbed the vial and pocketed it. "Thanks. We'll definitely go back. It was surprisingly cheap."

"Oh, I know. How do you think the Four Horsemen keep our saintly glow?"

Suzuki cleared his throat and stepped forward. He figured it was a good idea to just get the whole thing over with regardless of how awkward it felt. But then he remembered that asking for help probably wouldn't be nearly as awkward as having someone reset your DNA after finding out you were covered with Humpa Lumphad love juice. "I know you just did us a solid, but I was wondering if you could help us out with something else too?" Suzuki asked.

Diana sat down at the table in the center of the room,

crossed her hands, and leaned over her desk like a college professor. She was obviously interested, which the other people from her party hadn't seemed to be. "A quest, right?" Diana asked. "Why not just ask José?"

"We tried asking José. You were there."

"I meant one-on-one. Nines tries to be impressive when he's around other people, the whole 'little man' syndrome—except he's a fluffy cutie pie, so it's a thousand times worse."

"We just need—"

"I know what you need. I heard your sob story. It was actually a pretty good sob story, if I'm honest. I'm sorry José didn't want to help you guys. Me, on the other hand, I'd love to give you a chance. The only problem is, I'm all out of quests. The Chipmaster has a few, but trust me, you don't want any of hers, not unless you want to go pull dragon's teeth."

Stew eyes flashed with excitement. He pushed to get closer to Diana, his mouth moving before words even came out. "I could totally take a dragon! Where is it?"

Sandy pushed Stew back to restrain his excitement. "No, you can't. None of us can. So we're shit out of luck?"

Diana shook her head. "Not quite. José does have a shit-ton of quests. He collects them. You just gotta convince him to give one to you."

Suzuki shook his head as he folded his arms. "We already tried that. You saw how that went."

"He was just testing you," Diana said, putting the book back. "He pulls that shit all the time. He tells people it's their cross to bear, but he's really trying to figure out how badly they want it."

Sandy's hand shot up as if she were in school. She looked at it sheepishly as if she had no idea how it got there. "Like Buddhists do. My granny told me a story about when she was trying to become a monk. She had to hike hundreds of miles, and when she got to the temple, they told her that she wasn't going to be accepted, so she left. Then she found out that all the monks had had that said to them when they first arrived. Anyone who got accepted to the temple had to stand outside for almost a month before being let in."

"Like *Fight Club*," Stew exclaimed.

Sandy grabbed Stew's chin with her hand. "Sure. I mean, if you want to diminish a historical, cultural practice of over a thousand years, yeah. Just like fucking *Fight Club*."

Stew avoided Sandy's eyes as Suzuki burst out laughing. It was always good to see Stew get put in his place, especially by Sandy.

Diana chuckled before gesturing to Sandy. "By the way, you messaged me earlier about checking something out for you. Where is it?"

Sandy pulled up her HUD and the mask they'd found on the last mission appeared on the table. "Yeah, I wanted to see if you'd look at this before I used it."

Diana grabbed the mask and pulled out a microscope. She thumbed through a book that magically appeared in her hand without bothering to look at the pages. "I'll take a look at it. In the meantime, you three need to figure out how you're going to catch José's attention. Be creative. Unless you want to sit around for a hundred years. Pro tip: don't forget about Nines. He might be an asshole, but he can still be wooed, and the quickest way to José's heart is through Nines. Now get going. I've got research to do."

Diana shooed the Mundanes away, and they ascended the stairs. No one looked particularly happy with having to figure out how to catch José's attention.

When they got to the top of the stairs, Sandy's eyes nearly popped out of her head as she saw the number of books in the library. "Holy shit! I did not see all of this when I was Humpa Lumphad-ed. I'll meet you guys back at the Lion later tonight. I'm gonna do some reading, maybe find something to help us."

"All right," Suzuki said as he and Stew headed toward the exit. "Good luck."

Stew and Suzuki left the library, walking in silence as Suzuki tried to figure out what to say. He really wanted to think about what to do to make José help them, but he was exhausted from trying to get Stew and Sandy back to normal. He felt his whole body was made of chicken wire.

"Hey, buddy, you okay?" Stew asked.

"Just freaking out a little bit, that's all."

Stew pulled out the vial of purple liquid Diana had given them. "We could get a massage. It's really fucking relaxing."

"I swear to God, Stew, I will never understand you."

"Greatness is hard to understand, my friend. Even I don't get it half the time."

## 7

L ater in the day, the Mundanes gathered in the bar of
the Red Lion, and Suzuki noted that it was becoming
a habit for them to eat together, like a family.

Then again, there was nowhere else to eat unless they
wanted to venture to the Last Ale. Suzuki had persuaded
Stew to take a raincheck on their Humpa Lumphad man-
date. Instead, they had spent the afternoon brainstorming
how they were going to attract José's attention. Suzuki had
even gone the route of crowdsourcing the MERCs in the bar
about what past recruits had done to get a quest from him.

That yielded nothing. From what Suzuki had gathered,
José didn't like to waste time with recruits, or most anyone
for that matter. He seemed like a man who valued his time.
Suzuki could appreciate that.

Stew, on the other hand, had decided that José was to be
treated as a deity. When Suzuki asked how to impress him
then, Stew just shrugged, "Worship. Build a shire? Sacrifice
a goat? How the hell should I know?"

Suzuki wasn't sure how to worship a fellow MERC. It felt
like brown-nosing to him.

So Stew and Suzuki sat at a table, waiting for Sandy to show up. They were cleaning their gear in the meantime.

An assortment of weapons covered the table, most of them Stew's. Suzuki only had one sword and shield, as he'd been very careful to sell anything that he wasn't using for extra coin.

Stew, on the other hand, was hoarding as many weapons as he could. Suzuki would have said something earlier if it didn't seem apparent that Stew meant to use each and every blade that he had acquired for killing. Daggers, short swords, a few battle axes, and a heavy greatsword were covered in myriad kinds of dried blood.

Stew washed a short sword delicately with soap and a rag. "You know what I could go for? A mace. A *real* mace. None of these little tiny things. Something half the size of my body with a good swing on it. Then maybe something to actually use it on."

Suzuki buffed a scratch out of his sword. He held it up to the light to check its sharpness. He wasn't satisfied, so he took out a whetstone and got to work. He never would have thought maintaining his own gear would be one of the most satisfying parts of Middang3ard, but the simple act of cleaning and sharpening made him feel connected to his sword, to his shield.

"Dude, you got to upgrade," Stew said, handing him a longsword they had gotten on one of the useless missions. This one was similar to Suzuki's but had a gem on its hilt. When they got it appraised though, they'd discovered that the gem was worthless.

They had found a handful of other swords as loot, but none of them seemed to be worth trashing his first sword for, and Suzuki wondered if there was a way to enchant any of the gear he already had. That would make sense. Most of the veterans had enchanted gear, and it seemed unlikely that everyone just happened to find upper-tier stuff.

But like most of the magical world of Middang3ard, Suzuki was fuzzy on the details.

Stew appraised the menu on the chalkboard hanging on the wall behind him. "Grub's on me tonight. To say thanks for, you know, making sure that I wasn't punishing naughty children for the rest of my life."

"You mean like a krampus? I didn't know Humpa Lumphads did that?"

"Yeah, didn't you ever see "Willy Wonka." The Oompa Loompas ... aka the Humpa Lumphads—"

"Adjusted for copyright issues," Stew added.

"Exactly. Anyway, Humpa Lumphads only come out when a kid fucks up. Then they take the kid away to be processed into candy or something."

"Yeah, like, uh...Pete, Black Pete, or something. He was the one who punished the kids in the old krampus stories, I think. I'm a little foggy on my Eastern European folklore."

"Only you would say that like it was a bad thing. So you don't have anything in that giant nerd brain of yours to figure out how to convince Jesus to help us?"

"He's not Jesus, you idiot. His name is José. That's not even kind of like Jesus."

"They sound pretty close."

" 'Jesus' is etymologically closer to Joshua. And José is a Latin name used in cultures that often have the name Jesus as well. If he was meant to be named Jesus by his parents, he would have been named Jesus."

Stew tapped Suzuki's forehead with his oversized pointer finger. "Does your head ever hurt from being so full of useless shit?"

"Fuck you."

Stew picked up a dagger and threw it at Suzuki. It hit the wood to the left of Suzuki's chair. Suzuki didn't even flinch.

Stew whistled, impressed, reached over, grabbed the knife, and tossed it back on the table. "Damn dawg, you're getting nerves of steel out there fucking around with spider-babes. But seriously, what do you think we could do to catch not-God's attention? If you were God, what would you like?"

"A god," Suzuki corrected. "Even if José was Jesus, he'd probably be a part of a pantheon of gods. Fred's mentioned the Elder Ones a couple of times. And the elves have their gods too. I wouldn't be surprised if every race had tons of their own gods."

"Wait, what? I couldn't hear you."

"I was saying—"

Stew lifted his hands, cutting Suzuki off. "I couldn't hear you over all of the boring shit coming out of your mouth. Why don't you just ask your familiar if he knows about all these gods and things?"

"Fred said that if *he* were a god, he'd want all of Middan-g3ard wiped of infidels and false prophets. So yeah, that's not helpful."

Sandy walked up to Stew and Suzuki's table, balancing three beers on a plate. She slid the plate onto the table, kissed Stew, and grabbed a seat. "What's not helpful?"

"We still can't figure out how to get José to pay attention to us," Suzuki said.

"If he were a hottie, what would you do?" Sandy asked.

"What does José being hot have to do with anything?" Suzuki asked.

Stew dropped the sword he was sharpening. He picked it up quickly and fumbled with it again. His voice cracked when he spoke. He sounded like he was just about to start puberty again. "Yeah, what does it matter if he's hot?"

Sandy threw her arms up in exasperation. "For fuck's sake, Stew, I don't like José."

"I know, I know. You just think he's hot."

Sandy pointed at Stew and her eyes narrowed. She looked like she was ready to chop off an orc's head. "Do not start with me now, Stew. Anyway, if José was a hot chick you wanted to talk to, but she was too busy with her friends and shit for you, what would you do to catch her attention?"

Stew shrugged. "Can't help you there. That's unfamiliar territory for me."

"Stew, you messaged me for almost a month before I talked to you, and I only did that to stop you from annoying me."

Stew smiled smugly and crossed his arms. "Like I said, unfamiliar territory."

"I don't know," Suzuki said. "I'd probably try to make some big declaration of my feelings, like something that could fit in a decent 80s romance movie."

"You mean like *Sixteen Candles* or some shit like that?" Stew said. Sandy nodded appreciatively. "First off, I'm impressed you like *Sixteen Candles*."

"I didn't say I liked it."

"Sure, you didn't," Sandy chuckled. "Secondly, yes. I'd *Sixteen Candles* it."

"How?" Stew asked.

Suzuki scratched his chin as he nodded. That wasn't a bad idea. It beat just waiting around for José to decide that the Mundanes were worth his time. This way, they could show José that they had whatever it took to take care of any quests he might decide to give them.

"We've just got to impress him," Suzuki said. "If we can get him to understand what we're about, that we're serious about all of this, then we've got a better chance of him helping us."

"So we're *Sixteen Candling* someone who might or might not be Jesus." Stew shrugged. "Shrine?"

Suzuki shook his head. "No, Nativity Scene. Let's throw José a birthday party."

Sandy nodded. "Sounds like the best plan we've got right now."

Suzuki raised his tankard of ale, and the rest of the Mundanes clanked theirs with him. This was the plan. And they were going to find a way to make it work.

---

The Mundanes walked through the portal from the Red Lion and came out in the middle of a city. They had asked Wendy to send them to the closest one. Suzuki was instantly overwhelmed with the bustle of the city, regretting they hadn't done a bit more research about the surrounding area.

The streets were crowded with elves, pushed nearly shoulder-to-shoulder, trying to get to wherever they were trying to get to. He could hardly take it all in. It felt as if he had just been dropped in the middle of Times Square.

Horses galloped down cobblestone streets past the Mundanes, drawing carriages filled with elvish noblemen and women wearing ruffled shirts and elegantly-patterned dresses. The clothes of the people walking through the streets were plainer, mostly cotton tunics that hung loosely on their bodies, covered in the dust kicked up from the carriages speeding through the town. Feudalism was alive here.

Suzuki jumped out of the way of a carriage that screeched around the corner. He'd barely missed being trampled by a dozen hooves. "What the fuck is this shit?" Suzuki shouted.

Sandy grabbed Suzuki and Stew's hands and dragged them out of the middle of the street. She waved away the dust as she hacked up her lungs. "I guess this is what city life is like. Can't say that I like it much."

Stew jumped out of the way of a crowd of posh elves who rambled down the street. He shook his hands at them like an old, angry man. "Okay, what the hell are we here for and how fast can we get back home?"

Suzuki pulled out his map and looked through the notes that he had scrolled on it. The map was extremely detailed, pointing out the shops and residential areas of the town. This would be easier to navigate than the last few missions when they had been relying on sketchy maps. "This map is great," Suzuki finally said. "How did you even manage to set up a little field trip to an elf city?"

Sandy took the map out of Suzuki's hands and gave it a once over. When she was satisfied, she scanned the map into her HUD. She turned around, trying to find her bearings. "As I said before if you'd been paying attention, this isn't an elvish city. It's a refugee city the MERCs built. It's kind of like a pocket dimension that some upper-level MERCs have access to visit. I promised Diana few favors, and there you go. We can get supplies for the party from here. Or at least *some* of the supplies. This is the wine stop."

Sandy led the Mundanes through the city. The buildings were nearly as tall as skyscrapers. As they walked farther into the city, Suzuki noticed that there were more trees than on the city's outskirts. Many of the buildings were actually built into the sides of hulking redwood trees, stretching up the trees as if they were vines. All of the buildings appeared ancient even though, from the looks of their wares, they were trendy. "Pretty impressive for a refugee camp," he whistled.

Hats appeared to be in vogue. Elves paraded in the streets wearing a variety of hats, ranging from small, well-constructed caps to ornate witch hats with large brims, pointy tops, and something which looked like earrings which dangled nearly down to the elves' chests.

And everyone seemed to be in a rush. The elves hardly stopped moving, even when they stopped to greet each other. It was almost the opposite of what Suzuki would have expected to find. The few elves he'd met through MERC seemed to be much more easy-going.

The Mundanes turned a corner and stopped at a shop named Delicacies and Other Fare. It was one of the many shops built into the immense redwood trees.

Stew opened the door for Sandy and let it slam in Suzuki's face. He turned around to casually flip Suzuki off while trying to keep from smiling too widely.

"Real mature," Suzuki muttered, walking in behind them.

Bottles of wine and mead covered the walls. There was a display of wines and cheeses in the middle of the room. The smell of the cheese was almost overpowering, and it hit Suzuki like a wave of curds and spoiled milk. An old elf whose ears had started to droop somewhat sat behind a counter, his eyes closed. He snored quietly, murmuring in his sleep.

Suzuki and Sandy walked up to the front desk while Stew wandered around the store, picking up wine bottles and reading the labels. Sandy rapped her knuckles on the countertop and the old elf jumped. He wiped the sleep from his eyes and lazily looked at Suzuki and Sandy. "Welcome to Delicacies. Welcome, welcome."

The elf stood and extended his hand to Suzuki. His skin was nearly translucent, but his grip was firm. He puffed his stomach out and looked ahead, trying to look impressive, adopting a regal air. "My name is Antoine," he said. "This is my shop. These wines are the products of my family for centuries. They tell tales of elvish culture and history. Each note is a lesson in what it means to be elvish."

Antoine leaned closer, pushing up his spectacles. He appraised the two Mundanes in front of him in the way one looks at insects. "Hmm. Neither of you is elvish. May I ask what has brought you to my humble shop?"

Sandy scrolled through her HUD and selected an item which appeared on the countertop: a coupon for a forty percent discount on a bottle of wine.

Antoine picked up the coupon and stared at it. The bit of excitement he'd first displayed drained from his face. He sat down in his chair again and sighed as if he were expiring. "Oh, this. Yes, we still honor this. What would you like to get?"

Sandy smiled sweetly, trying to infuse as much class into her pearly whites as she could. Unfortunately, the number of small cuts and dust on her face made her look more like a street rat than a wine snob. "Well, we were wondering if you could help us with that. We're looking for something really good. A wine that says, 'this is for divinity.'"

A bit of that previous spark lit up Antoine's face. "Divinity, eh?" he mused. "I do have a few bottles that would conjure up those feelings, and might be in your price range." Antoine eyed the Mundanes again, not bothering to hide his disappointment.

Antoine came out from behind the counter and the Mundanes followed him as he meandered through the store, occasionally stopping at a bottle. He would hunch over and stare at whatever bottle was before him. He muttered under his breath as he stared at the wine bottles. "Hmmm. This would be too much for them. The stories are too old and too different, but if it's to inspire divinity, true divinity, perhaps this one. Yes. No."

Antoine snapped his fingers and chuckled, then walked briskly across the shop to the other wall. He grabbed a bottle from one of the top shelves and held it up for the Mundanes to see.

Suzuki took the bottle Antoine offered. There was no label on it, and the glass was black so that its contents were obscured.

Antoine pointed to the bottle and nodded as he spoke. "This is a fine bottle of elvish wine. It's a fairly new batch, so it'll be cheaper. Despite its youth, it still manages to convey a certain, what is the word, "gravitas" to its bouquet. It is based on the tale of Halsheriel, a renowned elvish warrior. It is said that he once defeated an entire army of orcs by himself. That is legend. It is a fact that he was the general who led the last stand against the orc rebellion of the Third Age."

Stew took the bottle from Suzuki. He nearly dropped it, and floundered to catch it as Antoine's eyes nearly jumped out of his skull. Stew narrowly caught the bottle between his legs. He sighed with relief as he looked closely at the wine. "What are you talking about when you say that the wine tells a story?" Stew asked.

"All elvish wines tell a story. With each sip, the story unfolds before you. They are meant to be enjoyed in one sitting and with multiple drinkers. Finishing a bottle by oneself has been known to cause month-long hangovers filled with nightmares. I'd recommend drinking this with at least three people."

"So you drink it and hallucinate?"

"It's not quite a hallucination. It's more like watching a dream that you are aware is a dream. You close your eyes and the dream plays across your eyelids."

The Mundanes talked it over for a moment before deciding to get the wine. Suzuki paid Antoine, who packed up the bottle in an elegant box which was decorated with a fine, green silk bow. He put the box in a pink bag which had Delicacies emblazoned on it. Suzuki thanked Antoine, and the Mundanes left the shop.

Once the door closed behind them, Antoine took a seat behind the counter. He was back asleep within a couple of seconds.

Sandy took a look at her map and pointed down the street. "Next stop is a cross, holy water, and a tabernacle."

"Those are pretty human things to find here," Suzuki said.

Sandy hit her HUD, and it flashed a holographic image in front of Suzuki and Stew. A shop with the name Oddities and Bizarrities was circled. "They specialize in other cultures' oddities," Sandy said.

"Are our religions our oddities?"

"Think about it. Wouldn't elf shit be kinda weird to humans?"

"If humans on Earth even believe in elves. No one seems to notice us here. I'm pretty sure someone would have already called a national emergency if these guys showed up in LA."

Sandy guided them to the next store. Much like the wine shop, it was built into the side of a tree, but this tree appeared to have been dead for some time. Its branches were gnarled and dried out. The shop was painted black, its windows had red crushed velvet drapes, and the door had a gargoyle knocker.

Suzuki pulled back on the gargoyle's nose ring and waited for an answer.

A small slot in the door materialized. Two bright red-and-orange eyes stared at Suzuki from the other side. "What's the password?" the voice asked.

"Uh, I don't know the password."

There was a pause, then they heard scuffling, and the sounds of large furniture being moved and a dozen glass bottles breaking. The eyes appeared again. "Good enough."

The slot closed and the door opened.

The Mundanes stepped into a shop of oddities indeed. Stuffed magical creatures hung from the ceiling, dangling over customers like some bizarre constellation. Shelves throughout the shop were filled with devices that Suzuki had never seen or dreamed of before. He wandered over to a shelf that was empty except for a book that he picked up. There was no title, so he put the book back down.

As Suzuki walked away, he heard a nasal voice whisper, "Hey, kid! Where you going? Come back!"

Suzuki turned back to the shelf. The book he had been looking at was sitting upright and was open. "Um, were you talking to me?"

"I was indeed. Why don't you just come over and have a quick read?" The book had a 1920s gangster drawl to it, sounding like it was trying to sell him drugs while on the lookout for Dick Tracy.

Suzuki warily made his way back to the book. He peered at it but kept his distance. "There's nothing written in, uh, you?"

"That's because you have to write it. I tell the story that you want to hear."

"How does it work? I mean you. How do you work?"

"Pick me up and find out."

Suzuki grabbed the book. He thumbed through the blank pages, hoping Sandy and Stew didn't see what he was doing. Then he heard a deep voice booming in his head.

*Beth leaned over to whisper into Suzuki's ear and licked his earlobe. With one hand, she started to hike up her shirt, her breasts aching to be released, while her other hand slowly unzipped Suzuki's—*

Suzuki dropped the book and stepped away. He checked to see if Stew or Sandy had seen him before he coughed loudly and adjusted himself.

The pages of the book began to ink themselves with a picture. Suzuki leaned over to see it. It was Beth and, from the outline, she was wearing less than Suzuki could have imagined.

Suzuki closed the book with his foot before picking it up and putting it back on the shelf.

The book shimmered and changed color as a title wrote itself on the book's cover. "No one can hear or see it other than you," the book said. "It can be our little secret. Whatever story you want to hear."

Across the store, Sandy and Stew were talking to an employee at the counter. Sandy caught Suzuki's eyes and waved him over.

"Whatever you want to read," the book repeated.

Suzuki grabbed the book and rushed over to the counter. He tossed it down next to a vial of holy water and a large wooden crucifix. The Christ depicted on the crucifix seemed to be in excruciating pain. "Do you think he's going to like this?" Suzuki asked.

Sandy picked up the crucifix and gave it a once over. She nodded, satisfied with the painful plight of the crucifix.

"Dude, it's his passion. If we're going to try to impress José, we gotta show that we understand what he went through. We don't want it to seem like we don't think it was important."

Stew took the crucifix from Sandy and held it up the way that children hold Christmas ornaments. "Yeah, we don't want it to seem like we just punked out of the hard shit. He's gotta know that we're as hardcore as he is. And this is a hardcore crucifix. What's up with the book?"

Suzuki shoved the book to the cashier and forced a weak smile. "Oh, this? Just a journal. I want to keep better track of my thoughts and shit. You know. Reflections and shit."

"Uh, okay, dude." Stew picked it up as if he were allergic to reading. "Sounds lame, though."

The cashier rang up the Mundanes' items, and they all forked over their coins. Once they had paid, they uploaded the items into their inventories and went back outside.

Outside, the sun was starting to set. The leaves of the trees the shops were embedded in looked as if they were on fire, the sky was all oranges and red, and the clouds were an eerie purple as the last of the day's light faded. Suzuki sat down on the side of the street and watched the few elves who were still out walking around, enjoying their city.

"I wish we could stay longer," Suzuki said. "It'd be cool to explore a little bit, you know. I've never been to another race's city before. I mean, look at this shit!"

Suzuki gestured to the shop behind him. "There's literally nothing like this on Earth."

Stew ran his hands over the bark of the tree. A piece came off in his hand, and he stared at it for a moment before handing it to Suzuki. "Here's a souvenir if you want to get all emotional and junk."

Suzuki took the chunk of tree and pocketed it before

shoving Stew away. "Fuck off," he said. "I'm just saying. This is pretty fucking cool. We should come back and check it again. Maybe some more elf shit. I know it can't all just be elvish shopping malls."

Sandy nodded as she sat down next to Suzuki and watched the horse carriages go by. "Suzuki's right. I remember when my grandpa was stationed in Japan, we used to travel all the time. See different temples and forests and things like that. It never got old. It was just, you know, not like home. It was pretty beautiful."

Stew sat down next to Sandy and put his arm around her. "All right, if we're going to be all emotional and shit, yeah, it'll be cool to see something other than bars and caves. And there's got to be a lot more than bars and caves for us in Middang3ard, no?"

Suzuki agreed. The little bit of Middang3ard that he had seen was beautiful and frightening, but that was just the tip of the iceberg. He bet there were hidden treasures in the world that even its natives didn't know about. "Beth would have loved this," he said. "She would have known how to appreciate what we're doing."

Sandy squeezed Suzuki's knee and smiled at him. "And she will. We'll make sure to show her everything, right?"

"Yeah. We'll give her the whole tour."

"Come on. We should get going."

Sandy led the Mundanes back to the corner that they had first been teleported to. There was another public tele-portation portal beside the one they had used. She stepped through it and Stew went in afterward.

Suzuki took a second, turning to admire the sunset. It was beautiful, so different from a sunset on Earth, yet still somehow similar.

He only wished he could share it with Beth.

---

## 8

Suzuki showed up at the designated party site in the middle of the afternoon. Stew and Sandy had already been there working for a few hours. They had rented a house in the MERC encampment a couple of blocks away from the Red Lion. The furniture had been moved out of the house's living room so there was an ample amount of free space.

The Ark of the Covenant had been set up in the middle of the room. It was something Sandy had paid a bit extra to have built for them. It was straight out of the Old Testament: a gold-covered wooden chest with a cherub on each corner.

Candles were lit around the Ark of the Covenant and incense was burning. The room smelled heavily of myrrh.

Suzuki walked through the room as he tried to take it all in. He felt like he was in church, or at least his idea of church. He hadn't attended much when he was younger. He'd gotten the gist of what was going on, though. Suzuki approached Stew while the barbarian was hanging up the Christmas lights. "Where the hell did you get these from?" Suzuki asked.

Stew pointed over to Sandy, who was tending to the incense burner. "That was all Sandy. She's taken care of all of the small things."

"I thought we were going with the Nativity Scene?"

Sandy jumped off the ladder she was using to hang Christmas decorations from the ceiling. "Oh, this is better. It's meant to be a Christmas Mass. You know, like a Catholic Mass. Super-ritualistic. I figured that would help show how important all of this is. I'm calling it Happy Belated Christmas Birthday Day."

"And you think he'll dig it cause it's a Mass?"

"Yeah, you know, cause of the whole ritualist part of it. Rituals aren't easy to do. At all. I've been reading about some of the ritualistic magic that MERCs use, and it's out of control. I figure if we go the extra couple of...whatever you'd go...it'd be pretty obvious that we were serious."

"And you guys have told José about all this?"

Stew and Sandy looked at each other. It was obvious from their blank faces that they hadn't bothered to tell José about what they were planning for him.

Sandy laughed as she wandered over to the Christmas tree in the corner of the room. "I thought you could tell José, Suzuki. You know, since you're the unofficial leader of the Mundanes. Leader talking to leader. That kind of thing."

Suzuki walked over to the Ark. It was covered with candles that were leaking wax onto its golden surface. There was a Nine Inch Nails CD sitting in the middle of the candles. Suzuki picked it up and held it for Stew and Sandy to see. "And what the hell is this?" he asked.

Stew grabbed the CD from Suzuki and put it down with the tenderness one would reserve for a newborn child. "This," Stew started, "is *The Downward Spiral* by Nine Inch Nails, the literal definition of gothic industrial music.

This album was revolutionary. After this album dropped—"

"All right, I got you. Why is it there?"

"We have the cross and holy water; that CD represents the nails used to crucify Christ. You know, symbolically speaking." Stew gave Suzuki a smile that the warrior-mage was sure the barbarian had used on his teachers when trying to pull a fast one. "It's the whole fucking thing. How could José not be into this?"

"And I have to bring him here?"

"Yep, O Fearless Leader. You're our only hope."

Suzuki looked at the hodgepodge of religious iconography. The room looked like something a kindergarten class would have organized for a Christmas pageant. Granted, there was a lot more gold than children could afford. The look was earnest, at least. Sincerity was as abundant as the Christmas cheer in the room.

Suzuki leaned over and casually blew out the candles. "Guess I'll go grab José."

"You got the easiest job," Sandy called from across the room. "I didn't see you having to hang anything."

Suzuki threw his hands up as he made his way toward the door. "Yeah, whatever. I'll take care of it."

---

It was the middle of the afternoon, so the Red Lion was practically abandoned. Suzuki walked to the bar, where Wendy was sitting, having a drink. She lazily looked up at him as she sipped her beer. Suzuki took a seat next to her and waited awkwardly until she paid attention.

Wendy downed the last of her beer and put it on the counter. "Can I help you with anything?"

"I was wondering if you knew where José was?"

"Up in his room. They're having some kind of meeting or something."

"Thanks."

"No problem."

Suzuki left the bar. There was a weird feeling in the Red Lion. He had never seen it this empty before. The few people who were in the bar were sitting by themselves, drinking quietly. He figured the rest of the MERCs were out on quests and missions. It was the middle of the day, after all. And that got Suzuki wondering if it was the weekend.

He honestly didn't know what day it was. Since he'd come to Middang3ard, the days had blended into each other. Now that he thought about it, he wasn't sure he had any idea how long he'd been in Middang3ard. It was hard to keep track of everything that was going on all the time. The concept of time had been the first thing to go out the window.

It didn't take long to find the Horsemen's room. None of the doors had any kind of marking other than room numbers. Still, Suzuki was able to figure out which room the Horsemen were in from the amount of noise coming from it.

Suzuki followed the shouting to a room near the back of the hall and knocked twice. There was a shuffling of feet and a couple of hoarse whispers before the door opened just a crack.

The Chipmaster's eyes peered out. "What brings you to these parts, young squire?"

Suzuki cleared his throat and tried to speak confidently. "Uh, I'm here to invite José to a party. And all of you, as well."

The Chipmaster swung the door open, grabbed Suzuki, and pulled him into the room. She twirled him around, and he was sitting in a chair at a table before he realized what was going on.

José, the Chipmaster, and Diana were playing cards. The table was covered in gold, armor, and weapons, and it looked as if the contents of a chest had just been dumped out for everyone to figure out who was grabbing what.

José was puffing a cigar nonchalantly, watching the clouds of smoke float up to the ceiling.

Diana was staring at her cards with an intensity that might have been reserved for cracking a dead language.

Suzuki assumed that the pile of gears had been the Chipmaster's contribution to the pot.

José looked up from his cards for a second before his eyes darted back. "Suzuki," José murmured. "What brings you here?"

Suzuki checked around the room quickly. "Is Nines around?" he asked.

"I do believe he's sleeping."

"I wanted to invite you all to a party. Something the Mundanes and I have put together for you."

Diana tossed her cards on the table and groaned loudly. "I fold," she whined. "This one is yours, Chip."

José drew a couple more cards and looked down at them as he chomped his cigar. "Not if I have anything to say about it," he muttered.

The Chipmaster didn't bother looking at her cards. She waved away the possibility of drawing anything else. She kicked her feet up on the table, leaned back, and motioned for Diana to hand her the pipe that was smoldering on the table. "Don't matter what you've got to say, Luv, you're still going down in a fiery explosion of guts and glory. I've only been teasing you, but once I'm done with this hand, there won't be nothing left of you to tell anyone about. You won't be betting in these halls for some time. Not unless you want me leaning over your shoulder to remind you how shite you are at the game."

José tossed his cards on the table. The Chipmaster took a look at the cards, curled her upper lip, and tossed her cards onto the table. José leaned forward to get a better look, then he slammed his fist on the table, practically cracking it. The gold and loot went flying as the Chipmaster and Diana burst into laughter.

The Chipmaster slithered out of her chair and started to gather whatever had fallen onto the floor, hoarding it in a massive pile of gold and shining armor. "Looks like another round for Ol' Chip," she sang.

"I say we play another hand. HUDs off," José growled.

"Are you accusing a moral person such as myself of cheating? The audacity! Truly, that's disturbing. And from such a confident and strong leader? The very idea of it is flabbergasting."

"Fuck it," José said as he stood up from the table. He turned his eyes to Suzuki. "What did you say you wanted?"

Suzuki felt his voice failing him. He swallowed and tried to stand as confidently as the other MERCs in the room. "Uh, I, my friends and I, we set up a party for you."

The Chipmaster leapt up from the pile of loot "A party! Where the hell at? Is that what you were on about the whole time? José! We have to go! It's a party!"

José folded his arms. He stared at the pile of loot . "I'm not sure I'm in the mood for a party."

"It's a birthday party," Suzuki squeaked, instantly regretting opening his mouth. "Of a sort," he muttered.

"For whom?" José asked.

"You."

José narrowed his eyes. "This, I have to see."

---

The Horsemen entered the room, led by Suzuki, his head low. Even more candles had been lit. The air was thick with incense, and it was nearly too heavy to breathe.

Stew and Sandy were still bustling around the room, trying to get everything set up properly.

José walked around the room, looking at everything the Mundanes had prepared, his manner cool and detached.

Diana and the Chipmaster, on the other hand, were nearly exploding as they tried to hold in their laughter. They were running around the room, looking at everything the Mundanes had prepared. "This is fucking awesome, mates," the Chipmaster shouted.

Diana stood beside the Ark of the Covenant and touched the wings of one of the cherubs. "This is exquisite craftsmanship. Where did you get this?"

"Oddities," Sandy said. "The shop you told me about. And I told the owner hi for you."

"Much appreciated."

Sandy and Diana instantly got into a conversation about the shop, exchanging anecdotes and product information faster than Suzuki could follow. *At least they'll enjoy the party,* Suzuki thought.

The Chipmaster seemed less interested than Diana, but not nearly as disinterested as José, who had already taken a seat in the corner of the room. He was holding the crucifix Stew had placed strategically. He rolled it over in his hand for a few moments before holding it up to peer at the Christ figure.

Suzuki walked up to José and took a seat next to him. He tried to hide the sense of failure that was building in his stomach. He had never been one for planning parties, but this was easily the worst.

José handed Suzuki the crucifix. "So," José started, "Christmas, huh? Let me guess, this is supposed to be my birthday party?"

"Yeah, we planned it just for you," Suzuki answered.

"And what about this is supposed to be for me?"

"Er..."

"Are you all still on the whole 'Messiah' thing?" José threw up his hands in exasperation. "I'm not *him*," he growled.

"No, no, not at all."

"I am not Jesus," José spat the Messiah's name like it was a curse. "I cannot express that strongly enough."

"We know you aren't Jesus. It's just that—"

"Then why the fuck is this a Christmas party? In the middle of August?"

"We just thought it was a fun theme."

"So you planned a Christmas party for me? In summer. Filled it with...with...I don't even know what."

"Yeah, it is."

"And a Nine Inch Nails CD? Don't you think it's in poor taste to theme a party after someone's death?"

"It's for Nines," Suzuki muttered. "We thought he might like it."

José stood and placed the crucifix back on the table. He stepped back to admire its golden luster. "But I get it. You're terribly misinformed, but I get it. So what do you want?"

Suzuki's eyes lit up. José wasn't totally dismissing them. They had a chance. "Just a quest. That's all we want," Suzuki said. "Something that will help us get gear so we can—"

"Yeah, yeah, I know. Fine. You got it. I've got a quest for you," José said, looking around the room. "I've got a whole lot of quest for you."

Even though José fell silent then, Suzuki was pretty sure the MERC was laughing maniacally.

## 9

A trapdoor behind the main bar of the Red Lion led down to a hidden hallway that José guided the Mundanes and the Horsemen through. It was a tight squeeze, and Suzuki was pressed up against Stew. They both tried to maintain distance, but Suzuki could feel Stew's muscles pressing against him, flexing uncontrollably.

Suzuki tried to push forward and shove Stew aside, only to find himself even closer to Stew. "Dude," Suzuki said, "your muscles are...cramping me."

Even though it was dark, Suzuki knew Stew was smirking with self-assuredness. "Yeah, they tend to do that. Can't really be helped."

The long, dark hallway led to a spacious room which held several comfortable, leather seats. A large table which was covered by a map and various clay figurines took up the majority of the room. The walls were covered with portraits of MERCs.

Given the nature of the portraits, Suzuki assumed that they were paintings of MERCs who had fallen.

José took a seat at the table and peered over the figurines

set up in various locations throughout Middang3ard. Suzuki stood next to him as the rest of the Mundanes found a place in the room.

Leaning over José's shoulder, Suzuki tried to angle himself to get a better look at the map of Middang3ard. In the whole time he'd been stationed at the Red Lion, he hadn't seen a full map of the realm. Fred had mentioned that each of the realms was identical to each other in geography, almost as if they had been interlaced on top of each other. The specifics of each region differed, but the natural geographical topographies were identical.

For example, each of the nine worlds had a Manhattan, but they were all developed differently. The imp had shown him what New York looked like for the dwarves: nothing but vast forests. The dwarves lived underground, so they had never touched the forests above. *Must make city planning easier*, Suzuki thought.

Whereas the gnomes' Manhattan looked like a scene out of a dystopic Steam Punk anime series, complete with black smoke billowing out of stacks and steam-powered zeppelins filling the sky.

Well, at least that's how the gnomish Manhattan had looked until it was conquered by the Dark One.

José moved around a couple of the figurines on the map. He stared at them for a bit before he turned to Suzuki. "So where did you say that your friend is?"

Suzuki pointed to the coast of New York, Ellis Island. He recognized the area from when he had triangulated Beth's position from her message. "There. Ellis Island. That's where Beth's message came from."

"That's not Ellis Island. Not here at least. It might be the same geographically, but it's a very different place in Middang3ard. We know that whole area was recently overrun with orcs. We also know that a host of the Dark One's troops have recently been stationed there. It's been hard to get any intel on the area recently. Most of the military that's stationed there has...well, you know. But at the moment, from everything we can tell, the island is being used as some sort of prison camp."

"So what's the plan?"

José swiped his hand over the map and a digitized screen popped up. The Mundanes were displayed on the screen, along with their gear and a bunch of ratings Suzuki didn't recognize. There was a percentage of success. It read .0007%. José pointed to the percentage.

"You three aren't going there yet," he said. "There's no way you'd even make it off the beach. We gotta figure out what you need to get so that you can at least make it a couple of feet without dying."

Suzuki wanted to object, but he kept his mouth shut. Across from him, Stew and Sandy's faces had sunk. There wasn't anything any of them could say though. They had asked José for help, and he'd finally given it to them. Suzuki knew that now was the time to listen.

José pointed to another section of the map, not too far from the Red Lion in the grand scope of things. "This," he explained, "is a good place to start. I'm guessing that the reason your percentage is so low is that you don't have the skills or the gear to make it there. The HUDs are designed to restrict MERCs from entering into areas they aren't prepared for. Back in the day, we lost a lot of good people because they were wandering into places where they couldn't possibly survive. So the HUDs have a built-in system to transport you back to the Red Lion if you step outside of your comfort zone. So what we have to do is send you someplace where we know that you'll get the tools you'll need to survive on this world's Ellis Island. This seems like a good place to start."

Sandy inched closer to the war table, swiped away the hologram of stats floating above the map and looked at the figurines on the table. There were three to represent the Mundanes. "So you'd send us here?" she asked. "Why here?"

"It's a quest that I've already been trying to get set up for you three," he said with a wink. "Christmas party or not, I've been planning this one for you ever since lover boy here came crying to me. As you know, it's the responsibility of the veterans to design quests for recruits who we think might actually make something worthwhile of themselves. We've been watching you three for a bit. Do you think Diana just helps every mage who comes to her? We've been scouting you. Or did none of you douchenozzles figure that out yet?"

Hearing someone else call them douchenozzles was like a punch to the gut for Suzuki. Still, it proved José's point. The only way he'd know that expression was if they'd been watching them when they were the Mundanes in the VR world of *Middang3ard*.

José folded his arms before going on. "This is a quest we all feel you'll be able to do, which will give you the loot you need to get to other areas."

Diana and the Chipmaster nodded in agreement with José.

José moved the three figurines representing the Mundanes closer to a large, gothic building. He stepped back and folded his arms over his chest. "It's going to be tougher than anything that you've done before. There are real risks. Any one of you could get badly hurt if you're not careful. You could die. And there's not going to be anyone to help you if shit goes south. Do you understand that?"

Suzuki didn't need to be asked twice. The risk didn't

matter to him. He knew that it didn't matter to Stew or Sandy either. If this was what they had to do to get to Beth, this was what they were going to do.

Stepping forward, Suzuki rested his hand on the hilt of his sword. "If you give it to us, we'll take care of it," Suzuki said.

"Then it's yours. I'll forward the paperwork to Wendy. She'll set you up with the rest of what you need."

"Thanks, José. We really appreciate everything you're doing for us."

José crossed himself solemnly. "Let the Lord...and *me* be clear about this, yet again. The Lord, not me, be with you." José held his hand out.

Suzuki clasped José's hand tightly. "We won't disappoint you."

"Let's hope not."

---

The Mundanes waited outside of the Red Lion as their provisions were being made ready. Stew and Sandy were leaning against the Red Lion, looking nervous. Stew was picking at his face, and Sandy was braiding and unbraiding her hair.

Wendy came around the side of the Red Lion, leading three horses. She came up to Suzuki and handed him the reins of the largest, a brute with a soft red mane. Wendy patted the horse's snout and fed it a carrot. "These guys'll serve you well. If you're going that far east, you need a mount that's up for the journey. These are three of our finest. They'll get you to your first checkpoint, and there you'll find something...more suitable for the terrain. José vouched for you."

Suzuki looked into the horse's eyes. They were deep brown and seemed to contain infinity. "We'll treat them well," he said.

Sandy and Stew came up, and each took a horse from Wendy. She nodded and walked off, turning only for a moment to watch the Mundanes as if there were something else she wanted to say. Instead, she walked back into the bar.

Suzuki mounted his horse and turned to watch Stew struggle to get onto his. Sandy hopped off hers and gave Stew a boost so that he could get onto the beast. Then she went back and effortlessly leapt onto her horse. She nudged it slightly, and the horse trotted over to Suzuki.

Stew's followed, causing Stew to lunge forward and grasp the horse's reins as if his life depended on it.

Sandy pulled the reins of her horse to slow it down and looked out at the sun hanging in its mid-noon comfort. "One more step closer," she said.

"One more step," Suzuki said. "Might as well get going and take that step."

The Mundanes rode out toward the East, leaving the Red Lion behind them. Suzuki did not know what it was that they were going to find in the East; he did not know what could be more dangerous than what they had faced already. All he did know was that they were getting closer to Beth.

That was all that mattered.

## 10

They had been riding for nearly three hours. Suzuki checked his map constantly for the first half of their trip. They had ridden a good distance from the Red Lion, and the swamp was fading behind them. Their first stop was to be at a ranch several hours away, where they were to switch out their horses.

Why they needed new horses, or even why they couldn't just use the teleport facilities, Suzuki had no idea. But it didn't matter. They were following José's directions, trusting the ancient MERC.

As the swamp disappeared, they traveled on grass. The trees were now less like hollowed out-ghouls and more full of life. Wildflowers grew along the road.

Suzuki led while Stew and Sandy rode side by side. He cast a look over his shoulder to see Stew singing softly to Sandy. She was giggling as she levitated a flower to Stew's ear.

He plucked it from the air and smelled it. "Feels good to actually get some fresh air. Smells better than the Red Lion and that elf city."

Sandy nudged her horse to catch up with Suzuki, and Stew quickened his pace to match Sandy's. "Yeah, I wasn't expecting the elvish city to be so...city-ish," she said. "It was a bit disappointing after everything I'd read about them."

Suzuki's interest was sparked. He hadn't thought to look into the history of any of the other races fighting in the MERCs. "What did you read about the elves?"

"Not much. I only started a few histories. Just to go along with all the elf magic theory I've been reading. Context, you know. One of the things that I had read, though, was that they had a vast empire back when none of the other realms even knew about each other. The elves were the only realm that managed to establish contact with the rest. They also had a huge spy network, and kept tabs on everyone else for thousands of years. But something happened, and their empire collapsed. I haven't been able to find out why. I'm not even sure the elves know."

"Fucking wild," Stew said. "All that history just lost."

Suzuki and Sandy stared at Stew in disbelief. "That almost sounds like insightful empathy," Suzuki joked.

"Fuck off. Just because I'm the very definition of manliness and valor doesn't mean I'm emotionless. It doesn't matter who you are, losing your history sounds tough. I can't imagine what it must feel like to not know anything about where you came from."

Suzuki nodded in agreement. He was preparing to launch into a lengthy lecture on the different groups of humans who had watched their history extinguish before their eyes when they reached the crest of a hill and he saw the ranch they were looking for in the valley below. At least he thought it was the ranch. Outside of the dozen or so horses grazing out back, it looked like a simple log cabin in the middle of nowhere.

They rode down to the ranch. It was little more than a small wooden affair off the side of the road, and Suzuki checked his HUD again to make sure they were in the right place. It seemed like an awful lot of trouble for a shack.

A large field of red wildflowers stretched out behind a meadow where dozens of horses grazed. As the Mundanes got closer, Suzuki could see that his initial appraisal of the horses and the meadow was wrong.

Those were not horses. As the Mundanes closed the distance between them, Suzuki could see that the creatures walking between the rows of what smelled like entrails were something else entirely.

The creatures were feathered and stood on two legs like ostriches. Their beaks were massive, shaped like axes, and cruelly sharp. There were at least a dozen of them meandering around.

Suzuki pinched his nose to try to block out the overpowering stench of death. "What the fuck are those?" he wondered aloud.

Fred unwrapped around Suzuki's mind. Somehow, Suzuki picked up that whatever was going to come out of Fred's mouth was going to be snide. *They are axbeaks, human,* Fred chided. *They are native to Middang3ard. I would have assumed that your exhaustive and useless knowledge of fantasy would have made that obvious.*

*I've never seen one before.*

*Your level of ignorance is never short of inspiring.*

Suzuki snapped his horse's reins, and the horse galloped toward the stable.

A dwarven woman was standing outside. She waved Suzuki over as he got closer to the stable. When Suzuki jumped off his horse, the dwarf took the reins.

"I hope you don't plan on dismounting like that with my

babies," the dwarf said. She spat, then wiped the spittle from her face as she eyed Suzuki with suspicion. "Name's Gwen. Those bad boys back there are my babies. You better treat them right."

One of the axbeaks looked up from its feeding trough, and that was when the Mundanes realized that they weren't eating hay, not unless hay bled red and was full of entrails.

The axbeak walked over to Suzuki, its head bobbing like a bird of prey as a piece of intestine hung out of his beak like a worm. When it close enough to Suzuki, it snapped at him. The crack of its beak let Suzuki know that it could have taken off his nose if it had wanted to.

Gwen came up behind Suzuki and pushed him out of the way. She petted the axbeak, whispering a soft cooing song under her breath to it. "Riding an axbeak isn't as easy as riding a horse. Those horses will listen to anyone wearing a HUD. My babies though, they only listen when you've earned it."

"So why did José send us here to pick them up? Why couldn't we just take horses the rest of the way?"

"Nothing's wrong with horses. But they ain't axbeaks. You take a horse into a fight, and you got as much of a liability as if you had a kid. My axbeaks, now; those are just as trusty as a fucking ax. They're lighter than horses too, which means they're faster. They should cut your trip time in half."

"If they're so great, how come you don't just give them to everyone then?" Stew asked.

Gwen reached into a pouch hanging on her side. She pulled out a severed orc arm and raised it to the closest axbeak. The axbeak reached over the fence and snapped the orc arm in half, catching one of the halves and instantly gobbling it down. "They're tough to take care of," Gwen said with a grin. "Gotta keep 'em fed, lest that be your arm."

Suzuki stepped forward and pulled out his coin purse. "Point made," he said. "So how much do I owe you?"

"All you owe me is bringing them back in one piece. As for the rental fee, it's on the house, courtesy of José. Thank him the next time you see him. And tell him Gwen says hi. Now let's get you situated."

Gwen led the Mundanes to the stable where the axbeaks were kept. She opened the fence and stepped beyond it before turning to the Mundanes and motioning for them to move slowly and to stay quiet. They all approached the closest creature. The bird was smaller than the rest around it. Gwen reached into her pouch, pulled out another piece of dismembered orc, and tossed it to the axbeak.

It snatched the bit of orc out of the air, threw it to the ground, and started to peck at it. Gwen looked at the Mundanes, sizing them up. She pointed at Stew. "This one will be good for Mr. Muscles over there," she said before whistling shrilly.

Two more axbeaks trotted over to Sandy and Suzuki. The axbeak that came up to Sandy's side nuzzled her face and nipped at her cheek, drawing blood. Sandy yelped and touched her face. As soon as she saw the blood, she smiled maniacally, cast Stoneskin, and headbutted the axbeak.

The axbeak stumbled backward before regaining its footing. Then it scratched at the ground as if it were preparing to charge. Sandy, still smiling gleefully, squared off with the axbeak and crouched. She moved first. Sandy dashed at the axbeak and tackled it to the ground as Gwen screamed in horror. The bird and Sandy tussled in the dirt, kicking up dust, as everyone watched.

Once the dust settled, Sandy had mounted the axbeak, and it reached back to nuzzle its beak against her chest.

Sandy slapped the axbeak's rear, and it leapt the fence separating the different sections of the stable. "I think he likes me," Sandy shouted.

Suzuki eyed his axbeak and approached it cautiously. The axbeak snorted loudly and pecked at the ground in what looked like irritation, but unlike Sandy's bird, it didn't attack. At least not yet.

Stew, meanwhile, was trying to grapple with his axbeak. The axbeak looked determined not to let Stew climb on. Out past the stables, Sandy was putting her axbeak through its paces.

Suzuki turned to Gwen, trying to hide how desperate he was. "How exactly am I supposed to get on this thing?"

Gwen was busy watching Sandy with her axbeak. "Huh? Oh," Gwen murmured. "Just don't be afraid. You gotta show 'em that you're not a wimp, so just get up on it."

"OK," he said and jumped on the axbeak, wrapping his arms around the beast's neck. It tried to take off running, slinging Suzuki around, but he managed to pull himself up onto its back.

Suzuki was mid-self-congratulation when the axbeak whipped its head around and tried to take a bite out of Suzuki's face. He hit his HUD, and his helmet shimmered over his face. The axbeak hit the steel of his helmet with a heavy clank before turning its head suddenly and screeching. With that, the axbeak was off, vaulting over the fence and taking off after Sandy.

The axbeak was fast. It took everything that Suzuki had to keep holding onto the flimsy reins attached to the axbeak's neck. Suzuki wanted to check how Stew was doing, but it was taking every bit of concentration he had to keep from falling off.

From behind him, he could hear Gwen laughing.

*Don't be afraid. Don't be afraid,* Suzuki repeated to himself. He clenched the reins tightly, dug his feet into the side of the axbeak, and pulled back on the reins. Hard.

The axbeak skidded across the grass and stumbled, but didn't fall. Its head cocked back and forth like a bored pigeon. "I think I'm getting the hang of this," Suzuki shouted as he finally looked back to see how Stew was doing.

Stew had mounted his axbeak, but the bird was refusing to vault over the fence. Gwen had opened the stable fence so that Stew and his axbeak could trot out. Stew gingerly snapped the reins, and the creature trotted off to catch up with Suzuki and Sandy.

It appeared that the barbarian had lucked out and gotten the most docile bird of the bunch.

*Sometimes life just isn't fair,* Suzuki lamented.

Gwen closed the stable gate and climbed on top of it. "You take care of my babies, all right!"

Sandy petted her axbeak's head and its rough tongue hung out of its mouth like a thirsty dog's. "What do they eat?" Sandy asked.

"What won't they eat is a better question."

---

The Mundanes rode off, steering their axbeaks away from the stables with Sandy leading the pack, Suzuki struggling to keep up with her, and Stew trotting behind.

Stew cracked the reins and the bird screeched, tossing him to the ground. As Stew scrambled to get to his feet, the axbeak slashed at Stew with its beak. "Guys," Stew shouted. "My bird is trying to fucking kill me!"

Sandy and Suzuki turned around and galloped back toward Stew. When Suzuki's axbeak saw that there was open mutiny, it tossed Suzuki onto the ground as well. Sandy's axbeak whined as if it were preparing to join in the fray.

She smacked it in the back of the head. The bird stared lovingly at her.

Stew was still struggling to get to his feet, as was Suzuki. The axbeaks were fast and much more vicious now that they were out of Gwen's watchful gaze. Their beaks rose and fell with frightening speed. Both Stew and Suzuki were only able to narrowly avoid their attacks.

*Fucking great,* Suzuki thought to himself. *We survive trolls and giants, and what does us in is a mutant ostrich.*

Sandy pulled up beside Suzuki and Stew, her axbeak stomping its feet as if it were irritated at Suzuki's lack of proficiency. Even if the axbeak wasn't annoyed, Suzuki was thoroughly embarrassed. He could deal with being attacked. But by his own steed?

Finally managing to get to his feet, Suzuki and the axbeak locked into a death stare as they circled each other.

They circled twice before Suzuki's axbeak dove forward, slashing with its face. Suzuki stepped to the side and got his arms around the bird. He squeezed as hard as he could and pulled down until the axbeak took a knee.

Then he slapped it in the face multiple times with his iron gauntlet-covered hand until it blinked its eyes rapidly in surprise. The bird cooed softly and leaned over for Suzuki to mount.

"Shit," Suzuki said, "these things only respond to violence."

"Sucks for Stew," Sandy pointed out. "He's as fangless as an earthworm."

Stew was still struggling with his axbeak. He hadn't managed to get to his feet and the axbeak was still coming after him. Suzuki figured that this was some kind of game for the birds. If it had really meant to hurt Stew, it probably would have chopped off his testicles by now.

Suzuki rode up to Stew's axbeak and punched it in the face. The axbeak sidestepped and shook its head, then it whistled like a parakeet before flapping its wings and kneeling for Stew to mount.

Suzuki could hear Fred laughing internally. *You think this is bad?* Fred snorted. *You should see them in the wild.*

*What's a bunch of them called?* Suzuki asked, directing his thoughts to Fred. *A violence of axbeaks?*

At that, the imp cackled. *That was a good one, human. I'll be sure to tell that one to my next human host.*

*So never, then,* Suzuki shot back. *You'll never get to tell that joke, huh?*

Suzuki could feel Fred contemplating this before saying, *I like you, human. You were a good choice.*

Stew, finally understanding that they needed to be rough with the axbeaks, punched his on the back of the head. It cooed. Shaking his head in disbelief, he cried out, "Who the hell thought it was a good idea to ride these things?"

Fred fielded that question, although because the imp was still inside Suzuki, only he could hear the answer. *Dwarves tend to raise them, and since dwarves are not often riders themselves, they can have the detachment necessary to harshly train them for other riders. Still, I have seen a level of brutality between axbeaks and dwarves that would rival even the Dark One. The only difference is that the axbeaks seem to like it. Somewhat akin to your human BDSM relationships.*

*You know about BDSM? How did you—*

*Some of us have lived, Suzuki. Some of us have lived,* Fred said with a cackle before withdrawing, leaving him alone, feeling like he was a constant source of pity and entertainment for his familiar.

Still, Fred had complimented him, so they were making baby steps.

Super tiny baby-fucking-steps.

---

The Mundanes traveled down the dirt road of the meadow for some time. Stew and Suzuki were still struggling to keep control of their steeds, but even Sandy was having trouble keeping hers on the road.

The axbeaks didn't like walking on the beaten path, and if they were not forced to, they would happily wander off into the thick brush of the surrounding area.

Suzuki wondered what it was that the axbeaks found so interesting about the meadows around them. If they were natives of Middang3ard, it was possible that they had an innate understanding of the world. They probably felt much more comfortable than Suzuki taking the untrodden path.

Suzuki's axbeak continually passed gas. It was a terrible smell of rotting eggs and old lima beans. The axbeak had been doing it for nearly half an hour. Stew's mount did the same, and Suzuki felt like he was traveling with a noxious gas cloud hanging over his head. "These things are fucking disgusting," Suzuki complained.

Sandy looked over her shoulder and laughed. "No worse than you when you're sleeping," she shouted back.

"I don't fart in my sleep."

"Everyone farts in his sleep. Yours just smell like you're dying."

Suzuki looked to Stew for support, but Stew wouldn't meet his eyes. "It's pretty bad, dude. That's why, as soon as we could afford it, you got your own room."

"I thought you guys got another room to be polite," Suzuki said.

"Polite about what?"

"Me hearing everything that you do."

"Oh, that? I don't give a shit about that. You could stand to get out of the room for an hour."

"More like a couple of minutes." Suzuki chuckled.

Stew reached out to grab him, but Suzuki clicked his tongue and his axbeak sped up. Stew almost fell off but caught his balance. Suzuki caught up to Sandy while she laughed at Stew's reddening face. "It's more than a couple of minutes, babe," Sandy called back.

The sun was setting. Suzuki pulled up his map via his HUD. He looked around the meadows and scratched his head. "We still have a long way to go. It's probably time that we started to look for someplace to camp. We shouldn't be on the main road."

"Why not?" Stew asked.

"Haven't you ever read—"

"I'm going to stop you there. No, I have not read whatever nerdy thing you're going to say to justify not wanting to sleep on the road."

"It's like Highwayman 101. Always rob the people who are sleeping on the road."

"And Animal 101 is always attack the people off the road."

"Sandy, what do you think?"

Sandy watched the setting sun. "Off the road," she

suggested. "There shouldn't be anything big and scary in the meadows. Niv was telling me that axbeaks are pretty sensitive to predators around them, and these guys seem fine."

Stew leaned forward to get a better look at the sharpness of his bird's beak. "I'd hate to see what eats these things. Well, lead the way, Fearless Leader. If you get eaten by a bear, I'm taking your gear."

"If I get eaten by a bear, you're the second course," Suzuki pointed out.

---

The Mundanes rode a mile away from the road as the last bit of light faded from the green and yellow meadows. They built up a fire and pitched their tents, and soon their small camp felt almost homey. Stew supplied the food: salted strips of hydra meat from the Red Lion. Sandy tossed a beer to Stew and Suzuki before cracking her own and opening a book.

Suzuki watched the sky, occasionally looking at his map. "What do you think Beth is doing right now?"

Sandy looked up from her book. She turned the page with a wave of her hand and shuddered. "I try not to think about it," she answered. "I've never been to prison, and I'd hate to think what an orc prison is like."

Stew bit into a thick piece of the hydra jerky. "Dude, we're going to get her back. She's going to be okay."

"Yeah, I know," Suzuki said. "It's just, you know, I wish we would have figured this shit out sooner. We wasted so much time with all those bullshit missions, all the fucking gear grinding. And the whole time, Beth is out there, and we don't even know if—"

"Suzuki," Stew interrupted.

Suzuki looked up from his map. Stew was staring at him, the fire casting shadows over his face. He looked confident; there was no doubt on his face. He had the certainty Suzuki wished he could feel. "Beth is going to be okay. We trust you. José thinks it's possible. It's going to be all right."

"Yeah, I guess so."

Suzuki laid down in the grass and looked up at the stars, the millions of small, shimmering lights. There were different constellations in Middang3ard. He didn't recognize any of them. Even if people had been living in Middang3ard for thousands of years, he was still discovering it. He tried to push thoughts of Beth out of his mind.

It wasn't that he didn't want to think of her, he just knew it wasn't going to get him anywhere. Sitting around and freaking out about Beth wasn't helping anyone.

Besides, he was here with the Mundanes now. They'd all be with Beth soon enough.

Sandy tossed a book over to Suzuki. He picked it up and read the title. *Tome of The Holy Hand.* "What's this?" Suzuki asked.

"Thought you might be a little interested in some more spells," Sandy suggested. "It's not as dry as some of the other books I got from the library."

"Thanks. I've been meaning to check out more magic stuff."

"And you should. Because you fight like a fighter, not a warrior-mage."

"And we already got a barbarian," Stew said. "It was nice to have another fighter when Beth was here, but what we need is a fighter with some spell-slinging skills."

Suzuki held his hands up as if he could ward off the criticisms. "I didn't know we were having a town hall tonight. I think I've been holding my own pretty well."

"No one's saying you aren't. Shit, you fight better than you ever did when we were playing. All me and Sandy are getting at is you need to be whipping that holy magic around more. You used to save the day with that shit before, with that and the plans. We're just saying we know you can do it. We got faith in you, dude."

"Thanks. That means a lot coming from you guys."

"Who else would it come from?"

"Point taken."

They talked a bit more through the course of their modest meal. The night was wearing on, heavy and tiresome. Sleep was starting to get at their eyes, and it was not long before Stew was dozing next to the fire, his head propped on his shield.

Sandy was still awake, reading as usual, curled up next to Stew like a giant cat. Niv was by the fire, snoring softly. Suzuki struggled to keep his eyes open. They'd close and he'd open them, only for them to close again. They remained closed longer each time.

---

Suzuki snapped awake. He was the only one sitting by the fire. He could hear giggling and whispering, and when he looked around the camp, he could see Stew and Sandy's shadows silhouetted in their tent. Suzuki groaned as he stood, stretched, and tried to ignore the sound of skin slapping skin coming from the tent.

He went to his own tent, zipped it behind himself, and cast an Alarm spell that should alert him of any attacks—not that he was expecting any.

Safe and secure...and alone. Nothing was coming in, and nothing was going out. So Suzuki pulled up his HUD and looked through his book section. Sandy's spellbook looked too boring since he was already tired. And there was that book that he had gotten from *Oddities*...

Suzuki looked over his shoulder as if there could be someone watching him in his tent. *Just a quick look*, Suzuki said to himself. *I don't even know what kind of story I want to hear, so it's not like I'm doing anything weird to begin with. Plus, it's a story. I'm just listening to a story.*

The book flipped open. Suzuki stared down at the blank pages as a voice whispered quietly in his ear.

*"I've been waiting a long time for this, Suzuki."*

It was Beth's voice. Low and sultry. Just the softest of whispers. Then the book started to speak.

*Beth danced over to Suzuki, her body moving as if she had intimate control over every nerve. She sat next to him and rested her hand on his knee. She kissed him, her tongue lingering over his lips as her hands reached down to his stiffening—*

Suzuki unbuckled his pants. He looked out of his tent one last time. Stew and Sandy were still busy with each other. They wouldn't even notice. He just had to be quiet and listen to the story playing in his ear. Suzuki lay back, closed his eyes, and let himself get caught up in the story.

*What the hell are you doing?* Fred shouted.

Suzuki jerked out from under his blanket as if someone had slapped him. He pulled up his pants and looked around the tent. *Fred?* he asked. *What the fuck?*

*Are you preparing to gratify yourself to that paltry sex tome?*

*Gratify myself? What the fuck are you talking about?*

*You know exactly what I'm talking about.*

*Shit, get off my case. I was going to masturbate, all right? Is that what you wanted me to say?*

*While your friends copulate a few feet away and you listen to a pathetic rendering of your love life?*

*I didn't know you were such a prude. People jack off and watch porn.*

*While listening to their friends fucking?*

*Okay, I'll give it to you. That one is kinda weird.*

*It is disturbing. Every time you...discharge...I have feelings of euphoria and happiness. It is...uncomfortable.*

*Wait? Are you saying you cum when I cum?*

*Just keep your hands off of yourself, you foul, talking primate!*

Suzuki sat in the silence of this disturbing news. He hadn't really thought much about the extent to which Fred could feel what he felt. Fred never mentioned being in pain when Suzuki was. That said, he had mentioned more than a few times that he enjoyed the taste of some meals Suzuki had eaten, so it wasn't a stretch to assume that he felt most of what Suzuki felt.

*You could at least use the book for something constructive instead of relieving your...physical needs.*

*What do you mean?* Suzuki asked.

*The book tells you stories based on what you like to hear and do. Granted, I understand your species has an unhealthy desire to...stimulate each other. But the book is only limited by what you choose to see. In essence, it has the potential to be a portal to many possibilities and is limited only by your own desires. It seems a waste to have such a powerful object be your designated jackoff tool.*

*There's nothing wrong with jacking off! But you do have a point.*

Suzuki turned to the book, closed his eyes, and focused. When he opened them, he saw ink forming on the blank pages. The ink took shape and became figures which morphed into illustrations of large-scale battle tactics. *Huh,* he said. *This could be useful.* Suzuki took out the book of spells adept fighters could use that Sandy had given him and set it next to the magic tome from *Oddities*.

*I believe this is a much better use of your time*, Fred said.

Suzuki looked out of his tent again. Sandy and Stew had gone to sleep. He turned back to his books. *Yeah, I think so too. But I'm still jacking off tonight. So you either need to check out for a little bit or figure out what you're going to do.*

*I will excuse myself.*

*All right. Then I'll hit the book.*

*Filthy primate.*

---

## 11

Suzuki struggled to get out of bed. He wasn't sure what time it was, but he had slept horribly. Stew and Sandy had woken up a couple times throughout the night as well. The constant rustling of their tent had made it a little difficult to sleep.

Sandy and Stew were already up, and Suzuki could hear their voices from outside the tent. He sighed, looked for his clothes, closed his books, and stumbled outside. The sun was bright and the air was crisp, full of the scent of wildflowers. Sandy was sitting next to the fire, reading. She looked up and nodded at Suzuki. That was all the good morning Suzuki was getting out of her.

Stew was cooking eggs and bacon in a small cast iron skillet. "Figured a hearty breakfast would give us a good start. I dig the jerky but, I don't want to be eating it for every meal. I made sure to pack a couple more things this time around."

Suzuki was immersed in the smell of breakfast. He felt drawn to the sizzling bacon. "I didn't know you knew how to cook."

"You should just assume that I know how to do everything. I'm fucking amazing, remember? Just chalk the cooking up to that."

Sandy looked up from her book and levitated the percolator and a cup toward herself. "He's actually surprisingly good at cooking. That's how he got off of dish duty at the Red Lion."

Stew dumped some eggs and bacon onto a plate and handed it to Suzuki. "Yeah, Wendy said she could use an extra hand in the kitchen, and I jumped at it. I fucking hated dish duty. The worse part about the kitchen is listening to Wendy yell, but I guess that's just working in a kitchen."

Suzuki took a bite of the eggs. They were cooked over-easy. He dipped his bacon in the runny yolk and sighed with satisfaction. "I haven't had eggs like this in so long. Why do they taste so different than the Red Lion's?"

"'Cause these are actual chicken eggs. Earth chickens. I had to beg Wendy to let me take some. I think she hordes them all for herself."

Stew cracked a few more eggs and smirked at Suzuki.

Suzuki finished his eggs, then got up and started breaking down his tent. Sandy continued reading while Suzuki finished tearing down his part of the camp.

"So we're heading farther east," Suzuki said. "I think we still have two more days of riding. Maybe less, since we're getting an earlier start than yesterday. Ready to get going?"

Sandy waved her hand at her tent. The tent spikes flew out of the ground and placed themselves in a pile while the tent neatly folded itself up. "Ready whenever you are."

They went to untie their axbeaks. Sandy quickly mounted hers.

Stew's axbeak snapped at him, locked eyes, and ruffled its feathers. He reached out to try and pet the axbeaks' head and the bird snapped again. "Sandy?" Stew asked. "How the hell did you get yours to like you?"

"Dominance," Sandy said.

Suzuki had the same problem as Stew. He was circling his axbeak, and it looked like the bird wanted to fight. Obviously whatever bonding they had done the day before was out the window. The axbeak scratched at the ground like it was preparing to charge. Suzuki unsheathed his sword and knocked the axbeak in the face with the sword's hilt. The axbeak shook it off but relented. Suzuki climbed on top of its back. "You just gotta give it a smack," Suzuki shouted as he trotted off to catch up with Sandy.

"It's so cute though," Stew shouted back. "How am I supposed to hit something so cute?"

Suzuki and Sandy waited for ten minutes for Stew to finally decide to hit the axbeak in the face. It took three lunges, one tackle, and a gash in Stew's thigh to force him to hit the bird. But when he hit it, he hit it hard. The axbeak instantly relented, and soon they were on their way.

The Mundanes followed the path for the better part of the morning. Suzuki let Sandy led the way. She was obviously better at riding than Stew and him. Besides, the axbeaks seemed more inclined to follow Sandy than either him or Stew.

Suzuki didn't mind at all. It gave him a chance to sit back and enjoy the scenery. The green, sloping hills were particularly fascinating. They were covered with a variety of flowers. Butterflies blanketed the meadow, and it was easy to confuse them for flowers. Suzuki was struck with the urge to climb off his axbeak and go running through the meadow more than a handful of times, and in that way, at least, he could relate to why the axbeaks were constantly trying to get off the dirt road.

Stew trotted up to Sandy and they started talking. Suzuki didn't bother listening. He'd grown so used to their one-on-one chats that he'd come to look forward to them. It was just more time to run through things in his mind.

*Hey, Fred?* Suzuki asked. *Did you see any of those spells I was reading through last night?*

*Unfortunately, I saw everything you did last night.*

*I told you that you could go for a walk.*

*I would prefer to stop speaking about this.*

*Gotcha, you little perv. But you did read through the book with me?*

*The spells seemed simple enough.*

*Sweet. I want to try some of them when the time is right.*

*I will help as I see fit. You also have a message on your HUD.*

Suzuki pulled up his HUD's display. There was a message from an unnamed account. Suzuki didn't know whether or not his HUD could get spam emails, but he figured it would be better to check the email.

He opened it.

The message was from Real_Deal, a player he had known back on Earth. Real_Deal had been one of the few *Middang3ard* players, or humans for that matter, who had taken the threat of the Dark One seriously. He had been theorizing over the purpose of the final *Middang3ard* expansion for months. Most people online had thought he was crazy. Suzuki initially had too. But he had a lot of good points about most of his theories.

As it turned out, he had been right about Middang3ard and the MERCs.

Earlier in the week, Suzuki had messaged Real_Deal, complaining about the area access issues he and the Mundanes were experiencing. He hadn't heard back, and had assumed that Real_Deal was too caught up in his life in Middang3ard to respond.

**Yo,** the message read. **Click here. Encrypted chat. TTYS.**

Suzuki clicked the link in the message. His HUD downloaded the program, and another message popped up. **What's up, Newb?** Real_Deal said.

**You gotta stop calling me that,** Suzuki replied.

**Stop newbing it up then. What's up? Your last message was filled with a lot of bullshit information.**

**We've been trying to find Beth.**

**I know that.**

**But we can't get close to her. We're locked out of most of Middang3ard.**

**Duh. Military does it to keep you from getting killed.**

**But we aren't military.**

**Your HUDs are. The Military and the MERCs are closer than you think.**

**Well, is there anything you can do to help us?**

**Nope, the failsafe is pretty...you know, failsafe. You get transported out of an area if your percentages are too low.**

**Yeah, I know. So you messaged me just to tell me that you can't help me?**

**Nope, I messaged you to give you something your whack ass might appreciate. Check it out.**

Real_Deal messaged Suzuki another link. He clicked it, and a program started downloading.

**So Middang3ard is all scoped out,** Real_Deal said. **It's part of the military recon. They've got hundreds of satellites floating above the atmosphere to help coordinate attacks on the Dark One's forces. Pretty good ones too. The images are solid. Crisp. I figure you could probably put it to good use. Like I said, there are a lot of satellites,**

and they're all named in code or another language or something. I didn't really care to find out. It seemed like too much work. But you can start going through them and maybe find something. I've been taking a look here and there. Anyways, I gotta bounce. Duty calls. Talk to you later, Newb. Good luck.

What duty?

The message deleted itself, along with the messaging program. The only thing that was left on Suzuki's HUD was the satellite viewer. Suzuki pulled it up.

The program's interface was bizarre. It took up the whole HUD. It looked like a 3D rendering of Earth projected onto another image of Middang3ard. There were patterns of broken lines streaming through each of the images. It looked like it might be satellite orbits. But Real_Deal had downplayed how many satellites there were. The map was practically covered with them. It was pretty obvious why Real_Deal hadn't figured it out. He'd tended to lack the resolve for big projects.

Suzuki clicked on one of the satellite feeds. Two images popped up onto his HUD. On the left, was the Grand Canyon. He wasn't sure exactly where in the Canyon, but he recognized it from pictures. To the right was another image of the Grand Canyon. This one was in Middang3ard though. The canyon was filled with thousands of orcs. They stretched on throughout the entire canyon, their torches burning so that the canyon floor looked like it was host to a tiny city.

*Are you fucking serious?* Suzuki thought. *This is the Dark One's army?*

*No,* Fred interrupted. *This is a fraction of the Dark One's army.*

*How the hell did he get so many soldiers?*

*No one knows for sure.*

Up ahead, Sandy cast a glance over her shoulder. She pulled her axbeak's reins and slowed down. "Hey, Suzuki," she called back. "You okay?"

Suzuki hadn't realized it, but he was trembling. He felt cold all over. The Dark One had more than an army.

He had a fucking empire.

There was no way the few MERCs he had seen had a chance, even if the MERC encampment were tripled. And how many did Middang3ard's army have? Suzuki tried to swallow, but his throat was dry. His head was swimming, and he felt he needed to sit down.

"Uh, nothing," Suzuki squeaked. "Just daydreaming."

Stew laughed and turned his axbeak around so he could face Suzuki. "He's probably just blue-balling," Stew said. "Fred wouldn't let him jerk off last night."

"What?"

"Yeah, the familiars got this whole familiar Skype or something so they can talk to each other. Sounds kinda weird to me."

*Either Fred respected my privacy and hadn't updated them or hadn't gotten around to it yet*, Suzuki thought, realizing he needed to be a bit more careful. He had no control over what Fred told the other familiars, and by extension, what the familiars told their hosts. It all made for a very messy situation.

"Talk," Sandy interrupted. "More like gossip."

Suzuki nodded and pointed to his crotch. "Yeah, that's it," he lied. "Just super horny."

Stew laughed and shook his head. "Come on, dude, you gotta stand up for yourself. You can't be getting pushed around by a giant lizard that lives in your head."

As Stew tried to turn back around, his axbeak took the

opportunity to balk, tossing Stew off its back. Stew hit the ground in a crash of steel and broken pride. He tried to avoid Sandy and Suzuki's eyes as he climbed back onto his bird.

Not that Suzuki was really paying attention. His head was still reeling from what he had seen. In real-time, too. They were fucked, and at that moment, it dawned on Suzuki that getting Beth was just the beginning. The war for Middang3ard would be epic, and it scared the shit out of Suzuki.

Sandy slowed down to match Suzuki's pace. She nudged him with her foot. "You sure everything's okay, Suzuki?"

"Yeah, definitely," he lied. "Ahh, so, how often does your familiar talk with Fred?" Suzuki asked.

"Just about every night."

"Hmm. I'd assumed he was as crotchety with them as he is with me."

"Nope. Seems like they get along fine." Sandy reached out a hand, placing it on Suzuki's shoulder (not easy to do while on the axbeaks, but Sandy seemed to have full control of hers). "Suzuki, you know if something is up, you can talk to us about it. Just cause you're the one making plans and everything doesn't mean you have to be up in your head the whole time."

Suzuki thought about telling Sandy. Sharing the images with both of them, even. But that would only rattle them like it did him. And they needed to stay focused if they were going to finish José's quest. "Yeah, I know. Trust me, nothing's wrong. Just enjoying the view. It's beautiful out here."

Sandy nodded in agreement. She looked out at the meadow they were riding through. "Maybe getting off the road for a little bit might not be a bad idea. 'Sides, I'm pretty hungry."

"Yeah, that sounds good."

Sandy led them off the road and up a nearby hill. They tied their axbeaks to a tree and sat around a small fire, where they cooked a quick meal of pork and fresh vegetables courtesy of Wendy's kitchen.

Suzuki tried to keep his mind focused on his friends as he listened to them talking, but he was still spacing out. Every time he closed his eyes, he could see the army of the Dark One marching through the MERC encampment, laying waste to everyone who stood in their way.

Stew tossed a piece of raw meat in Suzuki's face, snapping him out of his obsessing.

"What the fuck, Stew?"

"You looked like you could use some meat," Stew answered.

"I looked like I could use some meat?"

"Yeah. You know you're a growing boy and all."

Suzuki picked up the piece of pork and tossed it onto the skillet. He watched the porkchop sizzle as it browned. But he couldn't help thinking that the war was already in Middang3ard and if it spread, he doubted anyone would survive.

At least he had these idiots around to die with him.

Sandy snatched the piece of pork from the skillet and held it over the fire. "I've been working on my elemental resistance with charms. Check this out." She plunged her hand into the fire and pulled it out after a few seconds. Her skin was undamaged, and the pork chop was cooked to perfection. "I figure it might help if I could tank for us, too. I don't think that Stew can take any more axes to the chest," Sandy explained.

"Psh," Stew disagreed. "I'll take as many axes as are thrown at me. It's going to take more than an ax to kill me."

"You're right. Maybe three. At the same time."

"I'll manage."

Suzuki pulled out his map and checked how far they were from their destination. José hadn't told them too much about what they were riding toward, just that it was a small hamlet to the east. Suzuki wondered if they would recognize it when they got there. So far, there hadn't been any signs of civilization, just idyllic nature.

"You know, I don't really know what we're up against this time," Suzuki said. "I didn't even think of that when José sent us off. Even Milos told us a little bit about what we were getting ourselves into."

"Diana said that's part of how vets do the quests," Sandy explained. "Each quest is kind of like a test, I guess. They take assigning them pretty seriously. That's why we were given the run around so much before. I thought it was just MERCs being assholes. Turns out, nobody wanted to take responsibility for us getting killed."

"Guess that makes sense."

Stew bit into his porkchop as he dumped dirt over the fire to extinguish it. "Still feels like they were being assholes."

"What I'm trying to say is that we could get really hurt if we don't watch out for each other. Your head gonna be in the game, Suzuki?"

Suzuki nodded as he stood and walked toward his axbeak. "Have I ever let you guys down?" he asked.

"Not that I know of."

"I'm gonna keep it that way."

The Mundanes rode off into the afternoon sun. The little break was exactly what Suzuki had needed. Even if he was worried about the looming war, he knew that the

Mundanes were going to have his back. He was going to have theirs as well.

---

They rode for the rest of the day, hardly taking any time to rest. Their axbeaks were exhausted by mid-afternoon, and Sandy talked the guys into taking a break next to a river that flowed through the meadow. Then they were up and moving again.

The meadow faded around them, and they came to a village. The doors of all of the houses had been boarded up, and the streets were filled with glass. The smell of death and decomposition hung heavy in the air. As they went farther into the town, the smell got less bearable. The Mundanes stopped riding once they got to the center. There were piles of dead elves stacked as if they were going to be burned.

Stew jumped off his axbeak and approached the closest pile as he pinched his nose. "Holy shit," he murmured. "Guess this is why people don't go far from the Red Lion on a regular basis."

Sandy walked up beside Stew. She looked like she was going to cry or vomit or both at the same time. "Yeah, Chip told me most recruits hardly ever get sent this far out. This is fucked up. I wonder what happened."

"Looks like they were in the wrong place at the wrong time."

"It's fucked up when your home is the wrong place," Stew said.

Suzuki looked down at one of the piles of bodies. This was what the forces of the Dark One did. He knew it was them beyond a doubt. "We should get going," he said finally.

"Hold on," Sandy said. She looked around and raised her hands to the air. "Inferno," she whispered.

The piles of bodies caught fire, and the flies laying their eggs rose in a large black swarm. The sky filled with dark clouds.

Sandy walked back to her axbeak and mounted it. "It's the least that we can do. The dead shouldn't be left like that."

The Mundanes departed from the village and continued to ride until sunset. They hardly spoke to each other, ruminating on what they had seen in the village. When they stopped to make camp, they ate a silent meal, the flames flickering and their shadows growing long and strange.

No one said goodnight.

They each went to their tents in their own time, and Suzuki asked Sandy to cast any warding spells she knew. He also cast Alarm and Clairvoyance for good measure. The spells should warn them of any danger.

It took Suzuki a while to fall asleep. He couldn't get the sight of the dead elves' eyes out of his mind. When he did finally fall asleep, his dreams were black and frightening.

Not that he remembered any of them, for when sleep came, it took him as swiftly as death whisks away one's soul.

## 12

The Mundanes broke camp as the sun crested the green hills to the East, setting the sky ablaze in a spectrum of colors.

Suzuki hardly noticed it.

He packed up his tent, his sleeping bag, and his books, working in a haze. The world seemed dull around him. He felt like he was in the opening of the *Wizard of Oz*. He had stepped back into Kansas, back into a gray, sterile world.

Sandy and Stew were no better. Neither of them spoke during their quick breakfast: runny eggs and undercooked bacon. Sandy hardly looked up when Stew leaned over to give her a kiss before they mounted their axbeaks. The sight from the night before hung over them all like a guillotine blade ready to fall.

Suzuki knew he should probably say something. He was the leader of the party. He'd given rousing speeches to dig them out of a funk before, and this really wasn't that much different. Except it felt different. Something deep within Suzuki made him feel as if the carnage they had seen last night held some higher meaning. It was an omen of sorts.

They traveled in silence toward the East. Even the axbeaks didn't give them much attitude, barely acting up in their usual way.

The terrain of the country was changing as they made their way East. The flat plains had disappeared and there were rolling hills in the distance, some to the side. Suzuki pulled up the map on his HUD and tried to figure out exactly where they were.

Suzuki couldn't focus. He didn't see roads or terrain on the map. All he saw were lines that he knew were supposed to mean something, but he couldn't figure out what they were. His hands were trembling, and he shakily turned off his HUD.

Suzuki felt Fred uncurling from around his mind. *You humans seem to be lacking in banter this morning,* Fred said.

*Just tired,* Suzuki responded.

*You slept for ten hours last night. Are human bodies so frail that they require twelve hours of sleep?*

*I'm not in the mood, Fred.*

*No? All this week, you've wanted nothing more than to trade quips and sarcastic comments with me. Now all of a sudden, you're too tired to talk?*

Suzuki sighed. *Fred, I'm not in the mood.*

*Perhaps you aren't,* Fred hissed. *Neither are your companions. You all seem to be...disturbed.*

*No, we're cool,* Suzuki said, pinching the bridge of his nose. *Stop worrying.*

*Fine. Have it your way.*

The Mundanes rode until noon, crossing a valley and descending into a low field that was surrounded by hills on both sides. The hills were covered with a bloom of orange and pink flowers which filled the valley with a sweet, perfume-like scent which carried undertones of stone and damp moss.

Suzuki thought the scent was familiar. Something about it reminded him of home, of a time that he and his father had spent together camping up in the hills near his home.

If Suzuki closed his eyes, he could almost see the river that he and his father used to camp beside and the trees that stretched overhead in a canopy that filtered light so that it looked as if shards of light lay between each blade of grass. He could see his father, silhouetted in the rising sun, smoking a cigarette, face haloed in wisps of smoke.

Suzuki couldn't keep his eyes closed. His axbeak was trying to buck him off its backside. He tapped its forehead roughly and looked up ahead. Even Sandy's axbeak was giving her a hard time. It tried to veer off the road, and Sandy was barely able to catch its attention before it would have tossed her off. Suzuki wondered what all this was doing to their travel time.

The map Suzuki had been given was very concise in some areas and in others, completely lacking. What the map lacked in quest clarity was made up with specific notes on time and distance. According to the map, they should have already reached the village that they were riding toward. That was not the case. From what Suzuki could figure out, they were running a few hours behind schedule.

Suzuki snapped the reins of his axbeak and trotted to catch up with Sandy. "Hey, Sandy," Suzuki ventured. "How are you holding up?"

Sandy turned around. Her eyes were foggy. A smile hung on her face like a painting placed over a crack in the wall. "Huh? What am I holding?"

"No, I asked how you are holding up. You okay?"

"Yeah, yeah. I'm good. I'm just hoping that we aren't lost or anything like that. It feels like we've been riding forever."

"Ass sore?"

"Huh?"

"I asked if your ass is sore."

Suzuki desperately hoped that Stew would say something. He had set Stew up for the punchline. Even though Stew was riding next to Sandy, he didn't bother saying anything. His eyes stared blankly ahead as he absentmindedly thumped the back of his axbeak's head. Suzuki would have killed for a sex joke. It didn't matter how crass or awkward it was. Anything would have been better than the silence, the ever-growing, deepening silence.

It was a silence that echoed. Or rather, didn't echo...like the village they had ridden through.

There had been no sounds of children playing.

Suzuki pushed the thought out of his head and focused on the road. He tried to listen to the sound of the axbeak's claws as they dug into the ground. There was a rhythm to their movement, almost like a chicken scratching a beat.

The ground in the village had been scratched as well. Whatever had torn through that village was the owner of a particularly nasty, large set of claws. The ground surrounding the pile of dead bodies looked like a massive rake had been dragged through the dirt.

Suzuki forced his mind back to the present. They were riding East. They were looking for an ancient item José needed. They were the Mundanes, the victors of multiple battles, friends who cared deeply about each other, who were going to rescue...

No one had come to rescue those villagers. Maybe no one knew. Maybe no one cared.

It came rushing up before Suzuki realized what was

happening. He jumped off his axbeak and ran to the side of the road. He fell to his knees. All of his body was shaking. His skin was hot, it felt almost too hot to touch. He wanted to rip his clothes off, to crawl out of his skin, to run screaming into the hills.

He vomited instead.

Stew and Sandy dismounted their axbeaks. Sandy ran over to Suzuki and knelt beside him. She put her hand on his shoulder as Suzuki trembled. Suzuki was repeating something under his breath, but it was muted through his tremors. Sandy leaned forward to hear better.

"No one rescued them."

Suzuki repeated this over and over. It was boring itself into his skull like some kind of sadistic mantra. No one had saved them. There were piles of unmarked graves a mere two days ride from the MERC encampment—and there hadn't been one MERC body.

Sandy shook Suzuki, and they both tumbled onto the grass. The contact woke Suzuki up. He pushed Sandy away, rolled over, and stumbled to his feet. The haze was starting to clear, the heat was fading.

"What the fuck are you doing?" Stew shouted.

Suzuki whipped around as he closed his eyes as hard as he could until everything was black, and he took a deep breath.

"Suzuki, what the fuck are you doing!"

"What the hell are you talking about?" Suzuki shouted back.

Suzuki opened his eyes and took a deep breath. The air felt good in his lungs, almost like it was pure light.

Stew and Sandy were standing next to each other, clenching hands. Sandy's face was as white as a sheet of paper. Stew looked as if someone had slit his throat and bled him slowly.

Suzuki took a step forward, determined not to let their weird behavior get under his skin. Both Stew and Sandy took a step back when Suzuki approached them. "What the hell is wrong with you guys?" Suzuki asked.

Stew pointed to Suzuki's hand.

Suzuki looked down. His sword was gripped tightly in his hand.

"What the hell is wrong with *you*?" Stew asked.

Suzuki dropped the sword. It fell mutely to the ground. He backed away as the sword cracked and split into a million different pieces that disappeared. "What the fuck?" Suzuki murmured as he stared at his hand. Even though it had been said a couple times already, Suzuki couldn't help but think it again. *What the fuck was going on?*

Stew and Sandy were still watching Suzuki with alarm. Sandy was biting her fingernails, and Stew was picking at the skin on his arms.

Suzuki laughed. He tried to make it sound as natural as he could. It sounded phony even to him, and he covered it by coughing. "My fucking HUD," he stammered. "The fucker's been acting up all day." Suzuki smacked his HUD for added effect.

Sandy took a step toward him. She looked extremely calm.

Suzuki had seen that look before. It was how she looked at something she was about to light up, like he was a threat she was about to deal with.

Sandy raised her hand. Suzuki closed his eyes, waiting for the heat, the kiss of flames against his skin.

Suzuki felt Sandy's hand on his temple. He cracked one eye open.

Sandy had taken Suzuki's HUD off and was turning it over in her hand. "Fucking Chipmaster," she muttered. "I let her install an SD last week, and my HUD kept pulling my coin pouch out every time that I activated it. We should get her to check it out when you get back. You can just restart it for now. That should help." Sandy handed Suzuki's HUD back as Stew came up beside her.

Stew chuckled as he threw his arm around Sandy. "Fuck dude," he sighed. "You freaked me the fuck out. You better get that checked out when we get back. Maybe we should go back now. That thing could be tripping out on you the whole way. It could get you fucked up or killed."

Suzuki nodded his head, trying to focus on looking as casual as he could. His heart was still racing, and he was cold all over. He had drawn a sword on them. Even if Stew and Sandy believed him, he knew that his HUD wasn't malfunctioning. That sword had ended up in his hand because he had put it there.

Suzuki put his HUD back on and started toward the axbeaks who were surprisingly standing as calmly as broken horses. "We should get going," Suzuki's called, hoping that whatever it was wrong with him, it would go away in time.

They continued East. Suzuki stayed close to Stew and Sandy, rather than drifting back as he had before. He was worried that something similar might happen again. He wasn't quite certain what had happened though. Getting off the axbeak made sense, but drawing his sword? He could at least remember dismounting. He hadn't known that the sword was in his hand until Sandy had gasped.

There was something affecting him, messing with his head. A spell maybe? And if he was feeling its effects, then chances were, so were the others.

Nothing else happened until they broke for lunch. Much

like breakfast, they sat in silence, eating food that had barely been cooked. Stew didn't seem to notice. Suzuki choked down his morsels, while Sandy read and poked at her food.

Once they were finished, they led their axbeaks to a creek flowing between the hills and watered the fowls. Then they followed the road, occasionally allowing the axbeaks to meander from what had been paved.

The road and riders were silent.

They rode on for another three hours as the sky filled with swollen clouds looming apocalyptically in the distance. Suzuki thought the clouds looked like they were filled with whatever was going wrong in him, balloons filled with noxious gas.

Stew would have had a good joke about that. Most of the other MERCs too. The Red Lion was probably filled with MERCs, sitting and joking right now. They had probably been laughing and reveling that night when the orcs rode through and slaughtered the elves.

Suzuki had probably been there that night as well, he and the rest of the Mundanes, drinking and merry-making while the orcs' blades slit innocent throats.

Sandy leaned over from her axbeak and nudged Suzuki. "Yo, that's it ahead, right? The village we need to get to?"

Suzuki pulled himself out of his own head and swung around to meet Sandy's eyes. "What?" he asked.

Sandy pointed down the road. In the distance, between the black clouds and cracks of lightning, a large steeple stretched to the sky, with a thin, black cross which seemed to emit a descending blackness across the village which lay beneath the shadow of its arms as if it were a vulture stretching its wings.

As the Mundanes rode further toward the village, the colors of the sky stretched and changed until it seemed that the sun had set before them with hardly a gesture. Suzuki scanned the sky. The sun was still beaming brightly. Yet when Suzuki's eyes fell back to the land before him, the world looked as dimly bleak as a storm at midnight.

Lightning flared, ripping the sky open.

"Guess it is," Suzuki muttered, nearly too afraid to bring his voice above a whisper. This was a new fear, one that he had not felt before. It was unlike the cold shivers that had crept up on him the first time a troll stared him down. Nor was it the fiery heat shooting through him when he thought of kissing Beth. This was new—and it had started back at the village of the dead elves.

Here, it had only grown into completeness.

Suzuki turned his HUD on and surveyed the village ahead. His HUD read 35% chance of success. "We're fucked," Suzuki sighed. "We're only at 35%, and that town ahead is probably too small to even have a village elder. This is like walking into a mall and getting your ass kicked by a bunch of middle schoolers."

Stew pulled a spyglass from his HUD and peered through its lens. "Is that good or bad?" he asked. "The middle schoolers where I grew up were cut from fucking stone. I once saw a two 6th graders tackle a guy coming out of the gym. I didn't really think of it at the time. Then, like two weeks later, those kids were on the news. It was not a feel-good story."

Suzuki and Sandy looked at Stew blankly. Then Suzuki burst out laughing so hard that he had to lean over on his axbeak. Sandy managed to get down from hers to grab her stomach and roll on the ground in stitches.

"What the hell's so funny?" Stew asked. "These kids were straight-up serial killers. That could have been me. I could have been eaten by sixth graders for being too swole."

Suzuki forced himself to sit up, his sides still aching from laughing so hard. "Are you telling me that there were murderous sixth-graders killing off all the jocks in your hometown?"

"No, dude. Not jocks. They were coming after swole, adult gym bros. This was like last year. The swoler, the better."

"I swear to God, if you say swole one more—"

"I was terrified, dude. All I wanted to do was get the flex, but there were some fucking freak-ass kids running around, chopping people up and fucking their heads and—"

Sandy raised her hands to stop Stew from talking. "Did you just say 'fucking their heads?'"

"These kids were sick, dude. Next-level sick. I dropped so much muscle that summer. I wouldn't even go for a walk."

"You realize that you just told us a story about necrophiliac cannibalistic middle schoolers and your take-away was how you lost some muscle mass?"

"Babe, it wasn't some. It was noticeable."

"You are unbelievable." Sandy affectionately touched Stew's shoulder.

Stew shook his head. "Anyways, what were we talking about again?"

The Mundanes looked at one other. It was fairly obvious that none of them remembered what had prompted the story.

"Is the town filled with children?" Stew asked.

The sun was setting, and a heavy mist poured into the village. It looked like someone had cranked a fog machine up to high and left it on for a couple of hours.

Suzuki's HUD decreased the chance of success from thirty-five percent to sixteen percent. He muttered under his breath, aggravated, trying to figure out what he could do to change their odds. As he shook his head, pacing back and forth, he walked past the axbeaks, which were patiently nipping at each other. When Suzuki looked up, the chances of success had jumped up to sixty-eight percent. "What the fuck?" he mused.

Suzuki grabbed his axbeak's reins and looked at the fog-covered village. The success fell back to sixteen percent. "Hey, guys," Suzuki called. "I think if we tie up the axbeaks, we have a significantly higher chance of success."

Stew spoke in a nasal tone, imitating Suzuki. "A significantly higher chance of success. I also think the mating habits of adult gryphons is extremely exciting, and probably the closest I'll ever get to losing my virginity."

Suzuki glared at Stew. Something about Stew's tone irked him. Maybe he didn't like being imitated. Or it could just be Stew's general childishness. Whatever it was, Suzuki had to push down the urge to hit Stew in his smug, pimple-filled face. "Fuck you," Suzuki growled. "Let's just leave the fucking birds here and get this over with."

Then again, under other circumstances, he might have laughed, but whatever was affecting his mood was still there. Laughing had helped, but it hadn't taken it all away.

Stew shrugged and grabbed the reins of the axbeaks. "Whatever, dude," Stew sneered. "Don't know when you lost your sense of humor, but if you want to get all Gestapo, be my fucking guest."

Sandy snapped her fingers and a ball of fire flashed between Suzuki and Stew. They both jumped back, throwing up their hands and waving away the flames as they quickly dissipated. Suzuki had seen Sandy's face in the brief illumination from the fireball. Her eyes were stone-dead, and she had been biting her lip—the same look she often reserved for whatever monster she was going to sear alive.

"Let's just get this over with," Sandy said.

Suzuki marched over to Stew and snatched the reins from his hands. He walked the axbeaks to the nearest tree and tied them to it. Then he turned back. It felt like his body was moving through mud. His legs were heavy, and his arms felt like weights had been attached to them. Even blinking was difficult. "Anyone else really tired all of a sudden?" Suzuki asked.

Stew shrugged and scratched his face, his nail lodging in a particularly large pimple. Suzuki couldn't look away. He wanted to vomit or hit Stew. He didn't know which would feel better, or if it was going to make him feel better at all. The more he thought about it, the more he wanted to hit Stew.

But the rush of adrenaline at the thought was replaced with a sick feeling deep in his guts. "Maybe we should wait," Suzuki suggested. "Camp a ways out from the village. We could come through in the morning instead."

Suzuki checked the rate of success through his HUD as he looked out at the village. He hit variable option and wound the time forward to the morning. For each hour that passed, the rate of success improved. The HUD read at eighty-nine percent at roughly around 10 AM.

"We will have much better odds by then," Suzuki explained.

"How much better?" Sandy asked.

"We'd be at eighty-nine percent."

"We're at sixty-eight percent now," Stew said. "That's only a twenty-one percent difference."

"Twenty-one percent is a lot," Suzuki said.

Stew pulled out his sword. "We're still over fifty percent

to begin with. We should just get this over with. I don't like this place. It makes me feel sick. I don't want to be sleeping here all night."

"So you feel it too?" Suzuki asked.

Sandy nodded and pointed in the direction of the fog-covered village. "I can tell it's coming from there. I don't know what it is or what's happening, but I feel... I don't know how I feel, but it's coming from there."

So it wasn't just him.

Stew stepped up to be a part of the conversation, almost pushing his way between Sandy and Suzuki. They both looked at him as if they were ready to rip his head off. "What?" Stew asked. "Everyone was talking numbers, and I wanted in."

"You've never cared about percentages and success ratios before," Suzuki said. "If you had, we wouldn't have started calling you Leeroy."

"For the record, *I* started calling myself Leeroy. And I can talk percentages."

"There's a chance of success if—"

Stew groaned. "What the funkily fuckity fuck deal is it with twenty-one percent?"

"Are you fucking serious, Stew?"

"What a way with words," Sandy sighed. "That man, oh man, of mine."

Usually, the Mundanes would be smiling right now. Instead, the tension between them had thickened so it seemed palpable. He didn't notice that the fog from the village had stretched its way out to them.

After a long silence as they stared with murderous intent at each other, Sandy finally cleared her throat and woke them up out of their trance. "So we're going?" she asked.

Suzuki absentmindedly swatted at the fog swirling around his feet. "Fuck it," he growled. "Let's just do this."

Suzuki walked faster than Sandy or Stew. He wanted to get away from them. He wanted to lose himself in his thoughts. That was a bad idea. When he let his mind wander, he could see himself holding a rock, standing over Sandy's body, her eyes swollen and blackened, fully aware that the rock was coming down between her eyes. Suzuki shook his head and tried to drive the vision away.

The village was before them before Suzuki even realized they had crossed the field. The heavy fog he had seen from the hills of the plain was even thicker in the streets.

The village was empty and silent. The windows of the crudely-made thatch houses were mostly broken with shards of glass littering the streets.

Suzuki coughed loudly, trying not to inhale too deeply. His chest had suddenly grown tight, as if something had reached into him and gripped his lungs. He fell to his knees and clenched his heart as he coughed painfully, gasping for air, inhaling the fog.

At Suzuki's side, Sandy and Stew had also doubled over. They sounded like they were hacking just as hard as Suzuki was. The thought dashed across Suzuki mind before he realized: *I hope those assholes choke to death.*

The coughing fit passed after a couple of minutes. Suzuki was the first to his feet, and he was walking away before either Sandy or Stew stood up.

Stew called loud and obnoxiously, "Hey, where the fuck are you going?"

Suzuki spun and pointed toward the center of the village. "Would you mind keeping the fuck up?" he shouted before turning back and continuing on his way. He didn't care if Sandy or Stew couldn't catch up. Maybe they'd get lost. The fog was thick enough for that. Someone might be in the village, hiding in one of the shit houses. They might slip out and slide a knife into Stew's back.

Suzuki's heart raced at the thought of Stew dying in a pool of his own blood.

As the sun finally set, the amber-hued fire streaks in the sky faded to a starless night pregnant with a full moon. It cast a silver light that streaked through the fog, which was now up to Suzuki's knees. The fog was thick as storm clouds. Suzuki almost wanted to reach down and scoop some into his hand. Then he would shove it down Sandy's throat while she gagged on his fist.

Suzuki turned around. He was suddenly gripped with an intense desire to know exactly where his party members where. The village was too quiet. Sandy and Stew were being too quiet. Suzuki flipped down his HUD. "Cast Find Target," Suzuki said.

Fred unwrapped from around Suzuki's mind. *There is no target*, Fred said slowly. *There's only Stew and Sandy.*

*Well, then find them!*

*Suzuki, do you feel odd?*

*Me? No, I feel great. I feel like I could take on the world right now.*

*And your friends?*

*I could fucking murder them.*

*Something's not right, human. I sense...an offness in myself. Usually, I am filled with a slight murderous rage toward you. At the moment, I feel...well-disposed toward your squishy human body.*

Suzuki considered this. *Hmmm, yeah, that doesn't sound normal.*

*You and your friends. You keep fighting with each other. It makes me sad.*

*Jesus fucking Christ, something must be wrong. You sound like a* Lifetime *special. Are you going to teach me a lesson about the power of friendship?*

*No, I am only going to tell you that you are acting unnaturally, and I have found the source. The fog is bewitched. It is causing us to feel the inverse of our emotions. Rather than wanting to see you suffer for your poor decisions, I want to protect you. It is almost a compulsion. You have snapped at your friends multiple times since the fog rolled in, and you drew your sword on them both near the outskirts of the village.*

*There wasn't a fog out there,* Suzuki pointed out.

*Not that you could see. Your eyes aren't strong enough. But I could feel the magic back then. I just didn't think anything of it, since there was so little.*

Suzuki was relieved to hear that there was a bit of magic out in the plains. He had been sincerely worried that he was cracking around the edges. This made more sense. Granted, he was stressed, but he hadn't thought he'd ever get stressed enough to attack either of his friends. *So what are we supposed to do?* Suzuki asked.

*You are feeling hatred for your friends? Perhaps thinking positively about them would help? Then we must find the source of the fog.*

*What the fuck? You want me to think positively. Who the fuck are you? Tony Robbins?*

*I do not know who this Tony is, but if he is an advocate for thinking positively, then yes, I am Tony Fucking Robbins.*

Suzuki groaned in frustration. *Are you sure stabbing Stew and Sandy won't help?*

*Can you hear yourself?*

Suzuki closed his eyes and thought as hard as he could. He tried to bring up his memories of Sandy and Stew. He couldn't remember anything remotely friendly.

Mostly just memories of Stew annoying the shit out of him: cracking his stupid jokes, rushing into things without planning well enough, being nervous about the tiniest things, things that made Suzuki even embarrassed for Stew.

Suzuki chuckled. *Huh,* he muttered. *That's weird. I think you're right. I think Stew is my friend. A really close—*

An ax flew through the air, cutting through the thick fog and hitting the wooden wall behind Suzuki, where it stayed embedded.

Stew stepped through the fog, wielding two of his short swords.

Suzuki's sword was in his hand before he realized it. "Your aim has gone to shit."

Stew twirled one of his swords in his hand. He shrugged and took a step toward Suzuki. "I didn't wanna stab you in the back," Stew said. "I want to make sure to look you in the eye when I fuck you up."

Suzuki summoned another sword from his inventory. "Come at me, then...bro."

"So fucking cliché, dude. So fucking cliché."

Stew rushed at Suzuki, his sword raised high. He brought it down faster and harder than Suzuki had ever seen Stew do. That blow was meant to kill. Suzuki managed to pull his shield up in time and block the attack. He rolled to the side and slashed at Stew's ankles as Stew stepped forward to avoid Suzuki's blade.

Suzuki wanted to end this fast. He knew Stew's weaknesses. He'd watched Stew play for years and had been fighting beside him for at least a month. All he had to do was get Stew to stop thinking, to distract him enough that he'd make a stupid decision. And it wasn't going to be hard to distract him.

Stew rushed Suzuki again. *Typical,* Suzuki thought. *Just rush your target. I'm not even going to have to work for this.*

Suzuki slammed his sword to his shield, enchanting it with fire. Flames flickered across the surface of the blade as Suzuki took a parrying stance.

Stew hit Suzuki hard, their blades crashing together. The sheer strength behind Stew's blow was enough to drive Suzuki off his feet, but he held his blade, all the same, watching the heat from his sword force beads of sweat on Stew's forehead. It wasn't slowing Stew down, though; he was still pushing Suzuki as hard as he could. It became apparent at that moment that if Suzuki's knees went out, the fight would be over.

Suzuki tried to push forward while Stew pushed downward. They were caught in an uncomfortable stalemate. Stew was stronger, but the flames from Suzuki's sword were keeping Stew at bay. "Bet you were just thinking about how this fight was over," Stew said. "Just gloating over how you already got everything figured out and how fucking smart and put together you are. Weren't you?!"

It was happening. Just what Suzuki was waiting for. Stew's emotions were starting to get the better of him. It wouldn't be long until Stew was a screeching tank, incapable of slowing down or thinking things through. All Suzuki had to do was get out from underneath Stew. Then he could slide his sword through his chest and move on to Sandy.

*Huh,* Suzuki thought. *Where is Sandy?*

There was a giant crack of thunder and a bolt of lightning struck the ground a few feet away from Suzuki and Stew, sending rubble and bits of the ground flying through the air as the fog around Stew and Suzuki dissipated. In the clear air, Suzuki could see Sandy floating down from the night sky, the tips of her toes scraping the ground as she levitated.

Stew turned around to see Sandy.

This was just the chance Suzuki needed. He kicked Stew in the kneecap as he fell backward, rolling out of the way of Stew's sword as Stew fell forward, practically face-planting into the ground.

Stew scrambled to his feet and turned to face Sandy.

Lightning was crackling from Sandy's eyes. Bolts of lightning jumped out of her palms.

Suzuki was running through different contingency plans. He hadn't fought a mage 'in real life' yet. A straightforward, magic battle wasn't going to work. Sandy was a full-blown mage, not a battle mage. She had much more mana than Suzuki did, and she knew more magic than he did. There was no way around that, so the only option would be to play up his strengths. Weave his magic into his weapons, but rely on how much physically stronger he was than Sandy.

Stew screamed and charged Sandy. *Or I could wait for Stew,* Suzuki thought.

Sandy whipped a bolt of lightning at Stew, who barely managed to cast Stone Skin on himself before getting hit square in the chest. He went flying and hit one of the empty homes, crashing through the window, leaving a smoking trail. Then Sandy turned her eyes on Suzuki. "I have been looking forward to this for so long," Sandy said. "I'm going to melt your face and crack open your chest. I'm gonna pull your guts out and separate them one by one." Sandy raised her hand and drew it over her face. The death mask materialized as lightning flashed from behind her mask.

"Fucking bring it," Suzuki shouted.

*Stop this,* Fred's voice chimed in. Fred sounded very far

away, like he was yelling from another room. *They are your friends. Your friends.*

Suzuki's head hurt. "They are my friends," he muttered before looking up at Sandy and crying out, "What are we doing?"

"I'm going to kill you." She drew the Death Mask closer and put it on.

"The fog," Suzuki muttered. "It's the same fog that was in the last place, only less." Then a thought entered his fury-filled head. "Blow the fog away."

"I want to blow you away."

"The fog, Sandy. Then me. For honor, for glory. For XP."

"Fuck that." Sandy raised her hand to throw another lightning bolt, then she stopped. She looked at her hand for a second before crouching and bolting straight up into the sky, right into the cloud of fog that now hung over the entire village stretching up toward the moon.

Suzuki turned back to where Stew had landed. Whatever clarity he'd had was seeping away. Coating his sword in flames again, he figured that he could at least take care of Stew while Sandy was gone. Then he'd worry about her.

Across the street, Stew climbed out of the broken window. His stomach was still smoking, but the skin only looked chafed, as if two stones had been rubbed against each other. "Where'd my girl go?" Stew shouted.

A powerful gust of wind blew through the village, so strong that it sent Stew and Suzuki flying, along with a hurricane of broken glass and layer upon layer of thick fog. The streets were cleared out within a few seconds.

For the first time that day, Suzuki breathed fresh air. The murderous rage left him instantly. He stared at Stew, surprised. How could he ever have wanted to kill Stew? He was his best friend. He couldn't even imagine seriously raising his voice at the guy.

Stew was staring at Suzuki as well. He dropped his sword, ran to Suzuki, and threw his arms around him. "Fuck, dude," Stew sighed. "I was going to kill you. I fucking love you, man, and I was trying to kill you."

There was another gust of wind, this time weaker than before. Sandy landed beside Stew and Suzuki. "Jesus, Sandy," Stew started. "I am so—"

"Don't worry about it," Sandy interrupted "We can all pat each other on the backs and circle jerk later, but you need to pay attention right now. You were right about the fog, Suzuki. It was cursed. It's blocking our familiars from talking to us.

Suzuki nodded. "For some reason, Fred was able to get through, but barely."

Sandy pointed to her mask. There was a breathing apparatus built into the mouth. "And this mask is more badass than I thought. It also acts as a gas mask, and the moment I put it on, I could breathe, and all of those violent feelings vanished."

Sandy raised her hands and made a whooshing motion, and another gust of air blew through the village streets. "Fred told Niv that we gotta think happy thoughts," Sandy said. "I'm going to keep cleansing the streets, but the fog is going to keep coming back until we find the witch who's responsible for this. And I'm going to pull out her intestines through her fucking mouth."

Stew looked up at the mounting fog in the distance, dread palpable on his face. "Where are we going?" he asked. "Do you know where the mage is?"

"The church steeple. I can feel the magic coming from there. Happy thoughts, remember? Happy."

"So we're going to Neverland," Suzuki said.

Stew chuckled. "Dude, totes inappropriate."

"What? They think happy thoughts to fly! Didn't you ever—"

"Guys?" Sandy shouted.

Suzuki put on his game face as he sheathed his sword. He pulled Sandy and Stew close to him and shouted, "For Honor!"

"For glory!" Sandy added.

"For XP," the Mundanes shouted together.

## 13

The fog had not completely disappeared from the village. Wave after wave poured through the alleys and past buildings like a ghostly tidal wave as they made their way through the cobbled streets. Sandy led Stew and Suzuki down the darkened pathways, a ball of blue light flickering in front of them, occasionally raising her hands to cast a gust of wind to dispel the cursed fog.

With the fog being held back by Sandy's magic, it was easier to think, but not as easy as Suzuki would have hoped. He was getting annoyed at Sandy for taking so long to figure out where it was they were going although he knew that she was trying as hard as she could.

Even further in the back of his head, he knew that she wasn't lost, that they had not been walking that long, that she was leading because he couldn't at the moment. That didn't keep him from being severely annoyed.

*Think happy thoughts,* Suzuki thought to himself. *Just keep being positive.*

Suzuki couldn't help but sigh internally. Being positive had never been his strong suit. Being positive wasn't what helped him think of plan after plan, contingency after contingency. Being able to see the different ways that anything could go from simple to fucked was Suzuki's specialty.

Thinking positively was going to be a challenge.

Suzuki tapped the back of his neck as he tried to drum up a positive image. He turned to Stew and almost grabbed him until he thought better of it. Everyone was on edge. Being grabbed suddenly could have set him off in his current state. Stew probably wasn't any different. "Hey, Stew," Suzuki started. "What's your happy thought?"

Stew didn't bother looking at Suzuki. Instead, he was looking at his fingers as they picked the skin on the back of his hands. "Huh, " Stew murmured. "Happy thoughts?"

"Yeah, we're supposed to be thinking happy thoughts. You know, to keep the fog from getting to us."

"Oh. I'd forgotten."

Stew's eyes had gone a little soft. It was as if they had been shimmering stones before, but were now covered with a thin layer of dust. Suzuki had never noticed Stew's eyes before. Now that he thought about it, Stew's eyes were always bright, always dancing, as if there were a fire burning behind them. That fire looked as if it were going out.

"Sandy," Suzuki shouted. "Stew doesn't look right."

Sandy was waving her hands around, trying to steer the fog away with a small gust of wind. The fog detoured, but only after an extreme effort from Sandy, and when she turned around to address Suzuki, she looked exhausted. Her face had the complexion of someone who had just finished a triathlon after an inadequate training period. She swayed slightly as she asked, "What's wrong with him?"

Stew raised his hands defensively. He looked like he was trying to smile, but had forgotten how. "Guys," he objected.

"There isn't anything wrong with me. I feel...I don't know... okay, I guess."

Sandy didn't waste any more time looking over her shoulder. She turned back to the street and the new wave of fog barreling toward them. "The emotions of the fog are changing," Sandy shouted over the gusts of the wind. "This bitch of a witch couldn't get us with anger, so she's changing it up. It's sadness now."

Stew shrugged his shoulders with a motion that seemed to last for an hour. *Apparently*, Suzuki thought, *sadness completely sucks the life out of Stew.*

Sandy raised her fist and shook it in the direction of the church steeple they were slowly making their way toward. "Fuck you," Sandy shouted. "I'm on Zoloft, bitch! It's going to take more than a couple of sad feelings to keep me from ripping your fucking fingers from their sockets."

There was more than just irritation scratching at the back of Suzuki's brain. He didn't know what exactly Stew was feeling, but if it was anything like what was trying to sneak into his own brain, he hoped to hell that Stew was able to fight it off. There was something dark in there, something Suzuki had never realized was within him, something that he hadn't known was watching him. All that he could sense was a blackness so deep that it could swallow him up if he let it.

Then his feet went out from under him. He didn't know when he fell, but it felt like he was falling for an eternity, as if he had been born to fall and been falling since then.

"Suzuki, get the fuck up," a voice shouted.

The voice sounded far away. Maybe there wasn't a voice at all. Suzuki knew he could stand up and check to see where the voice was coming from, but he didn't see the point in it. The voice wasn't coming from within him, and it wasn't coming from the ground.

It didn't seem like anything else really mattered.

At least he didn't have to keep on walking, and the fog was actually kind of comfortable.

It was a thick blanket.

It'd be so nice to breathe in deeply.

Let it fill up his lungs and rock him to sleep.

"Get up!"

Suzuki felt his body lifting into the air. He put his feet down. Not because he wanted to, but only because they were up. He'd have preferred to have stayed on the ground, the soft place where he could just melt away into the stone. Then a bright flash of pain spread across Suzuki's face. His lips felt red and bloody, and he tasted iron in his mouth. When he looked up, Sandy was staring him in the eye, her own eyes bloodshot and rimmed with tears.

"I'm running out of mana," Sandy said. "We need to keep moving."

Stew was sitting at Sandy's feet. He was bawling loudly, his hands pressed so tight to his forehead that his skin had gone white. His whole body was trembling. Whatever sound was coming from him didn't sound human. It sounded like something small and frightened dying.

Even though Suzuki was watching Stew, it didn't feel as if he were really there. He could see Sandy too, but it was like Sandy wasn't there. Or maybe he wasn't there. Suzuki couldn't tell now. He just knew that it would feel really good to sit down. So he did. Sandy tried to keep him from squatting beside Stew, but she couldn't hold him up. Suzuki crashed to the ground, dragging Sandy along with him. They sat there, the three of them, the only sound being the rush of wind and Stew's animalistic whimpering.

Sandy took Suzuki's hand in her own and squeezed it tightly. "Suzuki, I need you to listen to me," she said.

Suzuki looked up dreamily, his eyes hardly able to hold themselves open. "What?" he asked.

"I can't do this alone. I thought I could, but I can't. I thought I was strong enough. I'm so fucking stupid. I keep trying to... I can't fucking do this. I need help. You need to help me."

Sandy's eyes were even more bloodshot. Her face was frantic. The edges of her lips quivered, and her pupils widened as her eyes shot back and forth. She looked like she was breaking apart, a porcelain figure cracking down the middle. "I can't do this! I can't fucking do this! We're going to die! I'm going to die, I'm going to die here, and I'm never going to see Momma or Poppa. I'm going to die. Beth is going to die. Oh my God, I don't want to die. I don't want to die like this, I don't want to die like this."

Sandy's words deteriorated to small whimpers as she cried.

Suzuki was staring at his feet. He couldn't imagine how they had ever moved before. "We are going to die, aren't we?" he asked. "Right here."

Sandy was blubbering and nodding her head, as Stew continued to pick the skin on his hands raw.

Suzuki nodded in agreement to whatever was conveyed in the blackness of each of their minds. "You know," he said, "I'd rather die here with you two than anywhere else. Period."

"Really?"

"Yeah, you guys are my best friends." Suzuki wiped away a tear. "And it's been an adventure. Something that no one's ever gotten to do before. Not like this. Not like us. Dying beside you both would be an honor."

Stew stopped crying. He was still picking his skin, but he was no longer trembling. The foggy wind howled around them.

"How many times did we die together in Middang3ard?"

Stew looked up and muttered, "Hundreds."

"More than hundreds. Thousands. We have been dying together for years."

"Yeah, dying after you hogging all the good loot."

Stew put an innocent hand on his chest. "Me? I hardly ever took any loot when I played with you guys."

Sandy chuckled. It was soft, hardly louder than a guarded sneeze. "Stew, you know you used to throw tantrums if you didn't get the gear you wanted."

Suzuki suddenly felt warm as if the blood had just started pumping through his body. It was like his heart had been frozen and had suddenly thawed. The warmth spread from his chest and to his feet and his hands. His whole body was warming up. He didn't know why he was sitting. For some reason, his legs were very tired. His whole body, really. He didn't think he'd ever been so tired in his whole life. But he was waking up. "Running into enemy territory right after you don't get the loot you want is throwing a tantrum," Suzuki lectured.

"That's not why I was running into enemy territory, ya dick," Stew said as he leaned closer to Suzuki, lowered his eyes, and spoke in a terrible Scottish accent. "It's the love of the fight, mate, of the glory, of the booty!"

Sandy and Suzuki burst out laughing. The peals of laughter bounced around them and spread into a barrier around them that physically pushed the billowing fog away. Their laughter spread down the streets and up the alleys, and the whole village looked golden for a brief second.

"I'm so glad you stopped doing that shit," Suzuki said.

"Do you know how stressful it was to pull you out of an undead boar's lair?"

"Well, I mean—"

"Or getting your ass unstuck from those giant red ant colonies?" Sandy chimed in.

"My ass was never—"

"And that was before we even got to the real thing. Christ, Stew how did you not get us killed already?"

Stew's face was solemn, the face of royalty, of one who had looked out into the world and learned great wisdom. "Badass is an idea. You cannot kill an idea."

There was silence, brief and sweet, then laughter so hearty it hurt Suzuki's sides. Hundreds of hours of videogames and online conversations, of late-night phone calls, of incomplete messages, of raids gone poorly and loot missed, of loss and triumph, of sincerely having known the others, to have seen them through the ridiculous and the painful, all of that erupted in laughter from the Mundanes as if it had been stored in their hearts for just this moment.

Their laughter seemed to chase away the mist.

The fog was gone.

Suzuki could feel his legs again, and he wanted to use them. The deep blackness had withdrawn. He knew it was still in there somewhere, but he also knew there was something else, something that Stew and Sandy shared with him. It was too corny to think about. There was still something else though, something else that they all shared as well: the desire to kill whatever was trying to stop them.

Suzuki pulled up his HUD inventory and selected a few mana potions. He passed them to Sandy, who swallowed them down. When she was done, she stretched out her fingers. A tiny, half-hearted flame floated in her palm. She shook her head and flicked the flame out of existence. "It's not going to be enough. I burned through everything pushing back that fog. And it's probably going to come back, so—"

Stew was already on his feet, running toward the church steeple, calling over his shoulder, "Are you guys gonna fucking move, or sit around talking all day!"

Suzuki knew Stew was right to keep moving. At most, the small bomb of positivity was only going to buy them a little time. It was, in fact, a small bomb. They were going to need something a whole lot stronger if they were going to take afternoon tea. It was better to keep moving and try to find the source of the fog.

It didn't take long for Sandy and Suzuki to catch up to Stew. The three of them sprinted as fast as they could, as if they were running from whatever dread had welled up within them earlier. Suzuki was curious to know what could have dragged Stew and Sandy into the depths of sadness. Now that he thought of it, he wasn't sure what had caused his downward spiral.

No one memory or emotion had stood out in his head. It was just an overwhelming feeling, one that had swept him up in its current before he had time to discern what was happening. There was no distinct image, no distinct point in time. Suzuki wondered if it was because he had had a relatively trauma-free childhood. So did Stew and Sandy though. So what could have caused them to sink so thoroughly into despair?

The church steeple was coming up fast. *Better to worry about it later*, Suzuki thought.

The church stood out oddly in the village, which on the whole had nothing particularly interesting about it. The houses and buildings look as if they had been pulled from a

How to Design Fantasy Worlds RPG manual. The black church was another story.

A long, thin, black steeple pierced the sky. It was covered in small spikes that stood out like fangs and was attached to a bell tower, where a cracked bell hung off-kilter. The rest of the church stretched out in a flat, monolithic fashion. It was also covered with the odd fang-like spikes, giving the impression that the church was the mouth of a dangerous creature that had been pulled inside out. Black flames flickered behind broken windows.

Suzuki came to a full stop, staring up at the church, hardly able to comprehend the sheer amount of dread pouring from behind its walls. There was something in there, something dark and dangerous, but it wasn't the source of the fog. Whatever was creating the fog was only a part of whatever had corrupted the church. "You guys feel that?" Suzuki asked.

Sandy was keyed into the church as well. She had hardly blinked since she had stopped running. Her skin had gone paler than usual, so much so that her cheeks looked as if blush had been applied. Stew was staring slack-jawed as well. His eyes were locked in a gaze of determination, as if the church were full of something which needed to be understood, but couldn't be grasped. "Yeah, I feel it too," Stew said. "Whatever we're looking for is in there."

"This isn't magic," Sandy added. "Maybe the fog, but whatever that feeling is, it's something else. Psychic, maybe."

Suzuki gave a Sandy a bemused look. "Wait, you're saying that there are psychics here as well?" Stew asked.

"Shit, do you ever read anything that I tell you to?"

"When it's not extremely boring," Suzuki admitted.

"Well, if you had, you would know by now that psychic here isn't the same as back home. We're not talking about moving things with your mind. It's deeper than that. Psychic is connected to something…other, something that permeates all of existence, something that sends out ripples that distort or alter reality. It's really not much different from magic. The only difference is that we don't really understand it, not how it works."

Stew started to pace back and forth, never taking his eyes off the steeple, rolling his shoulders as he fingered the hilt of his sword the way one imagines a gunslinger thumbing his six-shooter. "All right," he finally said, "that's a great history lesson, but when are we going to kill whoever is fucking with my feelings? This is worse than having a crazy girlfriend."

"And why the fuck does it have to be a crazy girlfriend? It could be a crazy anything, you sexist sack of—"

Suzuki stepped between Sandy and Stew. He had felt it too. Something hot in him, trying to leap up out of his throat. "Guys, focus," he said. "The effects of the fog must be stronger here. We gotta keep our shit together. So no fighting."

"I'd fucking win if we did," Stew argued.

"Earlier, when we all got depressed, what was it that you guys were thinking of?" Suzuki asked.

Stew and Sandy both looked at each other. For a second, Suzuki thought it might be some shared sore subject that had resulted in them spiraling into the black. Neither Stew nor Sandy offered any inclination that it might have been though. They both looked perplexed. Stew shrugged and earnestly looked at Suzuki. "I don't know," he offered. "I can't remember anything specific. Even just now, when I got pissed off, I can't remember why I was pissed. I don't even think I remember what Sandy said.

Sandy nodded as she thought it over. "Yeah," she agreed. "I can't really think of anything."

Suzuki snapped his fingers together and nearly jumped to click his heels. He got it. "When we were talking about dying together, you remember how we started to feel better, how we actually started talking again?"

"Yeah, it was like the fog was pulling back."

"It's because we were focusing on a specific thing, a specific memory. Everything that we said was about a single instance. All the negative feelings that are overwhelming us are generic, but the memories that we used to dig us out are very specific. That's how we can fight it off. Everyone concentrate on something that makes you happy or whatever. Just focus on the details."

"How do you know that's it?"

"It's worth a try. Now let's get to the top of that steeple and handle whoever decided to turn this into an afterschool special on feelings."

Suzuki approached the church gingerly. The doors of the church were massive, gothic things, a design that looked like it would be more suited for pre-revolution French cathedrals. Intricate designs were etched into the stone door. It looked as if they told a story. The etchings depicted a large fire, dozens of people standing around the fire. Then, by a trick of the light, one could see another group of people dressed in robes, lurking behind those near the fire.

Sandy and Stew came up beside Suzuki. "That's a fucking creepy-ass motif," Stew said.

"Since when do you know what a motif is?"

"Since I've been taking art history lessons, you ass."

Suzuki glanced at Stew out the corner of his eye and could see Stew smiling. The memory was keeping Stew grounded. "My bad, my bad," Suzuki said. "I keep forgetting that you're a modern-day renaissance man. Hope you're stronger than the average peasant revolutionary. Gimme a hand with the door."

"Not cool, dude. Revolutions for the equality of humankind should be praised, not get sidelined for a shitty punchline. The revolution is with the trampled masses."

Both Sandy and Suzuki stared at Stew with a mixture of incredulity and newfound respect.

"Just joking, guys. I don't give a shit about history," he said, digging a booger from his nose and flicking it on the ground. "Fucking nerds."

Stew leaned hard into the church door, along with Suzuki and Sandy. The door crept open, sending a shrill creak through the resonant chamber. The Mundanes crossed the threshold and entered the church, which smelled of mold and must.

The pews that had taken up the back part of the church were shattered, wood laying everywhere. There were pools of black liquid across the floor. The walls were covered in some kind of dark slime that oozed slowly down into the crevices in the wood. At the far end of the church, there was an altar.

It was gated off.

Suzuki went to the altar, making sure to avoid stepping in the puddles which smelled of rotten eggs and dried blood. He stood before the altar and stared at the large statue behind the gate.

It was not of a deity Suzuki recognized. Whatever was standing in the middle of the gated altar resembled a parody of holiness. It had the torso of a man, but the head was flattened as if it had been beaten in with a hammer. Its nose was an empty hole, and large leathery wings appeared to be sprouting from its back. The creature's legs were a mass of tentacles, goat hooves, and human legs. The posture of the stature was hunched, as if in some form of supplication, but to what?

Sandy and Stew came up behind Suzuki, both wearing similar looks of confusion and disgust. "What the fuck is that?" Sandy asked.

Suzuki opened the gate and walked behind the altar to get a better look at the statue. Now that he was closer, he could see that the details of the statue were obscene. He could see the individual hairs of the fur covering the sparse goat legs of the contorted mess of a lower body. "Whoever made it must have used magic," Suzuki mused. "There's no way that you could carve this."

As Suzuki walked around the statue, he noticed the candles on the altar had started to burn. He also had the distinct feeling that the statue was watching him from eyes that could not be seen. Suzuki did his best to ignore the eerie feeling crawling up his spine. He assumed that it was nothing more than the fog. If it could force him to feel anger and depression, how was fear any different? Besides, the statue wasn't that scary. It was unnerving, but it was only a statue. Suzuki continued to circle the statue until he noticed a stairwell carved into the church behind the statue.

Suzuki held up his hand and a small blue light floated out ahead of him, partially illuminating the pitch-black stairwell. "Hey, guys," Suzuki called. "We got stairs going up back here."

Stew and Sandy trotted around the statue, both taking time to eye the statue with suspicion and a slight sense of dread until they were next to Suzuki. The three of them quietly ascended the steps.

The stairwell was extremely cramped. The walls were barely wider than Suzuki's shoulders. He felt bad for Stew, who he imagined was trying to scoot sideways along the old stone walls. Suzuki was less worried about Sandy. She would have figured out an ingenious way to stay comfortable by now. Now that he thought of it, Sandy was always finding ways to do things without effort. Magic seemed to come so naturally to her.

Suzuki rested his hand on his sword as his mind wandered in a swirl of thoughts without any specific end. All that he could understand was that he felt miserable about being so shitty at magic when Sandy made it look so easy. He was an idiot. That's how simple it was. He could never be as good as Sandy was. Why the hell were Sandy and Stew even listening to his suggestions? Suzuki knew he wasn't fit to lead anyone.

The pace of the Mundanes started to slow. The walls felt tighter around Suzuki, as if they had come alive and were trying to crush the three small bodies. At least that was something that Suzuki knew he could do as well as Sandy: die.

Stew called from the back of the ascending queue, "Hey, guys, what's the holdup?"

Suzuki felt as if he had just been roused from a nap. "Huh," he murmured. "What are you talking about?"

Stew pointed at them. "You guys are moving real fucking slow."

"Are we?"

The barbarian shook his head. "Fuck, the fog must be getting to you, dude. You gotta push it out. Remember what you were saying about focusing. Come on, focus on something happy. Get it together."

Suzuki tried to turn his thoughts inward. It felt like diverting the course of a river. Still, it was less effort than when they had been outside. So he dove deep into his memories. He tried to focus on one moment with all his mind.

VR.

Work had been shit.

He signed on into the game...back when it was just a game. He went through his inventory.

A text from Beth.

There was going to be a raid.

Instant transportation.

Beth, Sandy, and Stew waiting for him outside of a cave.

He couldn't tell what they were talking about, but everyone was laughing.

Suzuki knew he belonged there, with them, laughing.

Suzuki could almost smell the dank moss of the cave.

He felt that if he closed his eyes, he could see Beth standing there, waiting for him.

Her and the rest of the Mundanes.

They were always waiting for him.

They never went ahead without him.

Like that one time they had been stuck running fetch quests for some glitched-out NPC.

The memories felt so strong that Suzuki didn't think of anything else for a while. He just reminisced about the hours sunk into *Middang3ard* and lost track of time. It was good to take some time and remember. Life had been so insane over the last few weeks. It was easy to forget about these things.

Suzuki finally came to the end of the stairs. A small, wooden door with a low arch stood in front of him. A thick fog slipped under the bottom of the door. "What's the plan?" Suzuki asked.

Stew tried to stretch, and Suzuki heard Stew's skin scraping against the stone. He must have cast Stoneskin to keep from rubbing himself raw. "How about we get out of the fucking stairwell?" Stew muttered under his breath.

"Seriously. What do we know?"

Sandy forced her way up to the door, close enough so that she was pressed uncomfortably against Suzuki's butt. "Uh, we know the source of the fog is here. The fog is magical and psychic in nature, so we can expect a mage at least. Also, Suzuki, you have got one hell of an ass."

Suzuki clenched his butt cheeks out of embarrassment and tried to move around, but realized that that would just result in pressing his crotch against Sandy's. From the rear, Stew could be heard chuckling. "Dude," Stew whispered, "what have I been telling you? Suzuki's backing an extra brain in his glutes or something."

"Can we just focus on killing whatever is in there?"

"All right. Whatever the fuck is in there is defs alone. And probably fucking tough as hell." Stew flexed his muscles as if saying, "I'm tough, too."

"Why do you think it's alone?"

"Homeboy has been pumping the town full of shit emotions. Can you imagine how terrible that would be to be stuck in a room with? I mean, imagine hotboxing all day, but you're just smoking resentment and that weird shame you get from your mom walking in on you jerking off. You, not me. I ain't ever been caught."

Suzuki scratched his chin as he nodded his head. "You know, that makes a lot of sense," he agreed. "That makes a whole lot of sense. So we have some kind of magic some-thing that's probably by itself. We get in there, disable it, and the fog clears up. Then we can find whatever the fuck José sent us looking for."

"If it hasn't already figured out that we're here. We have

been standing around and doing a shitty job of whispering for a while."

"Yeah. You're—"

The door exploded into a thousand cascading pieces. The force of the impact tossed Suzuki backward, widening the hallway he had been standing in. As the dust settled, Suzuki scanned the area to see if he could find the others or at least see what had attacked. He suddenly remembered that Sandy was already out of mana and was practically a sitting duck.

Stew had managed to dive into the bell tower and was plastered against the wall. Sandy was beside him.

Now that the dust was gone, Suzuki could see where the attack came from. The bell tower was a large room, with candle-covered floors and walls. A massive cracked bell hung in the middle of the room with an open expanse beneath it. A woman was hiding behind the bell. She had long black hair with white streaks. Her face was deeply wrinkled, her lips were blood red, and she was dressed in what looked like a black potato sack.

The woman shuffled out from behind the bell. She hung her head as she walked so that her hair covered most of her face. Only her wrinkled mouth could be seen. "Who comes to disturb the Bell Tower Hag?" she growled, her voice thick and violent as a crouching lion.

Stew drew his swords and stepped forward, pointing the blade at the hag. "Hey-yo," he shouted. "Are you the one who's making the sad fog?"

The hag bowed in a great show of false humility. "Most travelers would have killed themselves by now. Torn each other to pieces. But you three? How did you manage to move past my fog?"

"Less talking, more killing!"

Stew tossed his sword across the room with the accuracy of a throwing knife. The sword struck the hag in the chest, and she flew back. The blade pinned her to the wall, and she shrieked for a moment before her head rested against her chest and she was silent.

Suzuki crossed the room to join up with Stew and Sandy.

"Damn, dude," Suzuki said, "since when did you get so efficient?"

Stew tossed up one of his swords and caught it in midair. He had a smile as wide as a school kid's, obviously proud of himself. "Always been efficient," he said. "You two are just too busy with your heads up your asses to see my immaculate sick-ass skills."

Across the room, there was a sound like gas being forced from a balloon. Suzuki turned to look at the source of the noise. The hag was writhing against the wall. Her skin was covered in a thousand small gashes. She looked as if she were deflating.

Suzuki flipped his HUD on to check their percentage of success. He looked in the direction of the hag. His HUD read 50%. "Fuck," he muttered to himself.

## 14

The hag's skin ripped open as if a seam had been split, then fell away, and a skinny white thing that looked like a maggot slithered out.

"What are we fighting, a maggot or a hag?" Stew asked.

"Does it matter?" Suzuki responded, staring as the maggot expanded rapidly turning into a creature nearly seven feet long, its head covered in thick, matted hair. It had four arms, each of which was nearly the length of its body. It hunched forward using its arms to drag its body, leaving a thick slimy trail as spurts of mucus and gas shot from its body through oversized pores.

Suzuki drew his sword and cast Stoneskin. Stew did the same as he stepped up to stand beside Suzuki. "You can't blame me for this," Stew said. "I had no idea this hag was going to pull a Frieza on us."

The hag/maggot dashed forward faster than Suzuki could have imagined. She swiped Stew with her backside and sent Stew flying across the room. Suzuki turned to stab at her, but the hag was too fast. She bent low, slid under Suzuki's attack, and slashed Suzuki across the chest. His armor and his spell absorbed most of the force, but it was still enough to knock the wind out of him as he flew across the room.

Sandy was next and she was already on her feet, running behind the bell tower to avoid the hag, who was already scuttling after her like some de-shelled crab. "Kill it," Sandy screamed. "Will someone kill this fucking thing?!"

Stew came up behind the hag and grabbed its thick abdomen. The hag let out a yelp before her lower back swelled and a sticky white substance shot out and covered Stew's face. "Ah," Stew screamed, "I been cream-pied!" He tried to wipe the fluid off his face, but it was hardening quickly. "Suzuki, a little help?"

The hag was thrashing, trying to escape from Stew's grasp as Suzuki ran up from behind. He grabbed Stew's face and cast Healing and Remove Status Effect just to be safe. A pulse of white energy flowed from Suzuki's arm to Stew's face and the sticky substance on Stew's face evaporated.

Stew still held the hag's abdomen in his arms as she struggled. Suzuki saw his opening and brought his sword down hard on the hag's back, cutting her in half.

The screech that came from the hag was nearly unbearable. Stew let go as the hag's top half scuttled away, up into the rafters of the bell tower.

Suzuki pushed Stew to show his irritation, and Stew pointed to his ears, which were bleeding. "Maybe you should start wearing a helmet," Suzuki said.

"I'd rather lose my eyebrows, ears, and nose than look as big of a dork as you."

"Stew, it's practical. And I don't know what you're talking about, my helmet is fucking sick."

"Hey, idiots," Sandy shouted, "You're not done yet!"

Stew pointed at the hag's twitching abdomen that lay on

the ground. "Uh, I think we got her," Stew said. "Homeboy over here just cut her in half. *So,* I think we might be—"

The hag dropped from the ceiling, wrapping Stew in all four of her arms. The two of them rolled across the floor, toward the gaping hole in the center of the room.

Sandy reached out to try and help Stew, but she was too far away. She obviously didn't have enough mana to help either. "Stew!" she shouted.

Suzuki leapt and tried to grab one of the hag's arms, but he was too late. Stew and the hag rolled to the hole in the bell tower. Stew's head clanked the bell loudly as he and the hag fell through the hole.

Stew's screams echoed through the church and grew more distant as he and the hag fell through the church. Suzuki took off after them and jumped down the hole, casting Levitate to soften his fall. He hoped Stew had had enough sense to do the same. Below, there was a crunch and the sound of breaking bones and wood.

Suzuki plummeted into the darkness and landed with an impressive thud. He jumped to his feet and spun, looking for the hag. All he saw was Stew curled in a ball, and the hag scuttling off into the darkness. Suzuki rushed over to Stew and helped him to his feet. "Anything broken?" Suzuki asked.

"Just my pride."

"What's new?"

"Shut it, bro. How are we gonna flush her out?"

"Last time I checked, rafters were flammable."

Suzuki raised his hand and cast a fireball in the direction of the hag. The flames burst across the wood and Suzuki focused on keeping the flames from spreading. Now that the rafters were illuminated, he could see the hag scuttling across the wooden planks above. Her head spun around, and she let go of the rafters and fell toward Stew and Suzuki.

Suzuki managed to get out of the way. Stew, on the other hand, drew his other sword and prepared for impact.

The hag hit Stew hard and they both fell to the ground. Stew slid his sword into the hag's soft underbelly and she screeched in pain. Then she leaned forward and sank her fangs into Stew's neck. "Fucking A," Stew shouted as he rolled over, forcing the hag off him.

Suzuki had another fireball prepped, and he leapt, fireball in hand, and slam-dunked it into the hag's head. Her skin burst into flames. Stew grabbed his dropped sword, shifted under the hag, and lopped off her head. Her head went flying, and her body went limp.

Stew got to his feet and tried to wipe the blood off his face before sighing and giving up. Behind them, Sandy floated down from the bell tower. "Can't see why you said that was a fifty percent," Stew wondered. "Irritating, yes. Nearly deadly, definitely not."

Suzuki crouched down to inspect the hag's body. The blood that was flowing from her neck was black and congealing now. He poked it with his sword and, when he withdrew it, the blood trailed after like black syrup. "Gross," Suzuki said. "This crap looks like fermented bean curds or something."

"Is she actually dead this time?"

Suzuki stabbed the corpse a handful of times. Then for good measure, he set it on fire until there were only ashes. "Yeah, it doesn't seem like that fight could have gone either way. Something else must be up."

The skin around Stew's neck was bright red and inflamed. He kept scratching it, more vigorously than when he was picking at his face. There were rings of gray around the center of his pupils. Suzuki walked up and stared at Stew's eyes, trying to figure out what was wrong. The color of his eyes had changed as well. "Hey Stew," Suzuki ventured, "You mind if I look you over right quick?"

"As long as you keep your hands to yourself and I don't have to cough."

Suzuki pulled up his HUD. "Scan for ailments," he said. The HUD scanned Stew's body. After a few seconds, the HUD read "Ailment detected: vampirism."

"Holy shit, Stew, I think you just caught vampirism."

The color drained from Stew's face and his eyes went wide. Suzuki could tell that Stew was about to lose his shit and start freaking out. "Hey, hey, buddy," Suzuki started. "Don't worry. It's curable. You just got a little bit of it. You're gonna be all right. You should have a couple of dispelling potions. Sandy brewed them for us before we left."

Sandy smiled and nodded, obviously happy about her foresight. Stew opened his HUD and scrolled through his inventory, and a potion materialized in his hand. He downed it faster than a man dying of thirst in the Sahara. After Stew was done, Suzuki double-checked Stew's status.

That fast, the vampirism was cured.

Suzuki walked to where the hag's head had flown, knelt next to it, and opened the mouth to look at her teeth. There were more than just sharp. The hag had two rows of shark-like teeth. "That must have been why we were at fifty percent," Suzuki mused aloud. "The HUD was considering that we might also lose long-term by contracting the virus. So that's what we're up against, vampires."

Sandy and Stew came up beside Suzuki. Stew no longer looked like he was going to freak out but still did not look comfortable. Sandy knelt next to Suzuki to look at the hag's head as well. "That explains the psychic disturbance," she offered. "Vampires are in the group of undead who can affect the psychic plane. It looks like she might have developed that over time, though. I don't feel any remnants of the fog. It might be safe to assume that it was just this bitch who could manipulate our feelings."

"Thank the Godless Beings of Destructions," Sandy said. "If I had to focus any longer on happy thoughts, I was going to pull my eyes out of their sockets."

"What were you thinking about?" Stew asked Suzuki.

"Huh? Oh, I guess all the times that we used to play together. Basically you guys, I guess."

"That's sweet." Stew put his hands over his heart in the manner of one in love. "I never would have pegged you for a sweetheart."

"I'm not. That's why it was increasingly difficult. What about you?"

Stew nudged the hag's head with his foot so that her mouth lay slack-jawed and open. "Probably my sweet loving," Stew joked.

"You know it, you hunk of cock," Sandy quipped.

Suzuki tried to pretend he was in a soundproof room for a second. No matter how often he heard what Sandy and Stew counted as flirting, it still had the potential to turn his stomach. "Seriously," Suzuki said. "I told you mine."

Sandy braided her hair out of her face as she spoke. "It was you guys for a little bit. But it got distracting, so I started thinking about my dad. We used to go surfing a lot when he was stationed in Hawaii. He used to have to help me shake the sand out of my ears and hair."

"What about you, Stew?"

"I was just thinking about cartoons. You know, those old black and white ones. I always laughed at *Casper the Ghost.* That kid was *weird.*"

Suzuki didn't know where to start with wrapping his head around why Stew's best memories were of cartoons. That would have to be tackled another day. Suzuki inhaled deeply, held his breath, and then exhaled slowly. He felt normal. All those cursed feelings had ebbed away. Still, he felt something lingered in him. It could have just been the knowledge of what the whole experience had brought out of him. It was like they had all grown closer.

"It's like we survived an argument," Sandy murmured under her breath.

The words had been taken right out of Suzuki's head. Sandy stared at him, letting him know she understood. It might not have been the exact thing Suzuki was feeling, but it was close enough. Stew must have been feeling the same way because he'd been uncharacteristically quiet. "More like a thousand arguments," Stew then added on. "I can't believe that I thought those things about you guys. It's hard to imagine wanting to kill your best friends."

"Well, most people don't get to survive trying to murder their best friends. I say we're lucky. So what's next?"

The main section of the church where they were was nearly destroyed. The room had already been in shambles. Suzuki paced around the rubble, running his finger over the hilt of his hand ax. "It doesn't look like we're gonna find anything here," Suzuki thought aloud. "Upstairs was pretty empty other than shark-mouth over here. It's almost like she was caged up there."

Sandy crouched beside the head of the hag. She opened its mouth, withdrew a tool from her HUD similar to pliers, and started pulling out the hag's teeth. "Someone probably locked her up," Sandy suggested. "She was probably really fucking up whatever is here. Imagine a coven of vamps acting like us?"

Stew's face went white, and he shot a glance around as if he expected something to swoop down and snatch him up. "Coven," Stew said weakly, "That sounds like a lot. That sounds like more than one."

"Probably. You know how literature has been seeded to let humans know what's really going on? Social vampires didn't quite catch on, but from what I've been reading, vampires are pack hunters."

The fear had not left Stew's face. He didn't look reassured. If anything, he seemed a couple of shades lighter. "So nothing above. Nothing in the middle. Downstairs. We gotta go downstairs?" Stew's voice was that of a frightened child. The dark was beneath, and Stew did not look like he liked the idea of vampires.

"Yep. So we better find out how to get there."

They broke apart, each going their own way to look for a way downstairs. Most of the walls were covered in junk or falling apart. A secret entrance would have been obvious. After a bit of time, they all joined up in front of the altar. "Any luck?" Suzuki asked.

Stew and Sandy spoke in unison, saying, "Nope."

"Fuck. Where the hell could it be?" Stew asked.

Sandy knelt and scrolled through her HUD. "Hold on, I've got an idea." A large, musty tome appeared in her hands. "I figured I'd start taking what you said about trying new kinds of magic seriously. It doesn't make sense to have two offensive mages, right? So Niv has been helping me with this." Sandy raised her hand in front of the tome. She closed her eyes, and the book floated into the air. Concentric circles floated above her palms, intricate words forming the circle like a puzzle of fragile rings.

Obviously impressed, Stew leaned in to get a better look at Sandy's new casting trick. "What does it do?" he asked.

"It's more nuanced magic. Trap spells. I can give more support now. I'll still be able to hold my own, but I can work more ritualistic stuff. It's pretty cool. I've been going over it with Niv. Like this one."

Sandy raised her arms higher, and the book floated closer to her. "Dispel Illusion," she murmured.

Hot air pulsed through the room. Suzuki felt a wave of heat roll over him. Another sensation quickly followed. It was as if his eyes had suddenly started to see clearer. The room looked sharper, crisper. Suddenly, it was apparent that the walls were not nearly as dilapidated as they had initially looked. In fact, the church was in great condition. It appeared to have been constructed recently.

There was a staircase in the far right corner. Suzuki walked to the stairwell and peered down it. "How'd you do that?" he asked. "Aren't you out of mana?"

Sandy smiled innocently and flipped her braid over her shoulder. "There's more than one way to cast magic," she said. "Staves, wands, channeling magic into items and weapons...that all takes mana. A good book of ritualistic spells hardly burns any. The only downside is it takes longer to cast."

Stew peered down the dark stairwell. His voice slightly echoed as he spoke. "So we're going down there? It's kind of dark."

Sandy closed her book, squeezed Stew's butt, and kissed him on the cheek. "Don't worry, babe, I'll make sure no more old ladies give you hickeys."

The hilt of Suzuki's sword glowed as he pulled it out and pointed it down the stairwell. "Come on," he said, lamenting the fifty percent. Was that percentage also taking into account whatever was at the end of the stairwell? "We need to stop dicking around and finish this up. We still need to figure out what José wants."

There were no disagreements. Each of them stared down the stairwell, imagining what it was that lay waiting. Suzuki apprehensive. He hadn't forgotten that black dread that had welled up in him in the village. Nor did he forget the bizarre pagan sculpture profaning the church's altar.

Whatever was downstairs was going to be dangerous.

Cobwebs hung from the ceiling and walls of the stairwell, which was much larger than the one they had climbed to get to the fog hag. The stairs descended into the church in a spiral. Candles were burning on the walls, casting shadows that seemed to move independently. The air was dank and musty, the smell of old death, of decaying walls.

Suzuki couldn't help but wonder at the construction of the stairwell. The stairs themselves were metalwork so delicate that it felt as if each stair might crumble under their weight. The walls were covered with some kind of luminescent paint that caught the light and seemed to hold it in place. Suzuki noticed that both Sandy and Stew were also interested in the wall paintings. *At least it'll keep Stew calm,* Suzuki chuckled to himself.

Before this mission, there hadn't been much that rattled Stew. Over their last few missions, Stew was the one who had seemed the least fazed by the undead.

It was hard to tell, though. Sandy was always going on

about murdering their enemies. Part of Suzuki believed that was a way for Sandy to cover how scared she might actually be, a mask of bravado to hide her fear. There was a while he had thought Stew was doing the same thing, but seeing Stew frightened tossed that thought out of his mind.

Suzuki asked himself why he wasn't afraid. The last day had been such a flurry of conflicting emotions, Suzuki wasn't even certain how he felt anymore. Within a twenty-four hour period of time, Suzuki had gone from wanting to kill his friends to wanting to kill himself and everything in between. Walking into a nest of undead vampires seemed like a walk in the park comparatively.

There wasn't much Suzuki knew about vampires. He had skipped over vampire books and comics; he had thought them too juvenile, something that high-school goth pre-teens read. They seemed to be nothing but shimmering pretty boys and taut young women with ample cleavage. At the time, this seemed way beneath him, but now Suzuki felt a tinge of excitement. This was going to be a whole new experience. The most he knew about vampires was that they drank blood, were sensitive to sunlight and that fire, beheadings, and stakes to the heart would kill them.

Then again—beheadings and stakes to the heart would kill anything.

Maybe there was something about silver in the mix, too. Suzuki wasn't sure.

Down and down they went into the belly of the church. Suzuki lost track of time. It felt as if they had been walking down the stairs for hours, guided by the faint light of the flickering candles. *This could all be an illusion*, Suzuki thought. *Just like upstairs. Or it could be a trap.* Neither he nor Sandy had even bothered to check for any traps. In their excitement, they had rushed and forgotten to be careful. Suzuki made a mental note not to let that happen again. Leaving their bases uncovered could easily result in their deaths.

Being dead wasn't going to save Beth.

Finally, they got to the bottom of the stairs. A long hallway stretched ahead. There were no more candles. The halls looked as if they were generating their own blackness, not satisfied to merely be the absence of light.

The darkness ahead had a palpable existence, and Suzuki could taste it on the back of his throat. He asked Sandy if she too could taste the darkness. "I Guess all vamps give off that feeling," Suzuki said. "I wonder why they shoved the hag all the way up there."

Sandy stared up the stairwell as if she were retracing her steps along with her thoughts. "Maybe she got too old. Suck-head strength grows the longer they live, or whatever the fuck you want to call it. Maybe the longer she was around, the worse the feelings got."

"Yeah, this is much more manageable. I still don't like it though. You think swords will work as well as stakes?"

Stew nodded. "I don't see why not. They both have pointy bits."

Suzuki walked toward the entrance of the black hall, Sandy trailing behind him. The dread was building up. There was something dark and difficult for his brain to comprehend deep in the walls of the church catacombs. Stew hadn't bothered moving to catch up with either Sandy or Suzuki. He was standing further back, closer to the spiral stairs, watching the other two staring down the hall of blackness. Finally, he swallowed hard and came up to join his friends. The three of them stepped into the dark hallway.

At the far end of the hallway, there was a dull amber light that could only be seen once they started walking the length of the passage. The closer they got, the brighter the light. It did not take long until they exited the tunnel and stepped into a large room. The walls were covered with bookcases, and there were multiple leather chairs which looked older than anything Suzuki had ever seen in an antique store.

Chalices covered the tables. The floor had a deep-red carpet, and the walls were covered with red paisley wallpaper. A large, stone cauldron stood in the center of the room, a flaming chandelier floating above it, supported by some kind of magic. The room had the feeling of being an exposed chest, with a beating heart surrounded by blood.

Suzuki walked around the room, looking at each of its individual gothic components. It felt vaguely familiar, but he couldn't quite place where he had seen something like this. "I don't remember anything like this in-game," Suzuki said. "It feels kinda like that old D&D *Ravenloft* campaign."

Sandy was peering into the cauldron while Stew was inching his way into the room. "I thought you weren't into vampires?" Sandy reminded him.

"I wasn't. A friend tried to get me to play *Ravenloft* once, but I couldn't get into it."

"This is right out of *Hunter, in Darkness*."

"What's that?"

"It's from one of the *Middang3ard* Choose Your Own Adventure stories."

"Never heard of it."

"With a nickname like Suzuki, I thought you would have for sure."

"The name's Robert."

Stew shrugged. "Everyone calls you Suzuki, dude."

"Whatever," Sandy said, "It was an ESL supplemental. You know, for Japanese kids who were learning English, but didn't want to go through any of those boring modules. "Hello. How are you today? My name is Takashi." Blah, blah, blah. *Middang3ard* did a whole series. Now I'm guessing its part of their reaching-out-to-all-cultures-to-prepare-them sales pitch."

"Fuck, they thought of everything," Suzuki said. "Wait a minute? How do you know all that?"

"I taught English in Japan for two years. It was part of our supplemental learning material."

"When?" Suzuki asked.

"Back when we were exploring the Enzaro Realms."

"Oh yeah. You were always logging in late."

"Time difference is a bitch, my dude," Sandy said.

"Hey, where's Stew?"

Suzuki and Sandy turned to look around through the gothic atmospheric tension. Stew was nowhere to be seen. After a few seconds, a bloodcurdling scream cut through the air. Suzuki ran in the direction of the cry for help, kicking open a door, ax drawn, ready to hack away at whatever undead creature was waiting for him.

Stew was pointing at something, his finger trembling, and he was even whiter than he had been earlier. Suzuki followed Stew's finger, and he had to stifle the scream that quickly welled up in him.

They were in a kitchen. The walls were covered with blood-colored rust, and there were large washing basins like the sort you would find in a restaurant kitchen.

Steel tables were set up throughout the kitchen. That was not what Stew was pointing at though.

Stew was indicating rows of hooks hanging from the ceiling.

Skinned humanoid bodies hung from the hooks. Some of them had been ripped to pieces and were only hanging by a shred of muscle or tendon. Others had been gutted, their intestines laying on the tables or casually tossed to the ground. There were others that looked to be very fresh, the blood still glistening on their vivisected corpses.

Stew put his hand over his mouth and doubled over, trying to push down the sound of his dry heaving. "I think I'm going to be sick," he finally managed.

Sandy walked around the corpses hanging from the ceiling. She didn't seem distressed by the excessive gore. If anything, she looked interested, the kind of interest that she displayed when she was in the library, hunting for new books and spells.

"I would have thought that vampires were neater," she mused. "You know, they're billed as being pretty elegant killers. This looks like Leatherface's jack-off cave."

"Yeah," Suzuki agreed. "This is some sick shit. Guess this quest would have been rated R. Graphic violence."

"And sexual content. Vampires are supposed to be sexy," Stew said.

Sandy shook her head. "There hasn't been any yet."

"Patience, my young Padawan. Patience."

From the corner of the room came a sound not quite like a scream, but still an obvious plea for help. It came from the corner closest to Stew, and Suzuki motioned for Stew to check it out. Stew looked ready to bolt, but he pulled out his longsword and inched toward a wooden crate in the corner. He unsheathed his other sword and used it to pry open the box, his slashing arm raised, poised to kill whatever was in the box. Stew's sword stayed in mid-air though as a smile spread across his face, the sort of smile that crops up unconsciously when you see a baby or puppy.

Stew sheathed his swords and waved the rest of the Mundanes over. He pointed to the contents of the box.

A dozen or so large, brown eyes stared up at them. The eyes were attached to small creatures, covered in fluff with grubby noses and comical overbites. Their hands were short and squat, as was the rest of their bodies. Their fur was a subtle tan, and they looked like a cross between a teddy bear and an elongated Furby. The little furballs were trembling with fear.

Suzuki was not impressed by their cuteness. These things could easily be just as deadly as anything else in the catacombs. Stew was already won over though. He looked as if it were taking all his self-control not to reach into the box and grab one of the things to take home as a pet. "Guys," Stew started. "These aren't what I thought they were."

Sandy leaned over the box and started cooing at the furry creatures. Some of them stopped shivering and looked up at her. They mimicked her song. "They are so damn cute. They're Mogwais, right?"

Suzuki looked down into the box as well, taking a deep breath. "Actually, 'Mogwai' is the name for 'demon' in a Chinese dialect. The movie adopted the term because according to ancient Chinese legends, Mogwais reproduced when it rained, so the countryside would be littered with them during monsoon season. The addition of Mogwais turning into gremlins through—"

"Suzuki, will you please shut up and just look at the cute gremlins with us?" Stew said.

"They're called Mog—"

Fred unwrapped himself in Suzuki's brain. *Actually, these are gremouloons. A delicacy for vampires.*

Suzuki could feel Fred weaving through his memories,

tugging at the unconscious pool of things Suzuki wasn't even aware he knew. It was an uncomfortable feeling. He'd known Fred to have invaded his memories a couple of times already, and the longer he was with the imp, the easier it seemed to tolerate. The trade-off was that casting magic was also getting easier. They were forming a bond, even if it was mostly unspoken.

Fred relaxed and started his slow retreat back into Suzuki's pocket dimension. *They are very similar to gremlins on your world,* he explained. *"It seems that Myrddin has his magical fingers in everything, seeding your world with legends and then having another culture re-appropriate them for a massive, intellectually-devoid audience. There is a certain genius to the wizard's shrewdness.*

Suzuki had to fight the urge to pick up one of the gremouloons. It was almost a compulsion. He needed to feel their soft fur against his face, to stare into their obscenely large eyes, to press his ears to their lips so he could listen to that odd cooing sound they were now making. "They *are* pretty cute."

*No, they are not*, Fred argued. *They are disease-ridden, carnivorous rats pumping the air with pheromones that make you want to cuddle them until they can take a bite out of you.*

Sandy had leaned farther into the box, her braid dangling almost in reach of the gremouloons. "We gotta let them out," she pleaded. "They're trapped here."

Suzuki shook his head. He was tired of his emotions being manipulated by everything in this village. "Nope," he said. "They're dangerous. And we're much more liable to get caught if we do. I'm seeing a thirty percent increase of detection, putting us at eighty-three percent chance of failure if we let them out."

"Christ, when did you become a cyborg?" Stew asked.

Sandy clasped her hands in a pleading gesture. "We don't have to take them with us. We could just let them run wild down here."

Suzuki shook his head. "What if we swing back and let them out when we're done?"

"But...but..."

---

While Sandy and Suzuki argued the proper way to deal with the gremouloon situation, Stew wandered back to the red room. He found his way back to the cauldron, his feet moving as if he were compelled by some force.

The cauldron sat in the middle of the room. It looked as if it had grown larger. Stew leaned over to look into it. An eye slowly bubbled to the surface of the liquid. It rolled over so that it could look him in the eye. As a scream welled up in Stew as more bits of humans, elves, and orcs bubbled to the top of the cauldron. Now Stew did scream.

It didn't take long for Suzuki and Sandy to get back to the room, where the found Stew pointing at the cauldron. Sandy went to check it out. "So Stew's afraid of stew," she joked.

"I'm not afraid of stew! That thing is filled with fucking dead people."

Sandy smirked. "Hmm. Stew isn't very sophisticated. What are these, working-class suckheads?"

"Actually," Suzuki started, "stew can be a very complex, sophisticated dish. There are an array of flavors that can only be properly explored when given time to soak and come apart in the juices of—"

Stew pitched forward and vomited by a bookcase.

"Dude," he finally uttered after he had wiped his face. "Those are people in that thing."

Suzuki peered over the edge of the cauldron. "Shit, you're right."

"I can't be in here right now."

Stew stumbled back to the kitchen full of hanging bodies, and Suzuki and Sandy followed. They quickly passed through the kitchen, trying not to let their eyes linger on the corpses dangling like fresh-cut meat. Stew flung open the door at the end of the kitchen, and they walked into a small room with a few doors on opposite sides. There was a dirt floor, and there was hardly any light.

The room was filled with coffins stacked side by side.

The Mundanes stopped in their tracks. "Fuck," Suzuki muttered under his breath.

Sandy reached out and squeezed Suzuki's shoulder. "Don't worry," she said. "They should be out. We still have a couple of hours before sunrise. They should be out hunting."

"Well, let's get moving. I wanna get whatever the fuck José wants and get the hell out of here. Let's see what's behind door number one."

Suzuki approached the door closest to him. He fought the urge to go to the coffins and rip them open. He wanted to know for sure that they were empty. The suspense was making him jumpy. If the vampires were in their coffins, this could be a giant trap. They could just be waiting until he turned his back and they could sneak up on him, slip their fangs into the side of his neck. That being said, if they were sleeping in the coffins and hadn't realized the Mundanes were raiding their home, opening the coffin would be sure death. Moving forward as fast as possible seemed like the only option.

They crossed into the other room. The catacombs were taking on the feeling of a mansion that doubled as a maze. This new room was lavishly decorated, even more so than the red room they had initially stumbled into. There didn't seem to be anything interesting among the Victorian style furniture, so they opted to try one of the many doors in the room. There was another room, not too different from the one that they had just walked through with just as many doors.

*Lost*, Suzuki thought. *We're getting lost.*

The Mundanes continued to choose room after room, each one looking only slightly different than the one before. Suzuki didn't voice his suspicions but suggested that they check the room they had been in only a few seconds before. He made a mental note of the red vase that was sitting on a table with lion-motif legs.

When they reentered the room they had just come from, Suzuki noticed that this room had the exact same vase and table as the room they had just been in. "Guys," Suzuki ventured, "I think something's up with these rooms."

Sandy walked to the couch in the far corner of the room and collapsed into it. She kicked her feet up on the coffee table in front of her. "Yeah, I figured so too," she agreed. "Sometimes it feels like we're walking into a new room and other times, it's like it's a new room, but only slightly different."

"You think it's an illusion?"

Sandy nodded. "Probably."

"Can you dispel it?" Suzuki asked.

Sandy looked around. "I think so, but it's a really large space. It might take some time."

"Do you remember anything important from the books?

About large spaces and all?" Stew chimed in as he scanned the room for threats.

"Eh. Not really. Nothing like this. The book was mostly a gorefest. Pretty simple on plot and world-building. Just a bunch of scenes where you get to choose how you're going to kill the suck-heads. There was a lot of really cool vampire stuff though. Like, the design of the vampires in the book was pretty unique, and the feeding stuff was always cool. The vampires didn't just suck your blood out, but they'd torture you for hours first, making little cuts all over your body so they could do it slowly. They'd be, like, five to a person. It was gruesome. And uncomfortably sexy."

"And this was to teach English to kids?"

"Nah, ESL is for adults, mostly," Sandy said, shaking her head. "It's nowhere near as gruesome as *Clash of the Titans.* That's pretty fucking extreme."

"Yeah. It's got tons of really up-close munch shots," Stew agreed.

Suzuki cocked his head to one side in confusion. "What's a munch shot?"

Sandy used two fingers to mime a person running. Her other swooped down, caught the fingers, and she pretended to throw them into her mouth. She ended with a theatrical crunch.

There was a loud rumbling from somewhere deep within the mansion. Suzuki had to exert every ounce of self-control not to roll his eyes. Instead, he pulled out his hand ax and flipped it into the air as he checked with his HUD to see what the likelihood of his survival was going to be. "There's a fucking giant in here, isn't there?" He sighed.

The side of the room exploded, sending books and wood flying everywhere. A young, not-fully-grown giant barrel-rolled into the room. He was holding a club covered in spikes, and skulls and various bones hung from his body. It wasn't as tall as an adult, roughly standing seven feet. It was small enough to fit into the mansion, but still large enough to rip the Mundanes to shreds with its bare hands.

As was typical of its kind, the giant's face wore a dumb look of perpetual rage.

The giant swung its club at Stew, who managed to step out of the way as he tumbled forward, having overcommitted to the attack. "Since when do giants hang out with vampires?" Stew shouted.

The giant turned once it had stumbled to its feet and swung his club at Suzuki. "It must have something to do with the Dark One," Suzuki shouted as he moved to the side and dodged the attack. *I'm getting pretty good at this,* he thought to himself. The thought was premature. The giant landed the next attack, sending Suzuki flying and nearly shattering his HUD.

As Suzuki stumbled to his feet, he saw Sandy narrowly avoid the giant's club. Stew was trying to get in a good shot, but the giant never stopped moving. Because it was not fully grown, it had the speed and vigor of youth. The problem was that it was still very obviously a giant. The creature dominated the room, and it was all that Sandy and Stew could manage to keep from being crushed by the giant's stomping feet and swinging club.

Suddenly the giant stopped. It sniffed the air with its massive, mucus-filled nostrils. Then its eyes settled on Suzuki.

Suzuki checked his HUD. His SD upgrade had been deactivated when he'd been hit.

Now he smelled like a fucking Englishman.

The giant let out a terrifying roar as it turned its back on Sandy and Stew.

Suzuki turned and ran toward the open door in front of him. "Fuck me," he shouted as he sprinted. The giant was nearly running on all fours, foaming at the mouth like a rabid dog, deadly intent on crushing every bone in Suzuki's body.

The room Suzuki ran into should have been the same one they had come from.

It was not.

Suzuki noticed and made a mental note to check back into that problem later. It was going to be hell getting out of this mansion if rooms kept changing every time they switched rooms. None of that would matter though if he was a greasy stain at the bottom of a giant's heel.

The chase was on, with Sandy and Stew bringing up the rear, struggling to keep up with the giant's massive strides. Up ahead, Suzuki was running with every ounce of energy that he could. He flung doors open and stepped into them without so much as a care as the rooms of the mansion magically switched themselves around, creating a tangled web of déjà vu, disorientation, and foreshadowing of the immediacy of death.

Suzuki checked over his shoulder to see if the giant was any further away. He was greeted with a fresh roar from the encroaching juggernaut of a giant that turned his stomach sour.

*I cannot keep this up. Gotta figure this out quick.* But without his HUD helping him calculate his odds, Suzuki felt lost.

He'd have to wing it.

*Fine*, he thought as he made his way to another door.

This time, when Suzuki opened the door to a new room, instead of going for the room directly in front of him, he ran to the door in the corner on the other side of the room. As

Suzuki ran through the room, he noticed that it was different than the last fifteen he had Benny-Hilled through. Suzuki chose the same door this time as well. Now there was a new pattern. Once Suzuki crossed the threshold of the door, he let the giant barrel into the room. He raised his hand ax and concentrated. A blinding light flashed from his steel, blinding everyone in the room but him. As the giant stumbled around and Sandy and Stew covered their eyes, Suzuki slipped around the giant and grabbed his friend's hands. He ran through the door that he had come from, closed the door, and opened it again.

The room was empty. No giant anywhere to be seen.

Stew scratched his head, obviously confused, trying to wrap his mind around what had just happened. "There was a giant in here a second ago, right?" he asked.

Suzuki went farther into the room, holding his hands out as if he were worried that he was going to walk into an invisible beast. "Holy shit, I was right," he shouted as he pumped his fist.

"Care to explain?"

"It's a pocket dimension," Suzuki said, smug about figuring it out. "It's just like we have in us for the familiars, except since they're rooms and not people, they can keep replicating. Every time we choose a door, it creates an entirely different room. We're not lost. We're floating through a dozen iterations of the first few rooms we walked into."

Suzuki turned and spoke to Sandy. "Can you work on dissolving the illusion? You should have as much time as you need. I'm pretty sure if anyone opens one of these doors, they'll just be sent into another version of this room."

Sandy nodded and pulled out one of her massive tomes.

She sat down on the couch and started to thumb through its pages.

While Sandy figured out how to dissolve whatever magic had been worked on the mansion, Suzuki fiddled with his SD upgrade. Before they had left the Red Lion, the Chipmaster had gifted them all repair kits for their HUDs, in case anything happened. She had stood over them like an overbearing older sister, shaking her head, saying, "Head-shots are a dime a dozen out in the real world, ye lil' whelps. One to the noggin, and presto, you're knocked out to dream space and monsters get to have their ill-intentioned ways with ya. Ya know, in the most biblical of senses. Them fuckers loosen your noggin visor, and you won't be seeing straight enough to give 'em the good ol' ultra-violence. So take one of these in case you get a little unseen head trauma."

Suzuki had thought that it was overkill. He'd been hit in the head more than a couple of times, and his HUD had always been fine. Now, he was grateful the Horsemen had taken the Mundanes under their wing. Suzuki wondered how he could have been naïve enough to assume that every MERC was gifted with a piece of head armor that was nearly invincible.

Stew was standing by a bookcase with a sheet of paper, a pen, and a bottle of ink on it. He called Suzuki over to him.

The paper was crisp and cream-colored while the pen was an ornate feather piece. A single sentence was written on the paper.

*Eat Me.*

Suzuki picked up the paper and looked underneath it. There was nothing there. He didn't know what it was that this paper was referring to, but he was fairly certain that he didn't want anything to do with it. There could easily be a trap waiting.

Stew, on the other hand, had already dipped the tip of the quill pen in the ink. "What do you think it is?"

"A warning to leave it alone."

Suzuki placed the paper back in its spot as neatly as he could. He tried to line up the edges perfectly so that it did not look as if it had been disturbed.

The paper had hardly touched the surface of the bookcase before Stew leaned over and scrawled something underneath the sentence on the paper. He wrote *Alice in Wonderland*.

"What the hell are you doing, Stew?"

Sandy looked up from her book, her eyebrows low and her eyes narrowed. She looked like a very irate librarian. "Will you two keep it down over there?" she hissed.

"Sorry," they muttered.

When Sandy returned to her book, Stew leaned over the paper to get a better look at what was happening while Suzuki tried to pull him back. "We should not be fucking with this right now," Suzuki growled as he tried to wrestle the pen out of Stew's hand.

Stew fought back and stomped hard on Suzuki's foot. "Fuck off, dude," Stew said, "This is a fucking riddle. I love riddles."

The ink on the paper disappeared. Then, slowly, a new sentence bled out onto the parchment: "Yuletide cruelty sets spirits to flight."

Stew reached to pen his answer. "Don't," Suzuki interrupted. Stew didn't listen, and he wrote down his reply: *A Christmas Carol.*

Even though Suzuki was extremely annoyed, he couldn't help but look at the paper to see if the answer was accepted.

The ink disappeared, and a new sentence appeared: "Finale: A building, a war, a flower."

Stew delicately scratched his face as he stuck his tongue out of the corner of his mouth.

Suzuki noticed for the first time that Stew had a variety of different kinds of skin picking. He picked obsessively when he was nervous. But this one right here, barely touching his skin, was almost like an uncomfortable caress. Suzuki hadn't seen this before. He had the rising suspicion that this was what Stew looked like when he was being thoughtful.

Finally, Stew sighed and turned around to call to Sandy, "Hey, babe! What's that flower that your grandma uses with her blood thinners?"

Without looking up, Sandy shouted back, "Paris."

Stew scrawled the answer onto the paper before Suzuki could even ask why he had never heard Sandy mention her grandmother.

The ink on the parchment disappeared. Another sentence appeared: Please collect your reward.

The bookcase shook as the books on the shelves started to lean back or fall forward, some of them moving to the side, the whole bookcase rearranging itself so there was an empty shelf with a small wooden box on it. Before Suzuki could say anything, Stew reached out and opened the box.

Three SD upgrades sat on the velvet lining.

Stew snatched them and raised them in the air as he danced and shouted, "I got three new SDs, bitches!"

Sandy, still glued to her book, replied, "No, you don't. There are three of us. You have one SD upgrade. Don't be a dick."

"What? You guys didn't even do anything."

"I answered your question, so I deserve one. Not sharing

with Suzuki when we both get an upgrade is just poor form."

"Poor form?"

"A douche move."

"Fine. Fine, let's split them up."

Suzuki motioned for Stew to follow him back to the couch, where he took a seat next to Sandy, who hardly noticed. Stew passed Suzuki the SD's as Suzuki got to work repairing his HUD. The damage wasn't too bad. The SD card that he used to mask his scent (recently he'd been using it as a form of different colognes) was only knocked out of place. It only took a few moments to reset the SD card and change his scent back to Forest Greenery. Then he looked at the new SD cards. The information for the cards displayed itself on Suzuki's HUD.

**Critical Hit: Displays enemies' weak spots, allowing the user to better choose where to attack. Also increases damage when connecting a critical hit.**

**Clairvoyance: Allows user to open a small magical portal anywhere and another corresponding portal. The user may look through their portal and see out of the other portal, undetected by all but the strongest of magic users.**

**Spell Splitting: The user of this upgrade can effectively split a spell in two without consuming excessive mana. The spell will be split simply, such as casting a fireball that instantly doubles. Advanced casters may also use this ability to create spell hybrids, two spells cast simultaneously for the cost of the lowest mana-consuming spell.**

Stew snatched the three SDs from Suzuki's hand. "I call the Spell Splitting," he said.

Sandy peeked up from her book for a second, her face

showing she was already tired of this conversation. "Stew, you don't even use magic," she objected.

"Yeah, but this thing is gonna sell for *so much money!*"

"I'm taking the Spell Splitting." Sandy fluttered her eyes and touched the neckline of her shirt suggestively.

"Wait, but I totes... Fine."

"Which one do you want, Suzuki?"

"I don't know. Clairvoyance sounds pretty useful. Might give me the edge on planning something."

"Sounds good," Sandy chirped. "Stew, you get Critical Hit."

Stew threw his arms up in exasperation as he stood up from the couch. He looked like a child complaining that he never got his way. "That's so boring," he whined. "Both of your cards are sick."

Sandy's eyes darkened as she closed her book and stood up to confront Stew face-to-face. "Stop acting like a baby," she raged. "You literally hit things with different sharp things. All you do is try to get critical hits. Why would you want a card that gives you magic upgrades when you don't have magic? Or take an upgrade a Peeping Tom would want?"

"I don't know. They sound kind of cool."

Sandy stepped closer to Stew and wrapped her arms around his waist as she pulled him in. "Come on, baby, think of all the heads you can chop off. You can nickname it something cooler than Critical Hit. We'll have Chip edit it. Make it your own legendary SD."

The affection worked. Stew's irritation almost instantly left his face. He brightened up at the notion so quickly Suzuki would have thought Stew came up with the idea all on his own. "You're right," Stew relented. "I can make that shit so badass. Crit Hits every five—"

There was a crash of wood and falling furniture. Stew's eyes went wide as a slender black hand wrapped around his neck. He reached out to grab Suzuki, but the black hand pulled, and it pulled hard. Stew was snapped back to the wall and pulled into a massive hole. Suzuki and Sandy ran to the hole, reaching after Stew. There was nothing but blackness beyond the hole. The only sound that could be heard was Stew screaming.

-----------

## 16

S uzuki was still staring into the black void that stretched beyond the confines of the hole in the wall. There was nothing. The blackness went on and on; there was no light to be seen. He felt the distinct sensation of falling. Even when he looked at his feet, which were still solidly on the ground, it felt as if he were flying through the blackness of that space. He backed away from the hole very slowly.

On the couch, Sandy was rapidly flipping through the pages of her book. She stopped at certain dog-eared pages, and finally pulled a piece of chalk and a small wand out of her robes. "Gimme a hand," she told Suzuki as she started pushing the couch back.

Suzuki noticed that Sandy didn't bother trying to levitate the couch. Before he could say anything, she raised the wand. "I'm out of mana," she explained. "There's not much I can do with my own body, but I can still perform rituals, and the wand will help with the in-between."

Sandy knelt in the new space. She drew a series of circles on the ground, interweaving, interconnected orbs. Every couple of seconds, she would consult the book that was open by her side. She raised her wand once she was satisfied with the transcription. The tome that she was copying from floated up so that she could read from it. "There is that which is seen and that which is known," she murmured. "Let that which is true forever be shown."

A pulse of energy emanated from the circle in the middle of the floor. A blinding blue light flashed through the room, and Suzuki covered his eyes to shield himself. When he dropped his hands, he was still standing in the room with Sandy. "Did it work?" he asked.

Sandy raised her finger to her lips and shushed him. "Listen," she whispered.

There was a steady pounding from behind the walls, the sound of heavy footsteps. It was the giant. Suzuki pulled up his HUD and made sure that his scent was still set to Forest Greenery. Then an idea popped into his head.

"Do you think you could find a buffer spell?" Suzuki asked. "Like something to take my status effect and apply it to the whole party?"

"Yeah, I know one," Sandy replied as she started flipping through her book. She tossed it on the ground and started to draw a complicated network of runes. Even though she was rushing, Suzuki could see that she was well-practiced in the art. He wondered how long she'd been studying ritual work. It had never occurred to him to find out what other ways there were to perform magic. He guessed that was why Sandy had wanted to be a mage. It certainly looked like she had a knack for it.

Sandy stood up when she was done, the book floating up with her. She waved her wand, and the runes at her feet glowed an eerie green. "That which is within, let it be spread thick," she murmured, her eyes rolling back as if she were in a trance, "That which is yours, let it be ours."

Suzuki concentrated on his scent SD upgrade. He wasn't sure that he needed to be focusing, but it made sense to him. Once the runes stopped glowing, he looked at Sandy through his HUD and scanned her for status effects. An icon above her head read Forest Greenery. "Fucking great," Suzuki said as he scrolled through the infinite options for scents on his SD. Trying to conjure up the scent would be easier. He racked his brain for something that would slip past the giant undetected. "Change scent to vampire body odor," he finally said.

"Suzuki, are you fucking serious? Now is not the time to be fucking around."

"No, hear me out," Suzuki said. "The undead don't smell like us, but they don't smell like rotting flesh either. Or at least not only rotting flesh. They smell like something between. If this giant's been in here with these vampires for a while, it's probably used to how they smell. This way we can sneak past him, and he won't pick up on anything weird."

"Okay. Gross, but it makes sense. Come on. We gotta go find Stew."

Suzuki creaked the door open and peered down the hallway. Sandy's Dispel illusion spell had worked. He was staring down a hallway he hadn't seen since they'd started running through the mansion. The hallway was decorated with candles that cast an eerie light on the floor.

In the distance, Suzuki could see the giant turning the corner. "All right, we're going the other way."

A scream that sounded frighteningly like Stew's echoed down the hall. It was followed by, "Holy shit! Get that thing the fuck away from me! Once I get down from here, I'm going to personally shove my sword up each and every one of your assholes."

Suzuki and Sandy took off in the direction of Stew's voice. *Fuck being quiet,* Suzuki thought to himself. It sounded like something horrifying was about to happen to Stew. If the giant heard them, that just meant that they were bringing a giant to the slaughter.

They turned a corner and stopped in their tracks. Two massive stone doors which stretched up to the ceiling stood before them. The doors were covered with stone etchings like what they had seen before, but there was a difference.

These doors didn't tell any stories. There was only one scene. A creature of immense size and girth took up most of the upper section of the stone—the creature that was depicted in the altar at the front of the church. Its tentacles and feet combined and stretched toward the middle of the doors, where they trampled over thousands and thousands of bodies: elves, humans, orcs, and halflings.

The bottom of the door showed dead bodies, their blood forming a sort of structure near the base.

Stew's screams rang out from behind the door again.

Suzuki pushed all his questions out of his mind. He desperately wanted to help Stew, but barging in wouldn't help anyone. Helping Stew meant taking his time, planning this right. He only hoped the barbarian could hold his own for a few more seconds.

He pulled his HUD off, grabbed his tinker's tool, and quickly installed his new SD card. There wasn't enough time to do a proper installation, and, even then, it probably would have taken the Chipmaster to install the SD to work to its full potential. *This quick install should work well enough,* Suzuki thought. He placed his HUD back on.

The HUD read **New SD card detected. New SD card activated.** *Cast Clairvoyance in that room, Fred,* Suzuki ordered.

*There is something foul in there*, Fred said. *Something old. Something far too old to be played with.*

*Whatever it is, it has Stew, which means it's going to be more than played with. We're going to fuck it up.*

*As you wish, human.*

A portal slightly larger than Suzuki's palm opened in front of him. He brought his face close to it. He could see into the other room, but only faintly. There were a few discernable figures, but none appeared to be vampires.

Suzuki instinctively moved his hand, and the portal on the other side of the room turned so that he could get a better look. From this point of view, he could see Stew. He was hanging over a cauldron.

*Fuck it, we need to move. Help me with the door!*

"Wait, Suzuki, hold on," Sandy said. Change your scent to garlic."

"What?"

"Change it to garlic and let me amplify the smell. If the lore is right, and Myrddin made sure to teach us as much of it as possible, vampires can't stand that smell. It'll keep them away from us long enough so we can get Stew."

Suzuki mentally adjusted his scent to freshly-chopped garlic as Sandy knelt and covered the floor with runes as fast as she could. She waved her wand, muttering the words of the spell, and the hallway was filled with the overpowering smell of garlic. "All right," Suzuki said as he leaned against the door. "Let's get in, grab Stew, and get out fast."

They pushed against the stone doors until the doors finally started to budge. They were barely able to make an opening small enough for them to slip through, but they managed.

The main hall pulsed with magic, a kind of magic Suzuki had never come across before. Candles floated from the ceiling in elaborate patterns, and it seemed as if each flame had a face. The walls looked as if blood was running down them in steady streams. A row of seats circled the cauldron, which bubbled and emitted a foul-smelling odor as smoke wafted up toward Stew, who dangled from a chain that linked his wrists together. He was naked and covered in small cuts that dripped blood.

His eyes fluttered open when Sandy and Suzuki stepped into the room.

Stew fought the chains and they jangled loudly. "Get out of here, you guys," he shouted. "Get the fuck out of here! She's waiting for you!"

Suzuki looked around the room, trying to find whatever was causing Stew to freak out. His eyes didn't catch anything. Then he noticed a small hunched figure sitting at the foot of the cauldron, covered in sackcloth, rocking back and forth.

"Sandy," Stew shouted, "I told her I have a girlfriend! I promise! But she wants to give me the succ! I told her, Sandy. Get me down from here! I don't want it! I don't want her to give me the succ!"

Sandy couldn't keep herself from laughing. "He goes from 'get out of here' to 'save me' real fast," Sandy said. "Let's kill this old bitch and get some clothes on this kid."

Suzuki and Sandy stepped farther into the room. The mass of black rags looked in their direction. She did not have a face, only long black hair that hung over the blankness. A small slit ran from the top of her forehead down to where her mouth should have ended. She held small, bloody bones in her hand, and she tossed them to the ground as the two Mundanes approached her.

The faceless woman stood up, still crouching as if she had a bad back. Then the skin of her face slit started to part, to pull back like a wound being opened again. The slit filled with rows of teeth, lining what looked like a throat that stretched down to the pits of hell itself. The woman screeched and scuttled toward Suzuki.

Sandy slipped behind Suzuki and nudged him forward. "I'm still mana-less," she said. "You take Razor Deepthroat, and I'll get Stew down. Sound good?"

"That garlic didn't seem to do anything."

Sandy shrugged. "Not every idea I have can be a winner. Now go give her something to gag on."

Sandy made her way toward the cauldron while Suzuki ran toward the screeching maw of rotating teeth heading his direction. Suzuki enchanted his ax with fire, and the two hit each other with intense force. His desire to hurt the vampire instantly dissolved. When Suzuki looked at the vampire, all he could see was the way her body curved, the slight cleavage that had somehow appeared out of nowhere, and her slowly removing her robes until he could see how far the slit on her face went down.

Suzuki realized that he was erect, and he had no idea where the robed vampire had gone. Suddenly his lower torso flared up in an intense, bright burning that almost made him pass out. The world went hot, and Suzuki struggled to keep his eyes open. As he leaned forward, he found that he wasn't falling. He looked down. The robed vampire was crouched in front of him, her jaws firmly locked around his crotch.

"It's the succ, dude," Stew shouted. "She's gonna suck you to death!"

The pain had snapped Suzuki out of the spell. He raised his ax and brought it down on the vampire's head. There was a sickening thud, and the vampire's jaws relaxed. She fell, her head smacking the floor with a satisfying crunch.

Suzuki landed on his ass and scooted away from the corpse of the vampire. He looked down at his crotch as Sandy helped Stew hobble over to where Suzuki sat.

Sandy dumped Stew next to Suzuki before she ripped the robes off the dead vampire and tossed them onto Stew. "You know," she chided, "I remember you saying that you'd never turn down a blowjob once when we first started playing. I honestly didn't think you'd take that so far."

Suzuki stared at his blood-covered hands and showed them to Sandy. "Will you please stop being a dick and give me a potion?"

Sandy pulled two potions and status remedies from her inventory. She handed them to Stew and Suzuki. Both guys downed the potions as quickly as they could. Suzuki could feel the wounds on his crotch stitching themselves together. After a few seconds, it felt like nothing had happened. When he stood, he noticed something glinting on the table near the cauldron.

A beautiful gold chalice sat on the table. It was simply made, lacking the flash Suzuki had seen on other goblets in this realm, yet the craftsmanship was exquisite. Even from afar, it was obvious that this chalice had been made with something special in mind.

Suzuki knew in an instant that was what they were here for.

"Come on, guys," Suzuki said as he approached the table.

He grabbed the chalice and held it up to the light. He was right. The gold shimmered in a way that he had never seen gold catch light before. It wasn't particularly obvious why José wanted this chalice, but it was clear that this was what he had sent them for.

Beside the chalice was a small, glowing blue orb. There

was nothing particularly interesting about the orb. It looked like the kind of thing that you might find in a Best Buy. Suzuki was surprised by how unmagical the orb looked. Now that he thought about it, he hadn't seen anything that looked this techy, other than the MERCs' HUDs, since he came to Middang3ard. Without giving it any thought, Suzuki reached out and touched the orb.

He was instantly in a completely different room. He had been transported someplace, but not in the same fashion he'd been transported since Myrddin had first sucked him into a portal from New York to Middang3ard. This was smooth. It was almost like stepping off an elevator. He had felt a slight pull on his navel, but it had passed so smoothly that he had hardly noticed. Now he was in a dimly-lit room.

The room seemed to stretch on for some distance. Suzuki stood on a red carpet that ran up to a massive stone throne. Rows of pillars stretched alongside the carpet. Flags of different nations hung from the walls, nations that were unrecognizable to Suzuki.

Someone was sitting on the throne. The person rose and pointed at Suzuki. Somewhere in the room was a shriek, an ear-piercing wail.

Suzuki was standing in front of the throne. He didn't know how he had crossed so much space. He wasn't alone near the front of the throne, either. There was an orc kneeling beside him, head bowed. Next to the orc was a dwarf with red eyes. He was also on his knees. Suzuki quickly dropped to his knees and lowered his head as well.

The figure on the throne was draped in a deep purple robe with a blaze of gold that flowed to the ground. Her hood was pulled over her head, giving the appearance of a very gaunt wraith. Dust seemed to be pouring from the bottom of her robe. When she leaned forward to speak, there was a sound like the hiss of air rushing from crushed lungs.

The robed figure leaned forward so that her face caught the little bit of light cast by the blue orbs that the orc and the dwarf held.

The woman's face was scarred, but it was more than that. There appeared to be an infection on the side of her face.

But it was nothing like any infection Suzuki had ever seen. The skin was not rotting. It looked as if the skin had been peeled back, and instead of muscle and bone, there was only fiber optics.

The woman's right eye was gone.

Instead, there was a glowing red eye-piece in the empty socket. The decay was spreading from her eye as well.

The woman pulled back her hood. She was bald, and the techno-decay stretched from the back of her head down to her neck. Her skin was a sickly greenish-yellow, and when she smiled, her teeth were oddly white and straight. "The Dark One requests that you submit your reports," the woman growled. Her voice was deep, and it sounded as if her vocal cords been dragged through glass.

The dwarf held the orb above his head. "Viceroy Dominicus," the dwarf whispered, his voice trembling with each word. "I humbly offer the reports on the Dwarven continents. We have begun to furnish weapons for the orc troops that are set to descend upon the elvish cities in the third realm."

"How many weapons have you supplied?"

"Innumerable, my Viceroy. The upgrades the Dark One has blessed us with have allowed us to work faster than we ever have before. The furnace has not been shut down. We will make weapons until we are told to stop."

"Our numbers are increasing. Do not stop. You are dismissed."

The dwarf wavered and faded out of existence. As Suzuki watched the dwarf fade, he noticed that he was looking through the orc at his side. He looked down at his own body, which had a similar blue orb as the rest sitting in his hand, and he noticed that he was practically invisible. It was as if his spirit had been pulled from his body. *No, that's not right,* he thought. *More like an image of me is being projected.*

It was the orc's turn to report. "Viceroy, we have swept through the gorge that was formerly held by the human armies. We suffered few casualties, and we decimated the human army. Human captives were taken but, as the Dark One suggested, we have slaughtered all non-humans and left their bodies as an example of the Dark One's might. We have also received the boon that the Dark One promised us upon arrival. Many of the humans have already sworn their loyalty to the Dark One."

The viceroy laughed, a mirthless sound that sent shivers down Suzuki's spine. "Continue with the forward expansion," the viceroy said.

The orc dissolved, and the viceroy turned her eyes to Suzuki. "Report."

Suzuki fumbled with the glowing orb, trying to figure out what to say. "Uh, " he mumbled, "Our...efforts have been...consistent. Yeah, consistent."

"The reawakening of Hal-shoroth has been completed by now, I trust."

"Yeah. He's up and ready to...take care of business."

The viceroy leaned forward to get a better look at Suzuki. Suddenly, Suzuki felt his mind being ripped open. It was a similar feeling to when Fred went through his memories, but a thousand times worse. When the feeling passed, Suzuki fell forward, clutching his skull.

It felt like an eternity before the viceroy spoke again. "Hmm. A petty dungeon dweller. You must have broken into the mansion. No matter. You will be dead soon enough. Along with..."

Suzuki felt the viceroy invading his mind again. He screamed as he tried to shut her out of his head.

The viceroy sat back in her chair, wearing a smug smile that highlighted her freakishly perfect teeth. If she was concerned that Suzuki had seen their little pow-wow, she didn't show it. Quite the opposite. It was as if she wanted Suzuki to report back to the world what he'd seen.

"You and the other Mundanes," she finally said. "You will be swept under the tidal wave that is the Dark One, just as all else will be."

Suddenly, Suzuki was back in the room with Stew and Sandy. He looked around, trying to figure out where he was or what was happening. Sandy was looking at Suzuki, obviously confused. "Everything okay?" she asked.

Suzuki pointed to the orb. "The orb," he said. "That's how they're communicating with each other, and there's something—"

The sound of a creaking door cut Suzuki off. He whipped around, looking for another exit, but there was none. The most he could find was a few coffins stuffed against a wall in the back of the room. "Come on," he whispered as he ran toward the coffins.

Each of the Mundanes jumped into one of the coffins, closing the coffin lids behind them. Suzuki reached out to Fred. *Hey, Fred,* he ventured. *You and the other familiars can talk to each other, right?*

*Correct, human.*

*Can you link me to Sandy and Stew?*

*Very well.*

*Hey, guys?*

Even though Suzuki couldn't see the surprise on Stew's face, he could hear it in Stew's reply. *Dude, you're in my head,* Stew exclaimed. *How'd you do that?*

*Later. I just need you two to know what's going on. I'm going to check out what's going on out there and see if we can find an opportune moment to sneak the fuck out of here.*

Suzuki closed his eyes and cast Clairvoyance. The small portal opened in front of him again and he peered out at what was unfolding in the room outside of the coffins.

Robed vampires had filled the room. They were all carrying small candles. It was not only vampires in the room, though. There was a large number of orcs. The vampires and the orcs were eyeing each other with suspicion. The tension between them was palpable.

One of the vampires stepped forward and raised his candle. "Has the sacrifice been readied?" he asked. "With the rise of the Dark One's gift, we will march into the Shire and burn it to the ground this very night."

The vampires said nothing, but the orcs cheered.

Somewhere in the room, there was a quiet whine. The circle of vampires parted, and the vampire with nothing more than a slit for a face was walking toward the cauldron boiling in the center of the room. She leaned over the cauldron and began hacking and shivering until she coughed up a massive ball of coagulated blood.

It fell into the cauldron with a sickening plop.

The vampires crowded around the cauldron, whispering a chant.

The orcs watched uneasily.

Suzuki wiggled around, trying to get comfortable in the

coffin. *We gotta get out of here*, he sent Stew and Sandy. *There are at least a dozen vampires and orcs in there.*

*We can take them*, Stew shot back.

*No, we can't. Sandy's out of mana, and you just got bled for a ritualistic sacrifice to bring about some secret weapon. They've already finished the ceremony. We need to just get out of here.*

*So what's the plan?*

Suzuki wracked his brain. He wasn't coming up with anything. The thought of waiting until dawn came had crossed his mind, but that was before he realized that now there were orcs in the building as well.

They weren't going anywhere.

There was also the problem of the Dark One's secret weapon, which was apparently being birthed in the cauldron. Then it crossed his mind. *Sandy*, Suzuki said, *how good are you at sneaking?*

*Decent*, she replied. *I have enough mana to cast a stealth spell on myself. I'm pretty good with those.*

*All right. This is what we're going to do. Stew and I are going to bust out and create a diversion. You sneak back to the kitchen, grab one of those gremouloons, and bring it back here.*

*Uh, okay. Then what?*

*You'll see.* Suzuki looked at the group of vampires and orcs. *You're going to hustle your ass, too. I'm not sure how long Stew and I can—*

Stew kicked open his coffin and sprang out, two swords in hand, screaming, "I'm gonna gut each and every one of you motherfuckers!"

Suzuki could only shake his head as he opened his coffin. "Fucking Stew," he muttered under his breath.

Stew was already wading into the sea of orcs and vampires. He had the element of surprise. Within a few seconds, he had already knocked over two orcs and decapitated one of the vampires.

As he blocked an attack from one of the orcs, he leaned back and swung his sword arching backward, slicing through one of the vampires who was approaching him.

Even in Stew's stupidity, Suzuki could see that Stew had a certain knack for causing havoc.

Suzuki took a much more measured approach. He stayed to the outer ring of monsters and cast a fireball, which he held patiently in his hand.

Once he figured out a good spot, he lobbed the fireball over near the cauldron. The fire caught and forced the orcs and vampires toward the center of the room, which Stew was managing to turn into a killing zone.

Just as Suzuki was thinking that he and Stew might be able to finish off the vampires before Sandy made it back, the floor rumbled and the walls shook.

Vampires, orcs, and humans alike stopped for a moment to see what the source of the commotion was. An inhuman wail tortured the air, and a mass of tentacles spread over the lip of the cauldron and out onto the floor.

The distraction was just enough for an orc near Stew to reach out and slash him across the thigh. Stew fell to his knees, and the swarm of orcs and vampires threatened to overpower him.

Suzuki leapt across the room and landed in the growing dogpile of bodies, rolling around and slashing anything with legs and arms near him. He felt something against his neck, and before he knew it, he was sailing through the air, landing near the fire he had started. Suzuki slid straight through the flames along the cobblestone floor and bumped up against the cauldron, nearly tipping it over. He felt tentacles wrap around his neck and arms.

It took some heavy thrashing and slashing, but he was able to remove himself from the horror growing in the cauldron.

Stew was surrounded by vampires and orcs. He was backing up against the wall. With a scream and flourish, he slashed himself across the chest and cast Bloodlust. His muscles swelled, and his eyes went dark with concentration. He took a defensive stance and waited for the vampires to come for him.

The first vampire stepped up to Stew, wildly swinging a dagger. Stew simply stepped to the side, brought his sword up in an uppercut, and split the vampire in half. "Who else wants some?" Stew shouted.

More vampires were pouring through the doorways into the room. Some of them were climbing in through the windows like insects. Suzuki looked around in horror as the vampires flooded the massive room, each one of them coming for Stew. *It must be his blood*, Suzuki thought. *He had to fucking cast that spell.*

Suzuki took advantage of the vampires' distraction to rush into the crowd and decimate the orcs who were overrun by the sudden increase in bodies. His ax blade sang as he enchanted it with fire, slashing through any orc he saw, setting their bodies aflame.

In the heat of the moment, Suzuki turned around and felt a sword slip between a gap in his armor. He grabbed the sword, punched its owner in the face, flipped the sword around after he pulled it out of himself, and slashed the orc's face. Then he spun around, enchanting his new weapon, looking for something to kill.

Out of the corner of Suzuki's eye, he saw Sandy run into the room, holding one of the gremouloons. Suzuki cut a path toward her.

The vampires were overrunning Stew. He was hardly able to keep them at bay, still slashing at anything that got within a couple of feet of him.

Suzuki took the gremouloon out of Sandy's hand. He cast a glance at Stew, who was yelling at them to get away.

"Just go," Stew shouted. "Get out while you can! Get to the sun!"

It was out of the question.

Suzuki knew that, and he wished that Stew did as well.

Instead of running out of the room, Suzuki ran to the cauldron. He leapt over three orcs and landed right in front of the stinking, bubbling mess.

Curiosity got the best of him, and he couldn't help but look down into the cauldron. What he saw horrified him. The cauldron was filled with tentacles and cloven hooves. Beneath the mess of foulness, a crumpled head with deep red eyes stared up at him and bleated maniacally.

Suzuki screamed as he plunged the gremouloon into the cauldron.

Sandy's tome levitated in front of her as she waved her wand around. She shouted as she pointed her wand. A strong telekinetic pulse rocked through the room, sending the pile of vampires and orcs on top of Stew flying. The cauldron tipped over and the obscene creature being birthed skidded across the floor along with the gremouloon.

The gremouloon's body was shaking. It lay on its back and its skin was bubbling, little pus boils popping up everywhere. Suddenly, one of them shot out and landed in the pile of water next to the Dark One's secret weapon.

Then the boils started launching off like popcorn, just as the monster came to life.

Suzuki rushed over to Stew and helped him to his feet as

their enemies started to regroup. "Come on," Suzuki shouted, "Let's get the fuck out of here!"

The Mundanes turned and hoofed it. Suzuki ran faster than he ever thought he could. Behind them, the baby dark god Hal-shoroth was growing and expanding, his tentacles stretching out like heavy columns, falling on the orcs and vampires trying to avoid him.

At the same time, the gremouloons were multiplying at an unbelievable rate.

They nearly covered the floor.

None of this mattered to the Mundanes. They twisted and turned through the maze of rooms until they found themselves back in the kitchen. Sandy pointed to the stairwell that they had taken to descend into the church's depths. They ran up the stairs as an unearthly bleating chased after them.

Finally, the Mundanes burst out of the church and into the rising sun. It was just after dawn. Suzuki turned around and fell on his ass.

Sandy caught Suzuki's collar and tried to force him to stand. "Come on, you fucking idiot, we need to get the hell out of here," she shouted.

Suzuki smiled and leaned back, resting his hands in the grass. "Nah," he sighed. "Take a seat. This should be good."

"Are you fucking crazy?"

The air was filled with the sound of destruction. The fleshy mass of Hal-shoroth burst out of the church, a mass of disjointed body parts with a squashed human skull sitting atop it all.

Stew's jaw dropped. "This is what you want to see?"

Suzuki shook his head, smiling smugly. "Just wait for it."

As Suzuki was talking, the mass of the newly formed Hal-shoroth was overtaken by thousands of small scurrying gremouloons. They were gnawing on the newly-formed god as the sun shone down through the rubble, turning all the vampires to ash.

The great lumbering creature fell to the earth, trembling as the vicious gremouloons spread over its body. It did not take long until the abomination was reduced to nothing but bones.

The gremouloons scampered into the forest.

Suzuki brushed his shoulders off as he stood. "And that's called a fucking plan," he gloated. "You can both dwell on my awesomeness for as long as you need to. Take your time. Don't rush it."

Stew and Sandy were speechless. No one said anything as they made their way back to their axbeaks, which were sharpening their beaks against the trees out of boredom.

Finally, Stew cleared his throat and said, "Dude. That was fucking glorious."

Suzuki nodded as he cast healing on himself and Stew. Not that he had noticed his wounds. He was too high from the battle.

Once they were healed, the Mundanes saddled up.

This was a victory that dwarfed anything they had accomplished before. There was too much to be said, so they made their way back to the Shire, each replaying the last three days in their heads. They were the Mundanes. Suzuki felt like they had just made sure the Dark One would never forget that name.

## 17

The Mundanes arrived at the Red Lion to a flurry of celebration. The tavern was already in full swing for the evening. They were one of four parties returning from extensive quests. Most of the MERCs were already somewhat sloshed by the time Suzuki managed to pry the Red Lion's front door open. They were greeted with shouts and praises, although it didn't seem that many of the MERCs actually knew what they were congratulating the Mundanes for, which didn't bother the Mundanes at all.

They were glad to be alive.

After Suzuki, Sandy, and Stew finished a round of complimentary shots, they were guided to the backroom, where the Horsemen were waiting for them. José was playing cards with a group of MERCs. Diana and the Chipmaster were sitting in the corner, smoking. When Diana saw the Mundanes, she jumped out of her seat to greet them.

Diana threw her arms around Sandy, beaming brightly. "You guys made it out," she cooed. "How did you like the tomes? Did you dig the wand? What spell did you find easiest to cast?"

Sandy waved Diana's questions away and smiled breezily. "Too many questions," she laughed. "Grab me a drink, and I'll tell you all about it."

Sandy and Diana wandered off to find an ale while the Chipmaster stood there awkwardly with Stew and Suzuki. She finally cleared her throat. "So, uh, you young'uns find anything shiny to play with?"

Suzuki removed his HUD, handed it to the Chipmaster, along with the SD cards they had looted. "We got these," he said. "Would you install them properly for us?"

The Chipmaster snatched the HUD and SD cards out of Suzuki's hand like a greedy rat. "Oh, you bet, boyo," she exclaimed. "I been sitting around here all night waiting for something worthwhile and shiny to plop right into my lap. You three don't ever seem to disappoint. Oh, yeah, by the way, big ol' in charge is waiting to hear back from you." The Chipmaster looked at Stew for longer than was comfortable. "You, come with me. I got a feeling that you might need a doctor. You're looking a little on the pale side of the moon."

The Chipmaster grabbed Stew by his ear and pulled him away while he yelped his displeasure.

Suzuki shrugged his shoulders and pulled up a seat next to José at the card game.

José's eyes drifted over to Suzuki. The corner of his lips twisted up in a knowing smile. "I thought you guys were going to get killed for sure," he said.

Suzuki still couldn't hide the inner fanboy raging within. "You mean like died and resurrected like Gandalf the Gray?"

"No, I meant like killed, like the dead in the ground. You get the thing?"

Suzuki pulled out the golden chalice and put it on the table. José scooped it up and held it up to the light. "Now that is a good chalice," he praised. José passed the chalice to one of his acolytes sitting at the table. "Melt that shit down and make me something cool, all right?"

"Wait, you're just going to melt it? We almost got killed for that shit."

José grabbed Suzuki by the neck and pulled him close. "No, you didn't," he consoled Suzuki. "You almost died to put a stop to a massive raid on the Shire. And you also managed to bring me back some enchanted gold that I can put to good use for a sick ass weapon. That's why you almost got killed. So what did you find out?"

"Hold on, you knew about the attack? And you sent us in?"

"Last time I checked, you guys were the Mundanes. The second-most-talked-about-party in all of MERC."

"We are?"

"You are. I sent you to take care of something that I hoped you could handle. And you did. So what did you find out?"

Suzuki had hardly had time to process what had happened at the church. Even though he and the rest of the Mundanes had traveled in mostly silence, he had been so burned out from the last couple days that he had just given his mind a rest. He tried to focus and make sense of everything that had happened over the last few days. Suzuki started slowly. "There were vampires, but orcs too. They were working together."

"That's not surprising. The Dark One's been uniting all of the dark races."

"There was a dwarf too." Then it all came flooding back to Suzuki. "They were trying to resurrect some kind of god to attack the Shire. I accidentally dropped in on a meeting that was going on with the vampires and agents from the Dark One's army. I met someone called Viceroy, who was like a lieutenant or something. They used orbs to communicate with the different factions, that dwarf included. But the orb...that was the really weird part. It didn't feel like magic. It was...it was more like... I don't know, it felt like technology. Not human technology, but whatever they were using wasn't magic."

"What else?"

"The dwarf mentioned an attack on some realm. He said it was the sixth realm or something like that."

José stroked his beard and leaned back in his chair. "Sixth realm," he repeated. "I've never heard of anything like that before. We'll have to check into that. So what do you think your percentages at rescuing your friend Beth are like now?"

"Fuck me if I know. I just got back."

José pulled up his HUD. "Looks like you guys are at 18% right now," he said, his tone consoling and comforting. "Still looks like you guys don't quite have enough. You said it was near where Ellis Island would be on Earth, right? With Red Orcs?"

Suzuki nodded. "They mentioned something about capturing human soldiers. That's got to be more proof that Beth's alive."

José pursed his lips, deep in thought for a few seconds. "That checks out with what I know. I made some inquiries," he finally explained. "Sure enough, there were some humans being held captive there."

Suzuki jumped out of his seat. "Beth's still alive. I knew it."

José raised his hands, trying to calm Suzuki down. "Hold on," he cautioned. "That intel is at least a week old. We don't know what's happened since then. And in case you've forgotten, you're chances of success are still at 18%."

"That's enough. We'll take our chances. We aren't leaving Beth behind."

"The HUDs won't let you. They'll teleport you back the moment you step in there."

"Then we'll leave them behind."

José laughed and shook his head. For a moment, Suzuki was reminded of his father. "And go in blind," José chastised. "Are you fucking serious? Don't even bother with being able to gauge your actions based on your outcome. Just throw all planning to the wind? Go in there acting like a couple of fucking newbs? I was under the impression that you were the leader of the Mundanes, the MERCs who've come out over impossible odds because they're talented, well-led, and not a bunch of idiots."

Suzuki didn't have anything to say, so he just glared at José.

José cleared his throat and started again as he laid down his playing cards. "From what I've heard, you're a brilliant tactician. And that stunt that you pulled at the church is proof. So what's your tactic for this?"

Suzuki was still drawing a blank. But worse than being unable to think of a plan, he was growing more and more frustrated with José. "Listen," he shouted. "Every second that we're talking is one less second that I'm spending finding Beth."

"Ah, you love her, don't you?"

"Why the hell does that matter?"

"Love is a beautiful emotion. It causes people to try and be better than they are. Sometimes. Other times it makes people act like complete fucking idiots. Love is the kind of shit that can get you killed. Your percentage of success is shit. Lucky for you, the Horsemen are coming along for the ride."

José pulled up a screen on his HUD. He typed in a couple of keystrokes. "Looks like you're at thirty-eight percent." He sighed. "That's less than I expected. I figured we'd be worth more, but that just goes to show what we're up against. And like you said, she's running out of time."

Suzuki could hardly believe what he had just heard. The Horsemen were coming with them. José was coming with them. For the first time in weeks, Suzuki could see the Mundanes being able to pull this off. He was overcome with too many conflicting emotions. None of them truly mattered, though. There was one thought that was louder than all the rest.

*We're coming for you, Beth.*

*We're coming...*

## 18

The prisons on the outskirts of the red orc camp were barbaric. Orcs did not care for creature comforts for themselves, and even less so for their prisoners.

Brutality was still the only language they spoke.

Beth and the rest of her troop were being held in an underground prison mine. From the outside, the prison looked like a massive ant colony: dozens of different rooms interconnected with each other. Even if Beth could figure out how to escape their cell, she wouldn't have been able to navigate the winding paths of the orcs.

Orc capture had been covered extensively during boot camp.

So had will and perseverance, skills that were coming in handy at the moment.

The human prisoners had lost track of time. No one had any idea how long they had been underground. The Sergeant's beard had grown several inches, as had her hair.

One of the corners of the room was the shit and piss corner, and the cell reeked of urine and defecation.

Spirits were still high, however, even if hygiene was on

the decline. Most of the prisoners could hardly be distinguished from the dirt walls.

They were mostly quiet, as casual talking points had run out during the first hours. They had cycled through what their first meals were going to be when they escaped.

And they ran through escape plans, endless escape plans that simply weren't feasible. They were in the heart of the enemy camp, well-guarded and constantly checked in on. What was more, every now and then, one of them would be taken, never to return. Since arriving, that had been the fate of three of them.

Wherever they were taken and for whatever reason, it had been infrequent, with no rhyme or reason to it.

Sarge groaned as he stretched out. He scratched his beard and winced suddenly. After a few seconds of searching and separating his beard, he pulled out a tick. "Holy shit," Sarge muttered. "My beard's gone feral." Sarge popped the tick into his mouth and swallowed it.

Beth was one of the few in her troop to see the action, and her stomach instinctively turned, but she realized how jealous eating bugs made her feel. She found herself suddenly wishing she had some ticks of her own.

"Did you just eat that?" Beth asked.

Sarge nodded and sighed as he continued looking through his beard for more ticks. "Protein, girl," he said. "Gotta make sure to get that protein."

A soldier in the corner with dark eyes and a mischievous grin chuckled. "You know what else is protein?" he joked as he pointed at his crotch.

Beth shot him a look. "Tell you what, Myers. Get it up, and we'll negotiate."

Sarge popped another tick in his mouth, and there was a satisfying crunch. "Myers," Sarge growled. "If anyone is getting the sickly protein that you save in that sorry excuse for a pleasure stick, it's going to be your commanding officer. I can't leave you idiots to fend for yourself."

"Sir, no offense, but in all honesty, I would prefer to keep my love seed for myself. I have...a certain special ability. Besides, it's—"

The cell broke out in a chorus of "protein." The prisoners couldn't help but laugh, and Beth thanked God that she'd managed to be stationed with some soldiers with a sense of humor.

The Mundanes would have loved these guys.

Suzuki might have taken some getting used to as he was a little bit of a prudish nerd, but he always knew how to take a joke. She missed him. It felt like forever since she'd last gotten to talk to him.

And ever since her HUD stopped sending the repeated message because the system eventually figured out the error, Suzuki felt farther away than ever.

A red orc opened the cell door and the prisoners' laughter died off. The orc grabbed the closest prisoner to the door, dragged him to his feet, and smashed the prisoner's face against the wall, knocking out two of his teeth. The prisoner fell to the ground like a sack of wet clothes. Then the orc commenced to stomping on Myers who had been stupid and brave enough to come to their friend's aid. The unlucky soldier had stopped being able to scream long before the orc relented its attack.

Satisfied, the red orc picked up the prisoner he had first hit, unchained him, and dragged him out of the cell.

Beth glared with intense hatred at the red orc as he dragged her friend away, imagining sliding her sword into his spine. That was why she noticed the small microchip, hardly larger than a fingernail, lodged into the back neck fat of the orc.

*What the hell is that?* she thought.

Eventually, Myers woke up and forced himself to roll over. "Hey, Sarge," Myers whimpered. "I'm leaking a shit-ton of protein."

None of the prisoners laughed.

Outside, Beth could hear the marching of the red orcs. *Suzuki, how much longer are you going to take?* she wondered. *How much more of this can we take?*

## THE STORY CONTINUES

Book three in the Middang3ard series, It's My Party, is coming soon to Amazon.

# AUTHOR NOTES RAMY VANCE

AUGUST 10, 2019

Buffy saved my life. Twice.

I mean this as literally as one can when talking about a fictional character. The first time was when I was twenty-three and had just moved to Japan to teach English. You see, I had wanted to be a writer since I was eight, and I figured moving to the land of anime, samurais, and sushi would get my creative juices flowing.

It didn't.

It seems that creativity doesn't show up when you are alone in a small city where no one speaks your native tongue – in my case, English. And by no one, I mean, no one. And it didn't help that my smattering of Japanese was relegated to basic phrases like "Where is the bathroom?" and "My name is Ramy."

There are only so many times you can tell someone your name before they think you're weird. And as for the bathroom, I'm pretty sure the whole town thought I had IBS.

As the weeks turned into months, I experienced a loneliness so deep that there were times I thought I would literally turn into a wisp of smoke to be carried away by the wind. If you've ever experienced true loneliness, then you'll know what I mean. And if you haven't, well, then I pray you never do. There are few emotions so completely soul-breaking...

I think I might have faded away into that wisp if it wasn't for Buffy.

For some reason, local television played an episode of Buffy every Wednesday at 7:30pm. It was the only English I ever heard, and it became the one hour a week (well, forty minutes) where I could escape into a world that made sense (even when Darla was doing her thing). I built my week around that episode of Buffy, telling myself, "Only two more days until Buffy. Only one more day until Buffy..."

In between Buffy times, I would study Japanese, comforted that I would get that brief reprieve in the form of snarky dialogue and 90s-style choreographed TV fights. It gave me the strength to keep moving.

Eventually, my Japanese got better. Good enough that I actually started making friends, and even went on a date or two. And by the time I had completed my first year in Japan, I knew enough of the language and culture that I signed on for two more years.

Had it not been for Buffy, I would have quit after six months. Quit and missed out on some of the best times of my life.

Buffy saved my life. She gave me the strength to make it through that dark period in my life.

And she would save me again. Eleven years later, to be exact, when I'm living in Edinburgh, debating whether or not I should leave the company I started years earlier to pursue my dream of becoming a full-time author.

After all, it was what I had wanted since I was eight. And at (almost) thirty-eight, things hadn't changed.

But what to write? I started with the *GoneGod World*, my first series, and it did OK, but I was so far from a full-time income that I was starting to regret my life choices. It didn't help that my wife was pregnant (pregnant and still supportive, I might add. I married well. Very well, indeed.) But regardless of her patience, I needed to make money. Support my family.

Then, one evening, I was sipping some whisky (cliché, I know, but then again, what's better than sipping good whisky in Scotland, eh?), and thinking back to Buffy and the parts of her story I loved most. Those pleasant memories led to these words: When I was dead, all I wanted to be was alive. Now that I'm human again, all I want to do is die.

And from those simple words, my second series, *Mortality Bites*, was born. It was the story of a three-hundred-year-old vampire who was suddenly made human again, *mortal* again...and the series explores all the struggles that came with that transformation (or untransformation, I guess).

Mortality Bites quickly rose in the ranks, making me the income I needed to truly become a full-time author. And now, eight books later (and *Middang3ard* rocking the charts), I have achieved the one thing I have wanted since I was eight years old. I had finally become that full-time author.

So, thank you, Buffy. Thank you, Joss Whedon, Sarah Michelle-Gellar, and the rest of the Scooby gang. I owe you all for saving my life more than once through your amazing stories. You saved me in the most peculiar of ways, and I honestly do not have the words to express my deepest gratitude.

But I'd like to try...so, if any of you are ever in Edinburgh, look me up. We can talk about how stories save people from themselves and transform lives in the most peculiar of ways.

We can do so while sipping whisky, clichés be damned.

# AUTHOR NOTES MICHAEL ANDERLE

AUGUST 11, 2019

**THANK YOU for not only reading this story but these *Author Notes* as well.**

(I think I've been good with always opening with "thank you." If not, I need to edit the other *Author Notes*!)

There is a huge challenge with this series. Well, a challenge other than Stew and Sandy and the Humpa Lumphad stuff – that is just so different on so many levels I can't talk about it.

*Well, not without laughing, at least.*

Anyway, the challenge is the timeline between what I want to happen (the crew getting their rise in power and running across to save Beth) and how it would perhaps happen if we didn't write the story to my personal preference.

Like, having others not understand we need a Rocky Balboa sort of ending. (You know, where we see Rocky working out in a montage of shots that represents weeks of effort and finally runs up the steps to raise his hands in the air?)

But, Humpa Lumphad aside, the truth is, Middang3ard

isn't a good place. Not everything goes to plan, and frankly, there is a LOT of ass-kicking that needs to be accomplished. Good people die, and often can die horribly and quickly.

Further, I'm wondering if we can drop a nuke in the world to destroy a metric shit-ton of orcs.

Or a MOAB (Mother of All Bombs).

The problem is air superiority. Who has it, and what do we do with it?

On to the next story – it's time to get Beth back.

#BethBackNow
#DontForgetBeth
#StopPlayingWithHumpaLumphad
#HumpaLumphadArePeopleToo

**FAN PRICING**

$0.99 Saturdays (new LMBPN stuff) and $0.99 Wednesday (both LMBPN books and friends of LMBPN books.) Get great stuff from us and others at tantalizing prices.

Go ahead. I bet you can't read just one.

Sign up here: http://lmbpn.com/email/.

**HOW TO MARKET FOR BOOKS YOU LOVE**

Review them so others have your thoughts, and tell friends and the dogs of your enemies (because who wants to talk to enemies?)... *Enough said ;-)*

Ad Aeternitatem,

Michael Anderle

# OTHER BOOKS BY RAMY VANCE

<u>Mortality Bites Series</u>
<u>Keep Evolving Series</u>
<u>Fatebound Series</u>

# BOOKS BY MICHAEL ANDERLE

For a complete list of books by Michael Anderle, please visit:

**www.lmbpn.com/ma-books/**

All LMBPN Audiobooks are Available at Audible.com and iTunes

To see all LMBPN audiobooks, including those written by Michael Anderle please visit:

**www.lmbpn.com/audible**

# CONNECT WITH THE AUTHORS

**Connect with Ramy**

Join Ramy's Newsletter

Join Ramy's FB Group: House of the GoneGod Damned!

**Connect with Michael Anderle and sign up for his email list here:**

Website: http://lmbpn.com

Email List: http://lmbpn.com/email/

Facebook:
www.facebook.com/TheKurtherianGambitBooks